Crime Busters United

Sixteen connected short stories illustrating that AGE is not a synonym for USELESS.

by

Nigel Power

MAPLE
PUBLISHERS

Crime Busters United (Sixteen connected short stories illustrating that AGE is not a synonym for USELESS)

Author: Nigel Power

Copyright © Writer Sky Snow (2025)

The right of Nigel Power to be identified as author of this work has been asserted by the author in accordance with section 77 and 78 of the Copyright, Designs and Patents Act 1988.

First Published in 2025

ISBN 978-1-83538-452-7 (Paperback)
     978-1-83538-453-4 (Hardback)
     978-1-83538-454-1 (E-Book)

Cover Design and Book Layout by:
     White Magic Studios
     www.whitemagicstudios.co.uk

Published by:
     Maple Publishers
     Fairbourne Drive, Atterbury,
     Milton Keynes,
     MK10 9RG, UK
     www.maplepublishers.com

A CIP catalogue record for this title is available from the British Library.

CONTENTS

DISCLAIMER

With the exception of the names of two men who had a connection with the Soviet Union, all the characters in the stories that follow are fictitious and are not based on any acquaintances of the author.

INTRODUCTION

In 2021 a book was published by Arthur H. Stockwell Ltd under ISBN number 978-0-7223-5151-2 with the title 'The Adventures of an Elderly Gentleman and Other Stories.' The first four stories of seven in the book are about an 85-year-old gentleman, Mr James Willoughby, who had recently moved into a retirement apartment. He might have expected to live a quiet and sedate, and perhaps sometimes lonely, life. However, he gets involved in incidents that ensure that his observational skills are tested to the full. He also discovers that the police display a close interest in some of his activities and so also eventually does a gang of criminals. He realises that although he is now advanced in years he can make a positive contribution to the rural society in which he resides.

The last of the four stories concludes with these words spoken by another character, "Oh, no, he won't die, will he?"

Did he die? That is a question that has been posed to the author on several occasions. A further question often asked is, 'Are there anymore James Willoughby stories?' The answer to that first question is no, for he recovered, and to the second, yes there are a further twelve stories. All sixteen are included in this book.

PARTLY OLD

An eighty-five-year-old discovers that his observational skills prove that age is no barrier to making a contribution to society.

He assumed he must be old. His family and friends seemed to think so, but they hadn't got as far as using adjectives such as 'ancient' or 'vintage'. He didn't feel old. True, he had passed his eighty fifth birthday, but he had decided to live until he was at least a hundred. Admittedly, his hearing was not as good as it had been when he was younger, and he often couldn't hear what his granddaughters said to him. His eyesight, however, since he had had his cataracts done, was better than it had been for many years. He didn't need any support when he went for a walk and his teeth were all his own. Although there was a lift between his floor and ground level, he made a point of using the stairs at least once in a day, when he went down to collect his paper. Perhaps he was just 'partly old'. Yes, he'd accept that.

He hadn't liked the idea of moving out of his house, but the flat – no! He mustn't call it that – the apartment his children had found for him had much to commend it. It had four rooms – living room, bedroom, kitchen and bathroom – with a small south facing balcony off the living room. The views across the valley were splendid, and from his position high up on a south-facing hillside he could see for miles. On a clear day, with the binoculars (or should he call them field glasses?) given him by two of his grandchildren, he could see for several miles east, south and west. He had bought an Ordnance Survey map and spent many a pleasant hour identifying farms and landmarks as well as three villages that he could see from his window. In each of the three villages he could see their churches in prominent positions, two with spires and one with a tower. He could watch traffic on a dual carriage way making its way towards a town on the south coast and away to his right, the west, he could see trains on the hourly cross-country service. He knew the media delighted in quoting comments of members of the public about poor time keeping on the rail network, but his little trains, as he liked to call them, always seemed to be spot on time.

The patchwork of fields interested him. The farms he could see seemed to operate a mixed economy with both arable and pasture farming. The fields of oilseed rape had almost lost their golden sheen and those grown with grass were being harvested with tractors and trailers busy removing the cuttings from early morning till after dusk. In the fields with livestock he could see horses, cattle and sheep: in a field to the west he could see deer – he assumed that they must be at Buckland's Farm, if he had matched the fields to his map correctly.

With his field glasses he delighted in looking at the wildlife, particularly the birds. The summer visitors had now arrived and the house martins put on some spectacular aerial displays. He was sure that there was a nest above one of his windows which was visited regularly - not just by two birds, but by several one after another. Earlier, in Spring, he had watched blackbirds, robins and a thrush collecting nesting materials, while farther away he had seen rooks and jackdaws flying by with twigs in their beaks as they built high in the trees in a copse in the valley to his left. Also, in the copse, he had noticed woodpeckers, both green and spotted, hammering at the trunks of trees and, even with his poor hearing, he had been able to detect the rhythmic beat as they worked rapidly. Why it didn't give them headaches he couldn't imagine. Now it was feeding time and he could detect many small birds diving into the hedges with offerings for the young that hadn't yet fledged. Various titmice, including gatherings of long tailed tits, were especially busy. Sparrows, dunnocks, chaffinches, the pretty goldfinches and others he couldn't identify but which he classified as LBJs (little brown jobbies) were all intent on the same mission of filling empty stomachs. He had no difficulty seeing his friendly blackbird who came regularly for the raisins he put on the balcony, before flying on to his singing perch on the tree just below his window. Recently, a robin had started coming for the mealworms he put out.

On this beautiful morning, a Thursday, there would be a few farmers' stalls in the village. It was no more than a ten-minute walk away, even at his deliberate pace, and he might be able to buy a trout fillet for his lunch. He would have liked to make some parsley sauce to go with the trout, but now that he no longer had a garden he did not have access to fresh parsley, unless there was a vegetable stall with herbs for sale. He spent a few minutes thinking if there was anything else he needed to get while he was out. Then, taking a shopping bag, remembering to put on his shoes – more than once he had gone out in his slippers – he locked his door, set off down the stairs and out of the main entrance.

It really was a lovely day, warm with just a gentle breeze. Even though it was still quite early, there were several people about, some of whom he recognised. Most of them greeted him with comments about the loveliness of the day. There were five stalls, and he was able to buy fish and a bunch of fresh parsley. He also bought two pieces of local cheese and treated himself to a small box of chocolates made by the chocolatier in the neighbouring town.

On his way back he made a diversion into the local park and walked round the small lake where the ducks were standing on their heads, pecking at the weed under the water. He was then delighted to spot a pair of grebes that he hadn't seen there before. As he walked on he just had to stop and admire the roses. The warm sun inspired them to give off their perfume, which brought back memories of the roses he had grown.

Coming out of the park he decided to sit on the bench which afforded a view of the rising ground to the north of the village. There was little traffic on this minor road which would eventually wind its way through the valley he could see from his windows. He saw one very brightly polished car go past and noted that the three letters on its number plate were DOG. When, half a minute later a car with the letters FOX passed by, he wondered what might be next – would there be a CAT or a HOG? No, the next one was JXX, but the one behind it had EAD on its number plate. Now, he thought, you could make a word with those letters by adding another. So he began exploring the possibilities. Head, dead, mead. The first two rhymed, but not with the third. But what about lead and read. They would rhyme with all of them, as you could say them both ways. When you read a book, rhyming with reed and get to the end you will have read it, rhyming with red.

He was thinking about leading an animal or swinging the lead when he was interrupted by someone shouting. A tatty van had pulled up and the passenger was trying to attract his attention.

"Hey, mate," the man called. "Is this the way to Coltsford?"

He got up and went over to the van.

"Yes, this road will take you to Coltsford, but if you are not familiar with the road, be careful; there are one or two sharp bends, especially by the deer farm."

"Did you say deer farm? Thanks, old man – we'll look out for it."

Old Man! He didn't think much to that.

Turning to the driver, the man in the van said, with a note of excitement in his voice: "Did ye hear that, Al? A deer ...." The rest was lost in an explosion of noise from the engine and a belch of smoke from the exhaust as with creaks, groans and rattles the van went on its way. The vehicle had clearly had previous owners as part of its original light blue paint had been overpainted with dark blue, presumably covering up some original lettering. He looked after it and could just distinguish PYO on the number plate.

"Hmm!" he thought. "What could you do with PYO?"

The first thing that came into his head was 'Pick Your Own'. That reminded him of strawberries in the fields. Maybe they were farmers, but he thought that unlikely. Now, what else could you do with these letters? 'Spyhole' would work but P followed by Y needed an H in between, then 'physiotherapy' or 'physiognomy'. Was there a word 'physiology'? If you didn't start with P, what other possibilities were there? 'Eponymous' – yes that worked. Now, what did it mean?

"Deep in thought, Jim?" said a voice. Looking up, he saw his friend Ben standing beside him.

"Good morning, Ben. What a lovely day! I've been up to the village and I thought I'd sit here and look at the scenery and watch the traffic."

'Still looking at car numbers and making words out of them?"

"Yes! Today I saw a DOG followed by a FOX."

"That can't be right," smiled Ben. "The dog usually chases the fox in hunting, not the other way around."

"Hey, that's good. I hadn't thought of that. But we had a decrepit old van pull up a few minutes back. Did you see it – light blue with a great daub of dark-blue paint on its side?"

"I did see it, just disappearing in a cloud of smoke. Where was it going?"

"They asked the way to Coltsford. I don't know if it was a farm vehicle, or perhaps they were scrap-metal merchants."

"What, driving some of the scrap they had collected!" laughed Ben. "Any road up, I'm glad I've met you. My two grandsons are playing cricket for the village on Saturday over at Marchington and my son is going to take me to watch them. Do you feel like joining us?"

"This Saturday – yes, that would be grand as both my families will be away, one on holiday and the others have been invited to a wedding. If this weather holds it will be a very pleasant way to spend the afternoon. What time and where?'

'We'll pick you up outside your apartments around 1.30. Can you manage that?"

"No problem. Thanks for inviting me. But I'd better be going now – I've sat here long enough and I've some fish to cook."

So saying, he made his way home, but before putting his purchases away and starting his cooking he went out onto his balcony. The countryside was basking in the sunshine, but there was plenty of activity. Vehicles on the dual carriageway were reflecting the sun as they sped on their ways to he knew not where. He knew where the little birds were going though as they flew directly into gaps in the hedges. Looking to the west, with his field glasses, he was surprised to see the tatty old van parked in a gateway just round the corner from the deer farm. Perhaps they had broken down, but he felt a little uneasy about seeing the van there, although he couldn't think why.

After lunch, he sat in his chair facing his view and picked up his daily national newspaper, but before long the paper fell on the floor as he drifted off into his afternoon nap. He hadn't even turned to the puzzle page or the letters, which were often more interesting than the news items that were nearly all opinion or speculation. Nearly an hour later he was startled awake by the telephone ringing. Fortunately, the phone was within reach; on answering it he discovered it was a grandson checking that he was 'alright' and inviting him to Sunday lunch when they would tell him all about the wedding. He was given instructions about the time he was to be ready to be picked up.

Now that he was awake, he made himself a cup of tea and then decided to look at the local paper he had bought in the morning. He didn't have it every day, but he felt he ought to try to keep up to date by buying a copy occasionally. There were articles in which local councillors were pontificating on plans for development of the area and the need for more houses to be built on the edges of villages, summaries of national news and accounts of road accidents, village fares and garden parties. As he turned the pages his attention was caught by an account of sheep being stolen from a couple of farms. Police were appealing for witnesses or information about the rustlers. He wondered if any of the farms he could see from his windows had been affected.

In the evening there was nothing to interest him on television after he had listened to the news, so he sat and listened to the birds outside his window. He wished he was able to identify all the different songs they sang, but there were so many it really was a chorus with blackbird taking the role of lead soloist. Although he began to feel drowsy his mind was still active as he thought about the sheep rustling that had also been featured on the regional television news.

It was still light, being so close to the longest day, when he went to bed, but it wasn't long before he was asleep. It seemed only a few minutes when he woke again, although it was beginning to get light. He looked at his clock which showed 04.50. Half past four, he thought, then, no, ten to five. He felt something must have woken him, so he lay in bed not moving and listening attentively. Then he heard a scratching that seemed to be coming from the living room. He got out of bed and went to look for the cause of the noise and discovered that he hadn't shut the window next to the door onto the balcony and there was blackbird on the balcony tapping his beak on the windowsill and waiting for his raisins.

He could not deny such a friendly cheeky companion, so he fetched the raisin jar and went out on to the balcony. It was quite warm even though it was not yet fully light. He put some raisins on the balustrade, and he thought he would just have a look at the countryside before going back to bed. There was a steady stream of traffic on the main road, including a couple of cars towing caravans towards the coast – early arrivals on a Friday before the weekend rush. Everywhere else everything seemed quiet. He couldn't see any activity in the villages, but some of the grazing animals were having an early breakfast. As he turned from looking east and south to view how far the sun had reached in the west he saw there was movement in a distant field.

His interest aroused he retrieved his binoculars from their shelf in the living room. Yes, it looked like that old light blue van in the drive to Buckland's Farm and men and dogs chasing the deer. Two men were with the dogs and one man was by the doors of the van. And now the man opened the doors as the other men cornered a deer and pushed it into the van. As he watched, the procedure was repeated. Were these people the rustlers the police were after? Hastily he went back inside, found his phone and the local paper: he was sure there was a number for the police at the end of the article about sheep stealing. Yes, there it was. He went back onto the balcony while he phoned the number. There was a reply immediately.

"Sergeant Cartwright, Moleshire Police, how can I help you?"

"I think I might be able to help you. I think there might be some deer rustling going on at the moment, that I can see from my window."

"Please can you give me some details? Where do you think this is happening?"

"Buckland's Farm, near Coltsford."

"Can you give me your name and where you are?"

"I am James Willoughby and I live at Cloverhill Court at...."

The sergeant interrupted, "I know, my aunt lived in one of the apartments until about six months ago."

"I wouldn't have met her – I've only been here about four months."

"Then you may have moved into her apartment. It has a magnificent panoramic view of the valley."

"That's right – Number 4. It is a wonderful view. I don't normally look out at this time of the morning, only the blackbird woke me up looking for raisins."

"Oh, he's still at it, is he? Auntie will be so pleased he has found a new friend. Mr Willoughby, I've sent an alert out to a couple of patrols, and they are making their way to the area. Can you give me any more information?"

"Yes, it's an old light blue long transit-type vehicle with large splodges of dark-blue paint on the sides where the previous owner's name must have been. Perhaps 'clapped out' might be a better description of its age. I saw it yesterday when I was asked if they were on the right road for Coltsford. I told them to be careful on the road as there are some nasty bends, especially near the deer farm. I wasn't sure they would be able to negotiate the bends in that van, but they seemed to get excited when I mentioned the deer farm. I saw them later from my window stopped in a gateway near the farm."

"Thank you. Can you tell us anything else about the van?"

"Oh! I nearly forgot. The reg. number contained the letters PYO – I thought, at the time, of Pick Your Own and wondered if it was a farm vehicle."

"That's very helpful. Full marks for observation. Can you still see them, Mr Willoughby? Are they still there?"

"Yes, they are. Wait a moment – they have shut the doors. It looks as though they are calling the dogs and they have jumped into the front of the van. I think they are about to go. Yes, they must have started the engine – there is a great cloud of dirty black smoke – surely, that must be illegal – and they're moving."

"Can you see which way they are going?"

"I'm watching to see which way .... Ah! They have turned towards Coltsford and I shall lose sight of them soon, but if they stay on the same road I should see them go over the railway bridge, although only briefly as there are some big trees on that road. Oh! I can see a police car just down below me on the Coltsford road. The van is now out of my view."

"There should soon be another patrol approaching from Coltsford. We need to know if the van keeps on the same road."

"This is like being the 'eye in the sky'. Yes! There it is, approaching the railway bridge now. More black smoke as it climbs the hill to the bridge."

"Thank you, Mr Willoughby. The chase in on now and hopefully we shall catch them. I will let you know how it goes. You can go back to bed now. Sleep well."

He switched off the phone and went back to bed. He didn't know if he would be able to sleep after all that excitement. However, the next thing he knew was a bright light in his room as the sun pierced its rays through a gap in the curtains. Time to get up.

The morning was much as usual – he made his breakfast of scrambled egg on toast, went downstairs, collected his paper and fed the birds. He chose a ready meal from his freezer for his dinner, and put it in the oven. When it was cooked, he put the television on for the news and sat down to his meal. The very first item on the regional news was that suspects had been detained early in the morning on suspicion of stealing sheep and other animals. The police had acted on observations supplied by an elderly resident who was alerted by some strange behaviour at dawn. 'Elderly' was the adjective used – much better than 'old'.

He heard the rest of the news and then switched the box off and went through to the kitchen to wash up. The buzzer sounded suggesting that he had a visitor.

He picked up the intercom to ask who was there and a voice answered "It's Sergeant Cartwright – we spoke early this morning. Can I come up?"

"Wait a moment and I'll let you in."

When Sergeant Cartwright had been let in, she said, "It's lovely to meet you, Mr Willoughby. I wanted to call and thank you for your help this morning. It was a very successful operation. You were right about the van being clapped out: it broke down shortly after it passed over the railway bridge. Our patrols arrived at the same time from opposite directions, and we were able to arrest all three miscreants. They couldn't do otherwise than admit that they had taken the deer without permission, although they were prepared to deny all knowledge of sheep theft until one of them said he wasn't with them when they stole the sheep. They aren't a very bright bunch. We phoned the farmer: he hadn't heard anything, but he came with a tractor and trailer and was able to rescue all the deer. A few had superficial wounds and dog bites, but all will survive. He was most grateful and asked me to pass on his thanks to you. He said he would like to phone and thank you himself – do you mind if I give him your number? Now, I had an ulterior motive for visiting rather than just phoning. I'd like to feast my eyes on your lovely view for a moment."

"Many thanks for coming and giving me that information. I am so pleased the deer are safe. Now, if you have time for a cup of tea, I'll put the kettle on and you can sit on the balcony and look at the countryside. Blackbird might even come to see you – he often calls after lunch."

When the tea was served Sergeant Cartwright said: "James, you must have very good eyesight. I can hardly see Buckland's Farm from here."

"Ah, but the sun has moved round and it is not highlighting the west as it was early this morning. Try these." And he passed her the field glasses.

"That's much better and I can see the railway bridge and - my lucky day - there's a train just coming through. I had better go and find my bed. I'm on duty again at 11.00 p.m. tonight. There may be more news when I get back to the station. The thieves will get their day in court, but I think they will plead guilty, so we won't need you as a witness. They'll be charged with animal theft and a string of motoring offences. The van wasn't taxed or insured, the driver hadn't a licence and the vehicle wasn't roadworthy. We think they were taking the animals to a slaughterhouse near Birmingham. Our West Midlands colleagues have been concerned about that place for some time. So, goodbye and many thanks again. It has been a privilege to meet you. You're a valuable member of society."

After the police officer had departed, he felt it was time he had a nap. Such excitement was enough to last him a month and he must be able to keep awake the following afternoon at the cricket.

He woke to the telephone ringing.

"Mr Willoughby?" said a strange voice. "Sam Small from Buckland's Farm here. I just had to ring and thank you for your great detective work. I never heard a sound during the night and had you not seen what was happening to my herd I would have lost twenty-five of them. I count myself very fortunate. I have spoken to some of my colleague farmers and they are delighted that that gang has been caught. We reckon you deserve a medal or an award or something."

"That's very kind of you, Mr Small. I am glad you didn't lose any of your animals and I hope none was badly injured. Have they all recovered from their ordeal?"

"Well, they all seem to be eating well, although a couple have injuries I need to keep an eye on. Do you eat venison, Mr Willoughby?"

"I do, Mr Small, although I live alone, but often have meals with my son or daughter and their families."

"Splendid. I'll send some prime cuts that you can share with your families. Perhaps they'll cook them for you. Let me have your address and I'll see to it."

"That is most kind. A much better outcome for us than for those crooks!"

He had hardly put the phone down when it rang again. This time it was his friend Ben, checking he was still up for going to cricket the following day.

Then Ben said, "Did you hear that the sheep stealers have been caught near Coltsford? Do you think that old van we saw yesterday was involved? Did you see it again?"

He told Ben he had seen it in a gateway near the farm later that morning, then assured him he would be ready on the following day.

He thought he might make himself a sandwich before the early evening news came on, but he was only halfway through that task, when the phone rang again. He couldn't remember when last he had so many calls in one day.

As soon as he picked it up and said, "Hello" a voice replied, "Hello Grandad. It's Phil. We're at the airport waiting for our flight to be called, and Dad and Holly have gone to look for something to read on the plane. Are you alright?"

Before he could say more than "Yes", his grandson went on: "I've just seen on my phone that the police have caught those sheep stealers. Apparently, they were spotted by some old geezer who couldn't sleep. Got to go – the others have just come back. I'll take some pictures of Malta to show you. Over and out. Bye."

He sat still for a few minutes thinking he might be old, or partly old, but he could still be useful. The Sergeant said he was a valuable member of society. It gave him a warm glow. But OLD GEEZER indeed!

AN ARRESTING SUMMER'S OUTING

When two elderly pensioners attend a cricket match it is not only batsmen that are caught out.

James Willoughby woke to hear rain drumming on his bedroom window. He looked at his bedroom clock and was relieved to discover that it was not yet 4 o'clock, so he had time to go back to sleep in the hope that the rain would have stopped by the time he had to get up. When he woke again three hours later the sun was shining through a gap in his curtains. When he checked the time he realised that it was a Saturday and the fourth of July. Why did that date sound special? Of course, American Independence Day. Oh well, it wasn't special as far as he was concerned. But he was pleased that it was Saturday, the sun was shining and there would be plenty of daylight.

"Well, James," he said to himself, "We had better get up and enjoy this July day. At your age of eighty-five you had better make the best of such days left to you."

So saying, he got out of bed, put on his slippers and went through to the bathroom to have a shave and a shower. Then, just in dressing gown and slippers he went through to the kitchen to make his next decision – what to have for breakfast. The decision after breakfast would be what to wear. He would make himself scrambled egg on toast and, he decided after an argument with himself, a grilled rasher of bacon.

Having had breakfast and washed up, he went through to his living room on the way back to his bedroom, but stopped to open the curtains and go out on to his small balcony. Still wearing just his dressing gown, he could look out over the valley below him to east, south and west without being overlooked himself. This was the great advantage of living in an apartment on the second floor of the block located on a south facing hillside. He liked to watch the birds that had been busy for several hours already and check that all the farm animals were grazing peacefully. The road to the coast, twenty miles away, was already busy (probably had been since before dawn) with holiday traffic. He left a few raisins for his friendly blackbird neighbour and some mealworms for the robin, then continued to his bedroom.

He had remembered to check his calendar for appointments before deciding what to wear. Today, his friend Ben and Ben's son Mark would call for him immediately after lunch to take him to the cricket match, fifteen miles away, in which Ben's grandsons, Josh and Dave, would be playing. When he had dressed he left his flat and went down the stairs, avoiding the lift (worth a pat on the back), to fetch his newspaper from the entrance hall. After a few words of greeting with one of the other residents, he retraced his steps, again avoiding the lift (worth another pat on the back), and spent the next half an hour reading the paper. The main headline reported a massive drugs capture by a Border Force patrol boat two miles from a port in the next county. The drugs had a street value of several million pounds. They may not have seized the complete haul – there was a suspicion that some had been transferred to another vessel while still at sea and before the arrest had been effected.

There was also a report of new cases of coronavirus in two African countries. As he put the paper down he wondered how he would fare being locked down in the apartment that had been his home for less than a year. On the plus side, he had his wonderful panoramic view with continuous action to watch, but on the debit side he now had no garden of his own to work or laze in.

He spent the rest of the morning on a few minor tasks and then prepared a light lunch of soup and cake. The soup was watercress made by one of the lovely ladies who regularly checked on his health and well-being. He was very lucky, and most appreciative of the kindness of his four 'girlfriends' who ensured that he never felt lonely or forgotten, especially if they knew his family were unable to visit. He made sure that if he baked some bread rolls he made sufficient to share with one or two of the 'girls'. He thought of them as girls even though a couple were older than he.

He was ready when Ben and Mark called for him. They explained that today's match was a friendly with no league points at stake, so while it would still be very competitive it should also be good-humoured. The fixture between the teams went back many years, and honours were about even. As the weather was fine after the overnight showers, they anticipated that there would be a good crowd from both villages. Also, as the ground was adjacent to a busy road, but set well back from the road with plenty of car-parking space, they expected that some passing motorists would stop for a while and watch the match from their cars.

When they arrived at the ground and parked behind the pavilion Ben was quick to spot three seats in a good viewing position.

He called, "Come on, Jim – we are in luck. There are three good seats just over there. We'll keep one for Mark. I expect he will want to see if his boys have arrived safely. One or possibly both are bringing their girlfriends with them."

The match was due to start in ten minutes, so while they waited James had a good look around, noting the positions of the stumps (already pitched but bail-less), the outfield and boundaries and the cars parked along the opposite side of the ground with some spectators sitting in them. The pitch itself and the square looked as though it had recently been mown, but the grass of the outfield looked green and lush, perhaps having benefitted from the overnight rain.

There was a ripple of applause as the umpires and captains emerged from the pavilion to walk out to the pitch, where a coin was tossed to decide who would bat first. It appeared that the hosts were going to have the first innings.

As the visitors took to the field followed by the home team's opening batsmen, James, Ben and Mark settled down to watch. James had already noted the trees beyond the road in full leaf stirred just a little by a slight breeze, which tempered the heat of the sun and, to his mind, contributed to a quintessentially typical English country scene.

The batting side made steady progress, but James thought that the scoring rate was quite slow.

He remarked to Ben, "Have you noticed how few balls are getting to the boundary? Shots that should have been worth four are being chased and caught by the fielders and restricted to two runs. Too much grass has been left on the outfield and it is slowing the ball."

Ben replied, "Yes, there have been some good strokes played that didn't get the reward they should have. This is likely to be a low scoring match, I think. What do you think of the player facing the bowling now?"

"He has a good technique, a good upright stance, and has played some good shots. He is better playing off the back foot, but sometimes doesn't use his feet sufficiently when the ball is pitched up and so doesn't quite get to the pitch of it with the result that he is inclined to 'spoon' it up. Watch him this over. He has played back to three balls with good shots but all to fielders. Now, there you are – caught in the covers. He started to go back, then came forward, didn't get to the pitch of the ball and scooped it up to be caught. Let's see how many he made."

"I see what you mean. Ah, the score's up now! He scored 29 and the total is now 52 for three. Honours about even at this point, I think," said Ben.

A few more runs had been scored and the total had reached 69 for 3, when Mark and Ben exclaimed, "Josh is going to bowl! We must watch this."

James leaned forward and turned to Mark. "His mother's not here to watch him?"

"No, she's on duty nursing at the hospital today. A pity – she likes to watch the boys play."

They watched Josh's first over. The first ball was a long hop, hit to the boundary; the next four brought no runs; and the last was hit for two. In his second over, three singles were scored.

Ben turned to James. "Well, Jim, any comments?"

"Quite a nice action. Occasionally he drops his leading shoulder in his delivery stride and concedes runs, but when he stands a little taller the batsmen have to be careful."

The score had reached 83 for three when Josh bowled a ball that took the outside edge of the bat and was caught by the keeper. The score became 83 for four.

"Exactly the delivery he has been trying to bowl," commented James. "Shoulder up, ball left his hand a little higher and more attention given to accuracy and less to speed."

In his next over Josh took another wicket. This was well caught at slip by his brother; 89 for five.

Enthusiastic applause, particularly by the boys' father and grandfather.

Ben chortled, "That will look good in the scorebook – 'caught D Foster; bowled J Foster'. We could do with a few more like that."

When the score had reached 123 for six, another bowling change was made.

Mark leaned across and said, "Mr Willoughby, the new bowler is playing his first match with us. He is reputed to be a useful spin bowler. See what you think of him."

James watched the new man bowl two overs and then said, "From here I can't tell how accurate his direction is, but the length he bowls seems just about right and consistent. He is a bit square on when he delivers the ball. I wonder if he would be more sideways on if he bowled round the wicket. Oh, he is just going to do that." The next ball clean bowled the batsman and James commented, "Spot on! Much better round the wicket. He will be pleased with that."

The score was then 132 for seven.

Five runs later James exclaimed, "Oh no. I don't think the umpire saw it."

"What didn't he see?" asked Ben.

"There was a short run. In their eagerness to take two the non-striker didn't touch his bat down before going back for the second. The score should only have been credited one. I didn't see the umpire give any signal."

"Is there a signal for a short run?" asked both Ben and Mark.

"Oh yes," said James, and demonstrated by raising his right arm to the side and bringing his thumb up to his shoulder.

Another wicket fell. The score reached 148 and then an accident occurred. The ball was driven hard back, hit the bat of the non-striker before he could avoid it and ricocheted on to the head of the umpire, who staggered and collapsed. Mark, a paramedic, was out of his seat immediately and running on to the pitch to give assistance. After a few minutes the umpire was helped to his feet and professed that he felt alright to continue.

The end of the innings came fairly soon after the incident, when the hosts were all out for 156. The tea interval was signalled. Mark spent more time assessing the umpire while James and Ben enjoyed some refreshment and a chat with Josh and Dave and their girlfriends, Poppy and Lizzie. James took the opportunity for a visit to the toilet. When he got back there was news and a suggestion.

Mark had returned and had the two captains with him. Mark had advised that the injured umpire should not continue to officiate. The club secretary had taken him to A and E for a concussion check. This meant they were an umpire short. Would Mr Willoughby be willing to take his place?

James was somewhat stunned by the request and needed a moment or two to think before he responded.

"Oh dear!" said James. "It's a long time since I last umpired and I don't have a licence. My eyesight's fine, but my hearing is a little weak. I suppose I am fairly neutral; although I came with the visitors I don't have any real association with the club. Surely, there is someone else."

"As this is a friendly, you don't have to hold a licence," said Mark. "And you also know cricket and the rules, including the signal for a short run," he added with a grin.

James looked at the two captains. "Are you happy that I should substitute?"

Both looked at him and said, "We should be delighted if you would stand."

"OK," said James, "but you must just give me a revision course on the way batsmen ask for their guard when they come into bat. Things may have changed since I last umpired."

For the first over of the visitors' reply, James stood at square leg with his back to the pavilion, facing the cars parked along the opposite side of the ground. The first wicket fell with the score on 22, which brought Ben's grandson Dave in to bat. The score rose steadily until it reached 62 for two, which was when James was called on to make a judgement. Dave played a good on drive and set off for a run. He turned to come back for a second, but was well short of the crease when the keeper removed the bails. It was a very easy decision for James to make to give him run out, but he could not understand why Dave had chosen to go for such a risky run.

James looked around the ground in the direction in which the ball was played and then realised what must have happened. There was a small boy playing inside the boundary with a red ball. The match ball must have been held up by the lengthy grass in the outfield and Dave, when he looked to where he expected the ball to be, must have seen the little boy's red ball. While the new batsman was making his way to the crease James caught the eye of the other umpire, so that he didn't allow the game to continue. He walked over to where the small boy was playing and found the boy's mother. He advised her that playing inside the boundary was dangerous, and that with one accident already during the afternoon he didn't want to see her child hurt. Thereafter she kept her son and his ball well outside the boundary.

From 63 for three, when Dave was out, the score climbed to 129 for five. Then James had to make his next judgement and deal with a controversial situation. He was the umpire at the bowler's end when the batsman played the ball to a fielder, who threw it back to the keeper. The keeper failed to catch it, and the ball landed in front of the batsman's feet. The batsman bent down and picked the ball up to give it the keeper, who immediately appealed for 'obstruction'. Some of the fielders supported his appeal, others looked embarrassed and turned the other way. The batsman looked dumbfounded and there were shouts of 'No' and 'Never' from the pavilion. Everyone watched James to see what he would do. He didn't raise his finger. Instead he walked across to the other umpire and called the fielding captain to them. As other fielders started to join them he sent them away.

Then he spoke to the captain and the other umpire. "The appeal is for obstruction. The laws of cricket say that a player can be dismissed for obstructing the field if in doing so he impedes a fielder while the ball is in play. To all intents and purposes the ball was dead, but I had not called it so. I don't think any advantage was gained by the batsman by his action, so I cannot give him out for obstruction. As there has been an appeal I have also to consider whether he should be dismissed for 'handling the ball', which he clearly did. I think such a dismissal would normally only be given if the batsman handled the ball to stop it bouncing back onto his stumps after he had played it or if he stopped a fielder catching it. Again, I don't think the batsman's action on this occasion interfered with the passage of play. Much more important," – here he looked at the captain – "this is a friendly match and a fixture of long standing. If the batsman is given out, do you not think there is a chance of the relationship between the teams being soured? Would you like to withdraw the appeal?"

"I agree with you and I will withdraw the appeal," said the captain.

"Thank you," replied James. "I will leave you to explain the nature of the decision, but before the game continues I want a word with the batsman and the keeper." When they were brought to him, James said to them, "The appeal has been withdrawn. The ball had been returned to the keeper; if he had caught it, it would be regarded as a dead ball – that is, it is no longer in play. However," he said, looking directly at the batsman, "the batsman may only pick up the ball in that situation if he has first obtained the keeper's permission to do so. Now, I suggest you two shake hands and we'll have a two-minute break while I explain the situation to the scorers."

While he had a word with the scorers he noticed some strange activity amongst the parked cars. Seeing a paper bag blowing about on the far side of the field, he went over to pick it up and put it in his pocket, at the same time having a better look at the activity he had noticed.

When play was resumed, the batsman defended the first ball, but to the second he advanced down the pitch, swung at the ball, failed to make contact and was stumped. The score became 129 for six. There were no further incidents. Two more wickets fell before the score reached 157, giving the visitors a win by two wickets.

Hands were shaken, and players and umpires returned to the pavilion. Both the cars that had attracted James's attention had left independently before the close of play, and James, having handed in his borrowed umpire's coat, re-joined Ben and Mark. Mark had news of the injured umpire. After checks at the hospital he was allowed home, with instructions to take things quietly for a couple of days and to dial 999 if he had any adverse reactions.

Many of the players, including both captains and the batsman and the wicket keeper involved in the 'obstruction' incident, approached James and thanked him warmly for being a superb substitute umpire.

On the way home Ben and Mark wanted to know what he had said to the mother and how he had resolved the controversial appeal. James had just finished telling them when they had to stop because the road was blocked by two police cars. A female police officer came up to the car and told Mark that a car had left the road and it might be blocked for some time and they would be advised to seek another route. When Mark said he was an off-duty paramedic he was immediately welcomed as the driver was still trapped in the car, which was on its side with the front smashed into a tree. The ambulance had not yet arrived. After Mark had gone to see what help he could give, Ben and James got out of the car to look at the scene and enjoy some fresh evening air. It was then that James saw the crashed vehicle. It was one of the cars he had noticed at the match. He also recognised the female police officer. He had to cudgel his memory for a while before he remembered her name. Having done so, he approached her.

"It is Sergeant Cartwright, isn't it?"

She turned and looked at him and she recognised him immediately and exclaimed, "Mr Willoughby, what are you doing here?"

"I am one of the paramedic's passengers. We were just returning from watching a cricket match. I think I recognise the crashed car. It's a blue Peugeot, isn't it? I noticed it at the match we have just come from. There was some strange activity going on between that car and a green Vauxhall Corsa – it looked as though something was being exchanged at the back of the cars. A reflection of the sun on the windows of another vehicle enabled me to see what looked like some plastic bags and some scales being used. Might this driver have been under the influence of drugs?”

While speaking he had been facing the sun, now lower in the sky, and felt he was about to sneeze. He put a hand in his pocket for a handkerchief and discovered the bag he had picked up earlier. As he held it he noticed a strange smell. He passed the bag to the Sergeant and explained how he had come by it.

“Mr Willoughby, I wonder if you have been in the right place at the right time again. I think it has contained cannabis resin. Now, I wonder if you can give me any other information about the green Corsa?” She said this with a conspiratorial grin.

“Indeed, I think I can help. How about an 08 plate and the letters AEG?”

“Now, how did you remember that?”

‘Easy, they are the first, fifth and seventh letters which give 157. That was the number of runs needed to win the match and the match was won for the loss of eight wickets.”

“Well, thanks – that’s great. We’ll send an alert out. I’m sure a crew somewhere will spot that car and have a ‘friendly’ word with the occupants.”

“Jim,” said Ben, “did you say that the letters were AEG, because I saw that car arrive during the tea interval when I went for a walk round the ground. I only saw the back as the driver drove past several places where he could park as though he was looking for someone. I thought the letters were AEC – that’s what many of the London buses used to have on their radiators. Did you just see the front number plate?” Realising the Sergeant was also listening, he went on: “Do you think they could be false plates and the person who made them up didn’t make them identical?”

“It’s possible,” said Sergeant Cartwright. “Jim, what sort of activity did you see that caught your interest?”

“The activity was by the blue car. Two men were bending down and looking under the car and reaching just behind the nearside rear wheel. I don’t think the petrol tank is on that side.”

"We will have look as soon as we can. It shouldn't be too difficult as the car is lying on the driver's side, but as the ambulance team is now on the scene we shall have to wait until they have finished. It seems our paramedic is coming back to us."

"Well, the driver is alive and conscious, if he could be so described. He is as high as a kite, probably from cocaine. I think he has a broken leg and possibly some internal injuries or broken ribs. He wasn't wearing his seat belt, but he was saved by the airbag, which will have given him some bruising. The ambulance crew will see to him, but they may need help from the fire brigade to get him out."

"Thank you for your help," said the Sergeant, who had been joined by another officer. "Was there anyone else in the car?"

"Not now," said Mark.

James then made another contribution. "Shortly before we reached the accident I spotted someone walking, or rather staggering, towards us. I looked back after we had passed him and I saw him sit down by the side of the road. I wonder if he came from the car and if he is still around and injured."

"Good point," said Sergeant Cartwright. And turning to the other officer, "What do you think, Robbo?"

"A dog car has just arrived, Jane. I'll get the dog and his handler to have a walk up the road."

When he returned, Sergeant Cartwright introduced him to James and Ben: "This is DC Robinson." Then to the officer. "James and Ben saw some unusual activity earlier at the back of the crashed car. We need to investigate behind the nearside rear wheel when we can, which should be fairly easy as the car is on its side. The car was in company with another, of which we have details thanks to Mr Willoughby and his friend. We have an alert out for the other car."

"Mr Willoughby! You are the gentleman that tipped us off about the sheep and deer stealers, aren't you? I think we should recruit you as a part-time detective – don't you agree, Jane?"

Before Jane Cartwright could reply Ben said to James, "So you were the elderly resident who saw the van. I did wonder who it was, but you never said anything."

The driver was released from the crashed car and taken by ambulance to hospital accompanied by a police officer. The dog handler and dog returned with another male, looking far from well, and arrangements were made for him also to go to hospital. A low-loader arrived to take the car away for forensic examination; but before it was loaded, Sergeant Cartwright and DC Robinson examined the area behind the rear wheel and discovered what looked like a bolted-on compartment with a lever by which it could be opened.

As they stood up they looked at James and Ben, smiled and shouted, "Bingo! Just as you suspected. It will need some persuasion to open it as the impact has twisted the frame of the car, but we'll see to that when we get it to the pound."

The Sergeant's phone rang and after she had held a short conversation she reported, "They have found the green Corsa with a significant quantity of drugs on board. Driver and passenger have been detained and are being brought in for questioning. The car has been seized."

She then turned to James, Ben and Mark and said, "Very many thanks for your assistance. You have done a great job. I hope the cricket match was as successful."

Ben replied, "The match contained some surprises: an umpire was injured and Mark had to attend to him and send him to A and E for observation, and Jim took over as umpire for the second half, during which he had to deal with a controversial incident."

"James Willoughby, is there anything you can't do?" Sergeant Cartwright exclaimed. "You are certainly a man of many talents. We'll maybe call for you when we get another difficult incident."

Looking around, she said, "The road will be open again shortly and I'll be in touch to let you know how we progress. Goodbye for now."

THE DOG RESCUER

A seventeen-year-old girl is attacked and left unconscious, but her dog summons help from two passing strangers.

At 2.45pm on Wednesday 10 August, the second Wednesday of the month, James Willoughby was sitting on a bench in the central square of the village of Compton St Philip, having just exchanged his library books at the Mobile Library that parked in the car park next to the Church of St Philip. He was enjoying the warm sunshine and watching the few shoppers, some of them probably holiday makers, who hadn't completed their shopping in the morning. He thought he could indulge in a few minutes of idleness before walking back to his apartment.

His interest was aroused when he saw an elderly lady, probably more advanced in age than his own 85 years, pushing a wheelchair seated within which was a man likely to be older than her. They came steadily on until they reached where he was sitting. "Good afternoon," said James. "You have made valiant progress; are you going to have a rest now?"

"Thank you, but no, not just yet. I must go into the library first, but could I leave my husband here beside your bench? He is only allowed a little exercise each day as he had a heart by-pass operation last week, and stairs and steps up into the library van are certainly out of bounds."

"I shall look forward to his company, so take as long as you need. It wasn't very busy when I went in."

"Thank you," said her husband. "Don't worry, Marjorie – I shall be quite alright here. See if you can find another Agatha Christie."

The two men chatted about the weather, the pleasantness of their surroundings, the range of shops in the village and the prospects of the English cricket team due to start a Test match the next day.

When Marjorie returned, she sat down on the bench and said, "I hope I wasn't too long, but I found you a murder mystery to solve, Roger. I hope he has behaved himself and not talked about politics, Mr er.. ?"

"Willoughby, - James Willoughby. Now, your husband has been very well behaved - we have talked politics, the politics of English cricket. Is he good at solving murder mysteries?"

"Oh yes. Well, he thinks he is. He always finds a list of suspects and occasionally he gets it right – after he has found that all the others have alibis." Without a breath, she continued, "We are Roger and Marjorie Webster. Do you live in the village, Mr Willoughby?"

"Just outside the village at Clarence House in Cloverfield Road. I have been there about six months."

"Oh, I know where that is. Our home is in that direction, but only about half the distance. We live in Waterfall Close - do you know it?"

Roger eventually managed to get a word in: "Do you answer to James or Jim, Mr Willoughby?"

"Both. There's a rather di…, sorry, a rather pleasant police lady I have met a couple of times recently and she has used all three forms of address to me."

"We had better be getting back," said Marjorie. "I must make sure Roger doesn't get overtired."

"I am concerned about you getting tired, Mrs Webster. Would you like me to take a turn as helmsman?"

"I really would appreciate that, if you think you could manage. And call me Marjorie. I did find the outward journey a bit hard. I haven't pushed him so far before; but it will be another two weeks before the library comes again, by which time Roger might be walking."

James pushed Roger as far as the end of their close, when Marjorie invited him to join them for a cup of tea. He declined but said that he would be willing to take Roger for a 'walk' in his wheelchair on another occasion if that would be helpful. After a short debate, it was agreed that James would take Roger out two days later and they would follow the tarmac footpath that went out of the end of the close and on to a paved country footpath.

When he arrived at Roger and Marjorie's chalet bungalow, just before ten o'clock on Friday morning, James was asked if he had seen the short story that Marjorie had picked up in the library. It was called *Partly Old*.

"It is about James Willoughby helping the police to catch some animal rustlers," said Marjorie. 'Have you seen it and is it about you?"

She showed him her copy.

"No, I don't think I have seen this. You say you found it in the library. I didn't notice it. It probably is about me, but I wonder who wrote it. How extraordinary! It's quite nicely presented, isn't it? I shall have to read it. I wonder why it has that title."

"You can borrow this copy if you like. We have both read it."

James and Roger made steady progress to the end of Waterfall Close, but had to stop briefly on two occasions as neighbours wanted to check on Roger's recovery. Eventually they reached the little passageway between two properties that gave access to the country footpath. They talked about the neighbours they had met, and Roger said they enjoyed really good support from the other occupants of the eight dwellings in the close. Then they discussed the first day's play in the Test Match and pondered whether England had made a strong enough start to be able to set a competitive total.

James asked, "Have you made a start on the murder mystery Marjorie chose for you? She found an Agatha Christie novel, didn't she?"

"Yes, she found a Miss Marple story. A body appeared in the first chapter and after about sixty pages we already have six suspects."

"It sounds as though you are going to have your work cut out to solve that one. Miss Marple spends much of her time sitting knitting while she watches, listens and sifts thoughts in her mind. That should suit you while you are required to take things easy. Now, if your detective had been Hercules Poirot you might have had to be more energetic, especially if Chief Inspector Japp was striding about the place or Captain Hastings jumping to wrong conclusions or occasionally coming up with vital information without realising its relevance. It would be enough to wear you out. Let's hope your sleuthing can be confined to the written page today."

"Agreed, James – we'll hope for a peaceful trip enjoying the sights and sounds of the countryside. Do stop and take a rest whenever you need to. There is usually something to observe and we can forget about murders, although I did once see a sparrow hawk catch a small bird in the field to our right."

To the right of the path, behind a hawthorn hedge, was a field where the grass had recently been cut, probably for silage, and on the left there was a wood with no form of fencing. There didn't appear to be any paths going into the wood and it looked as though the land fell away some six or eight metres from the path. The only tracks were probably those made by small animals – possibly rabbits, foxes or stoats. Most of the trees were deciduous and there was sufficient light near the path for the undergrowth to establish itself with a few young hawthorn bushes and brambles near the path. The cow parsley that skirted the hawthorn hedge was no longer in flower and it looked as though the farmer had cut most of it back, which had allowed some of the later small flowers to bloom. This was clearly a place for chalk loving species and James was delighted to see patches of delicate harebells creating a blue haze against the green background of the grass.

Roger pointed out a piece of cloth caught on some brambles and one or two strands of sheep's wool attached to the hedge, but there were no sheep in the field yet. Maybe they would be brought in when all the hay crop had been gathered. They had stopped to think about the way in which the fields were used when they heard a whimpering.

By then they had travelled about 150 metres along the path and the gate by which they had entered was out of sight. Behind them, however, was a dog alone – a black cocker spaniel. As they looked at it the dog ran towards them and then turned back and went a couple of feet into the wood and then came back, whimpering again. Again, it came towards them and then turned back again and repeated its part entry into the wood.

James had turned the wheelchair round so that Roger could see the dog. "He seems in distress," said Roger.

"Certainly, strange behaviour" agreed James. "I think he might be trying to tell us something. I'll see if I can find out if anything is the matter."

Having made sure the wheelchair brake was on, he took a few steps towards the dog, who immediately came to him.

James stopped and bent down to talk to him: "Is something the matter, boy? Do you need help?"

The spaniel barked, wagged his tail and ran off a few paces, and then looked round for James. Then he came back again, grabbed at James's trouser leg and tried to pull him.

"He obviously wants me to go with him," said James. "Will you be alright if I leave you here? I think there is something in the wood that is bothering him."

"Yes, you go. I have my phone if we need to summon help. See what you can find out."

James followed the dog, who ran ahead, turned to check James was following, then ran on, again turning to check he was being followed. In this way they went several metres through the undergrowth and then James noticed a woman's shoe, then another, then clothing and then the naked body of a young woman. By now the dog was whimpering again and running round the body in distress. When James looked into the dog's eyes it was clear that the dog was appealing to him to help.

He went over to the body which appeared to be quite still. She was lying on her back, with bruising on her neck and eyes closed. He felt the girl's arms – she appeared no more than about eighteen – and felt some warmth, although initially he didn't think she was breathing. Nevertheless, he felt her neck to see if he could feel a pulse, and when he detected a slight movement, he knew he had to work fast. He was wearing a light jacket, which he had put on, because there was a cool breeze when he left home.

He took this jacket off and placed it over the girl, then turned to the dog and cried, "We've got to get help, come on." Making as quick progress as he could, he yelled to Roger, "Phone 999 for police, ambulance, possibly air ambulance as well. We may just be in time – there is a girl in there near to death."

While Roger phoned and provided their location, James bent down to the dog. "Well done, lad. We'll have some help here in a few minutes and we'll do our best to see she is alright. You have been very, very clever." He patted the dog and stroked him and was rewarded by some almost joyful tail wagging.

Roger had done a good job with his phone call, giving clear information about their location and with prompts from James like, 'clever dog', 'naked', 'about eighteen', 'weak pulse' and 'possible sexual attack', provided a clear picture of the situation. Within six minutes they heard sirens and, incredibly, four minutes later they heard the sound of a helicopter.

The ambulance team and the police arrived almost at the same time. James met them and took them immediately to the casualty, where the paramedics took over, checked and found the faint pulse and prepared the girl to be carried on a stretcher to the air ambulance, which had been able to land in the field beyond the hedge. With drips and oxygen and all the paraphernalia needed to keep her alive, she was soon on her way to the hospital.

While the girl was being attended to on the ground, police officers started examining the scene and James looked around. He saw more of the girl's clothes and the dog's lead. He drew the attention of one of the police officers to the lead: he wondered if the girl had been able to free the dog from his lead so that he might seek help. If this was the case the dog had not gone far, but rather wanted to stay near the girl.

When another police officer arrived, James recognised him as DC Robinson, whom he had met at the scene of a traffic accident about five weeks previously. DC Robinson did a quick double take and exclaimed, "Well, hello, Mr Willoughby! Incidents do seem to follow you around or rather you stumble on them. I don't suppose you can keep up your record of being able to give us a car number."

"I doubt it, but as I was walking towards Waterfall Close just after a quarter to ten a white BMW went past on its way out of the village at what

I thought was excessive speed. I only saw the letters SPD, which I thought appropriate for a car at speed."

"I'll make a note of that. You never know it might have some bearing on the assault on this girl, which I hope will only turn out to be *attempted* murder."

"Do you think you will need the dog's lead for forensics, or should I use it to take the dog home if we can find out where he belongs?"

"Yes, we do need to look after the dog, although he seems to have attached himself to you and will probably follow you wherever you go. Has he got a collar with a name or any ID on it?"

James bent down, stroking the spaniel, who seemed delighted to be the centre of attention, while he felt and found a collar and a name tag without a name but with a number and a postcode. James read out the details and said that it was a local postcode. DC Robinson called his office to see if they could identify the post code. He was given the name of the road and was also told that they had just received a telephone call from a worried lady who said that her daughter, Melanie Hardy, and her dog had not returned home when they were expected. She had heard the sirens and put two and two together. On this occasion DC Robinson thought that her two and two didn't make five. James thought he recognised the name of the road, but wasn't certain of its location. However, when he mentioned it to Roger he knew where it was. He also suggested that Roger should phone Marjorie to let her know that they were all right and the police and ambulance had not been called for them.

DC Robinson agreed that James and Roger should take the dog to its home, with a police constable to give the worried mother more details. In the meantime the 'scenes of crime' team would search for more evidence in the wood. James remembered that Roger had spotted what appeared to be a piece of cloth on some brambles. When they found the place, the police looked at the cloth and realised that it was a woolly hat. The ground around it seemed disturbed, as though a struggle had taken place there, during which the hat may have been lost. The hat, which had some black hairs attached to it was placed carefully inside an evidence bag for forensic analysis later. As the girl had fair hair, the police considered that this could provide an important lead to finding the attacker.

James, Roger and the police constable made their way to the address provided by the dog's collar tag with James looking after the dog and the Constable pushing Roger, who guided them to Melanie's home. Mrs Hardy saw them coming and met them on the doorstep wringing her hands, agitated and fearful as to what she was going to hear.

James tried to calm her. "Mrs Hardy, I am James Willoughby. My friend Roger and I were stopped in our walk by this very clever dog, who asked, in his way, for help. We don't know his name."

"Pepper," said Mrs Hardy.

Hearing his name, the dog jumped up and wagged his tail.

James continued, "I followed Pepper into the wood, where I found Melanie. It looked as though she had been attacked. She was unconscious. Roger, here, immediately rang 999 and the emergency services, including the air ambulance you probably heard, arrived within ten minutes. With the helicopter it was possible to take her quickly to hospital for a proper assessment of her condition and treatment. Melanie was far enough into the wood for us not to see her from the path, and if it had not been for Pepper we would not have known she was there. PC Porter, here, will give you more details as to where Melanie has been taken, and he will want to ask you some questions about your daughter and if you have any idea of who might have attacked her this morning."

While they were talking, a message came through to PC Porter to say that Melanie had regained consciousness and her condition was being stabilised. She was going to be kept in hospital for a few days under observation. Mrs Hardy seemed a little reassured by the news, but wanted to know where her daughter was and if she could go and see her.

Leaving Pepper with Mrs Hardy, James and Roger left PC Porter to ask his questions and make arrangements for Mrs Hardy to go to the hospital. But before they parted from the Constable, he asked them to keep their ears open for any information about strange cars or vans that had been in the area earlier in the morning. In response to a question from Roger, he also gave them a number to phone if they had anything to report. He also asked Mrs Hardy when Melanie had left home with the dog and was told about eight thirty.

As the Hardy's home was on the other side of the village to their own homes, James and Roger had to pass through the centre of the village. It was while they were crossing the village square and passing the cars parked there that they met James's friend Ben Foster.

Ben had just come out of the village store and post office, and James was surprised to see him shopping so late in the morning; so he said as much, "Hello Ben. You're shopping late today. You are usually one of the early birds."

Then he introduced Roger and Ben to each other before Ben replied,

"'I don't know, Jim. I must be getting old. This is my second visit today. I had just finished getting a few things, but still had to call at the Post Office to send a letter by recorded delivery. When I got here I collided with a young man in a hurry. He just called a quick 'Sorry, mate' and ran on. I watched him. He suddenly stopped, felt his head, then looked back at the way he had just come. He felt his head again, as though he had lost his hat, then got into a car and drove off at great speed."

"Was it a white BMW by any chance?" asked James.

"Yes, it was. I got a good look at it and did your trick and tried to get the number, but he was so quick I only got part of it. The first two letters were too dirty to read, but it went on 02 S something."

"Well done, Ben. That sounds like it, doesn't it, Roger? I can add the other two letters – PD. There was a nasty attack on a young girl earlier this morning – you may have heard the police and ambulance sirens and the air ambulance. We found her at about ten fifteen – your man may have been the attacker, especially as a woolly hat was found near the scene. Did you get a good look at him? We have a number to phone the police if we have further information."

"Oh, yes, he was clearly agitated and that made me look at him. I think I could give a good description. I was so busy observing him that I completely forgot my letter, which is why I have had to come back again."

James pondered. "I wonder if there are any police nearby. How about trying that number, Roger?"

Roger got a response immediately. He explained that they thought they had some information and where they were, and was asked if they could wait and someone would be with them shortly. In less than five minutes a police car arrived. James introduced Ben, and explained that he had been in the area at about nine forty-five and had probably seen the same car, as well as the man who drove away in it.

Ben then took up the story and described the suspect. The officer made a note, complimented Ben on his description and phoned the further details of the BMW in the hope that it could be traced. The policeman thought Ben's observation about the man appearing as though he might have just realised that he had lost a hat and that he had dark hair could provide an important clue. He expected that the hairs on the hat would be checked for DNA. He also said that the investigation of the area where the girl was found and the girl herself could provide additional clues. He thanked them again and said that he or one of his colleagues would be in touch again as the investigation progressed. As part of that investigation he said he was going to ask in the shops if anyone had seen the car and its driver. He hoped to find out what time it arrived.

James, Roger and Ben continued their journey, with Ben offering to take a turn at pushing. When they reached Waterfall Close, Ben continued on his way home for the second time that morning and Roger and James went to Roger's home to tell Marjorie about their exciting experience. Marjorie insisted on making coffee for everyone and then settled down to hear the account. They agreed that it must have been a terrible ordeal for the young girl and hoped she would make a full recovery and be able to continue with her life without severe mental scars. They also thought the dog, Pepper, should be recognised for his part in the rescue.

The three of them hoped that the police had sufficient evidence to be able to solve this near murder mystery quickly.

Roger then remembered something one of the policemen said and asked James, "What did that policeman mean when he recognised you and suggested you had a habit of stumbling on incidents and something about car numbers?" Before James could answer he continued, "In that story that Marjorie found in the library, you – if it is you in the story - spotted the number of the thieves' van. Is that what the policeman was referring to?"

"Very good, detective Roger! You found the answer without knowing that five weeks ago the police apprehended some drug smugglers after I had again noticed part of a car number. That incident was so recent that DC Robinson recognised me."

"Do you think that incident will go into print as well? If it does we shall have to make sure we read it."

"I don't know. I didn't know the rustlers' arrest would be written about and I haven't read it to check for accuracy. And I think, Roger, you have had more than enough excitement for one who is supposed to be recovering from surgery. Marjorie, I think you will have to keep him in sight. I won't offer to take him out for a few days, but I might call next Thursday after I have been to the market, unless we get any news before then."

"Here is the book, James. Let us know what you think of it."

"Many thanks. I am very curious to read it. I think I know what I shall be doing this afternoon."

By this time, midday had passed, so James bade them good-bye and made his way home.

When he arrived at his apartment block he discovered a rather battered large brown envelope in his pigeon hole, marked 'Private and Confidential'. He took it upstairs with him, pondering what it could be and noticed that it had been posted at the end of July, two weeks earlier. He wondered where it had been in that time – stuck in the bottom of a post bag or wandering around the country. He would have his lunch first and then examine his two curious items.

He warmed some soup and made himself a ham-and-lettuce sandwich, then sat down to read the story, thinking the battered envelope could wait a few minutes longer before being opened. He was fascinated by what he read. Most of the facts were accurate, except that his address had been slightly changed and the descriptions of what he might have been thinking matched his character very well. But who was the author or was there more than one person responsible for it?

Next he opened the envelope and discovered that it was from Sergeant Jane Cartwright, the police officer whom he had met on two occasions.

With the letter was another copy of Partly Old. He was asked to read the story and let her know in a week if he had any objection to it being published. Sergeant Cartwright wrote that she had had some assistance in compiling the story from two of his grandchildren and she hoped it might be a means to flushing out two collaborators of the thieves who were on police radar, but were still at large.

Well, it was a bit late now for him to object, but while he was thinking what the implications of its publication might be the telephone rang. It was Sergeant Cartwright with a message from DC Robinson to say that the driver of the white BMW had been traced and arrested pending further enquiries. There was also news of Melanie: the hospital thought she would make a full recovery, but she may not have survived if she had lain in the wood undiscovered for another hour.

While she was on the phone, he asked her about his story, which he had just read and what impact the police thought it might have. He explained that he had only just become aware of it, so she arranged a date when she would come and talk to him about possible scenarios that might follow and tell him more about the information they already had.

Nearly four weeks later, when he was sitting on the bench outside the library a cocker spaniel and its owner and her mother found him there. The dog greeted him with glee, wagging his tail and jumping up on the bench to sit beside him. When the dog had quietened down, Melanie and her mother thanked him profusely for helping her. This was Melanie's first day out since coming home from hospital. When James looked at her he realised what a beautiful girl she was – so vibrant, altogether different to the near-corpse that Pepper, the dog, and he had rescued.

The following February Melanie's attacker was convicted of sexual assault and attempted murder, and seven further sexual assaults on other girls, and sentenced to twenty years in prison.

REVENGE IS NOT ALWAYS SWEET

A gang get more than they bargained for when they try to get even with the elderly man who interrupted their illegal practices.

By the middle of September summer was drawing to a close and in a week's time the autumn equinox would have arrived. Although the Meteorologists had said the autumn had already begun James Willoughby, having lived through eighty-five summers, preferred to stick to the seasons determined by the passage of the sun rather than dates that fitted neatly into the calendar. Therefore, on the morning of Saturday 18 September he was to be found sitting on a bench in the square of Compton St Philip enjoying some late summer sun having shopped for the few items he needed. To passers-by he might have appeared to be dozing, but he was quite alert and responded immediately to a cheerful 'hello' from a lovely young lady.

The young lady was Melanie Hardy, whom he had rescued, with the help of her dog, after a vicious sexual attack five weeks earlier. If he and her dog had not acted so swiftly she would have died.

"Good morning, dear. How are you? Have you nearly fully recovered from your ordeal? And where is my little canine friend Pepper?"

"I have had to leave Pepper at home. He was scampering madly around the garden when he trod on a sharp thorn on a rose cutting that Dad had missed when he was doing some tidying up. We managed to get the thorn out, but it is still sore. We put some cream on it given us by the vet, but he has to rest it for a day or two. Trying to get Pepper to rest is not easy, I can tell you."

"Have you much shopping to do or could you spare a few minutes to have a coffee with an old man?"

"I'd love to. I only came down for a paper, mainly to see if I felt capable of going for a walk on my own. It will be like having morning coffee with a surrogate Grandad."

Melanie fetched her paper from the shop next door to the baker's. At the back of the baker's there was a little coffee bar area.

When their coffees and biscuits had been served James remarked, "You appear to have made a wonderful recovery. Are you fully healed physically and what about psychological scars? I doubt if you have been near that wood again."

"I am still a little sore in places, but nearly all the bruising has gone and I can breathe properly now. I am not sure about going down that path again – certainly not on my own. Have you been there since?"

"No, I haven't; it's a pity because I was enjoying that walk. I keep thinking I will venture that way while the weather is still pleasantly warm. If you feel you wish to try to lay a demon to rest, perhaps we could take a walk there together."

"That's a lovely idea, but I can only go at the weekend as I am returning to school on Monday. I have missed a few days already and A levels will come round quickly. I am a little apprehensive about Monday as I think my friends will want all the details."

"Melanie, my dear, if I may offer some advice, I suggest that if you think it will help you to talk about it then tell them. It may be cathartic. But if you feel you are not ready, just tell them it was a horrible experience and rather than reliving it by talking about it, you would prefer to fill your mind with other matters. I am sure they will understand, particularly if they are friends worth having. Now, tell me what subjects you are studying for A level and what other interests you have."

"Thank you for that advice. My A level subjects are English, history and mathematics. I also completed a one-year course in biology. I'm not sure what I want to study if I go to university or indeed what career I want to pursue. I am trying to keep options open. I also liked music and religious studies before I joined the sixth form."

"Do you play any musical instruments or sing?"

"Yes, I have passed Grade 5 in both piano and 'cello. I play the piano now mainly for pleasure, but I play the 'cello in the school orchestra. I used to sing in the church choir, but I fell out with the choir-mistress. I think I might re-join now that they have a new organist."

"If you re-join the choir I shall look out for you on a Sunday. I'm afraid my choir singing days are over, but it sounds as if you lead quite a busy life. Any sporting prowess?"

"Well, last term the girls were allowed to play cricket. We played two matches, winning one and drawing the other. I did quite well in that as I had played with my two older brothers, so I had developed some skill, although ......"

"They wanted you to field while they batted and bowled?" suggested James.

"Absolutely! How did you guess? But they soon realised that if they didn't allow me to take a full part I wouldn't play, and my dad backed me up."

"How old are your brothers?"

"Tom is twenty-two and at Exeter Uni, while Luke is twenty and at Bristol. Another week and then their terms start. They both played cricket for the village team during the vac. The club only has a men's team although there is talk about starting a ladies' team next year and there may be winter nets. I shall go to those if they manage to get them organised."

"It's possible I may have met your brothers, because I was asked to substitute for an umpire who was injured during a friendly match."

"Oh, it was you! I didn't go to that match, but my brothers told me about it. Didn't you have to deal with a controversial situation? They were full of praise for the way you handled it."

"Thank you." They finished their coffees and James said, "It's been lovely chatting with you Melanie. I hope we have not been too long. Do you think you had better phone your parents to let them know you are alright, but have been talking to an old bore or, if you prefer, a friend?"

"Not an old bore, Mr Willoughby – a friend, yes."

"You needn't call me Mr Willoughby. It's a bit of a mouthful. Call me James or Jim. And it might help to make the differences in our ages feel a bit less."

"I'm not sure about that, but may I call you SG? That stands for Surrogate Grandad. Both my grandfathers died before I was four and you aren't all that old, are you?"

"That sounds a grand idea. As to being old, somewhere recently I was described as 'partly old'. Time to go, I think."

"Can we meet next Saturday and, if the weather is OK, go for that walk?"

"Sure, Melanie. Meet by the bench at ten thirty? Perhaps Pepper will be recovered so that he can come with us. Here's a card with my phone number if you can't manage it."

"Great, SG! See you then. I'll phone you in any case and give you my number. Bye," she trilled, and was gone.

"Well," thought James, "that girl seems to have made a remarkable recovery. I hope her youth and resilience will help her to avoid a delayed reaction to her ordeal, particularly when the case against her attacker comes to court. I'd like to keep in touch with her so that I can give her support if she needs it – as much, that is, that an old man can give. Perhaps encouragement is the key."

While he had been thinking he had been making his way home and didn't immediately notice Marjorie and Roger Webster walking towards him, but when he looked up he recognised them.

"Good morning," called James as they got nearer. "You're walking well, Roger. Have you been able to dispense with the wheelchair?"

"That's right," said Marjorie, before Roger could get his breath for a reply. "The consultant is very pleased with his progress and I don't have to push him any longer. How are you, James?"

"Very well, thank you, I have just spent a pleasant half an hour with Melanie – the young girl we rescued. She seems to be making a very good recovery and will be going back to school to resume her A level courses on Monday."

"That's really good news," said Roger. "With the attacker in custody until his trial, it's a much better outcome than we feared at one time."

They bade each other goodbye, and James continued on his way, this time trying to remember if he had decided what to have for lunch and if he had, what it was. He was nearly home, passing the park with its small lake, when he was reminded that he had a fishcake in the fridge, and that he was planning to cook a couple of new potatoes to go with it and a green salad.

The following week was pleasantly warm, but on Friday it rained most of the day and the following day was expected to bring in a wet start to autumn. In the evening Melanie phoned and it didn't take long for them to postpone their walk for a week.

Melanie went on to tell him, "When I arrived home last Saturday humming, Mum and Dad wanted to know how I felt about walking on my own and who I had had coffee with, so I said I had had a lovely chat with SG. "Who is SG?", they wanted to know, so I told them and that we had planned to go for a walk together as a further step in my recuperation. They hoped it wouldn't be too tiring for an old man – no, they said an "elderly gentleman" – so I said "SG is only partly old." Dad pricked up his ears at that and said that he had been sent a short story called *Partly Old* by the police, and it is about someone called James Willoughby. He was sent it because he runs a security firm and may be called to provide protection. Is that you and are you in danger?"

"Oh dear," thought James, "I had better tell her."

Then he answered her, "Melanie, you are not to worry about me. If you read the story, which has got my name in it, you will see that I played a small part in the arrest of some criminals. The police think there could possibly be some repercussions, so they are making sure that none of us is taken by surprise. They may even be able to catch other members of the gang. Don't say anything to anyone else and I'll tell you more when we go for our walk next week. Sleep well tonight and have sweet dreams."

After he had put the phone down, he admonished himself, "James, you are getting forgetful – you never asked her about her week back at school."

The following Saturday was bright and sunny. Several of the trees had started to turn rich autumn colours, although a few had lost leaves during the wind and rain of the previous weekend. As the daylight each day was getting less and the temperatures cooler, James decided to wear a quilted anorak and a cap. Next week it would be October. He would have to look out his gloves and perhaps a scarf.

Arriving at the bench he had not had time to sit down when a car pulled up and out got Melanie with her dog. When Pepper had finished his excited greeting, Melanie introduced James to her father.

"I am very pleased to meet you, Mr Willoughby. I am Stuart Hardy. My wife and I would be pleased if you would come back to our home with Melanie for coffee after your walk."

"That's very kind. I don't think we shall be more than an hour."

Melanie, James and Pepper set off, with the cocker spaniel keen to get going.

James asked, "Well, my girl, how has the past fortnight been for you, particularly at school?"

"Oh, OK. I took your advice and deflected questions about my ordeal, but later I was able to give some info to my closest friends. It's been alright. I gather the teachers have been given some details, but they have not probed and we are well into term now."

It didn't take many minutes for them to leave the houses behind, and shortly afterwards they came to the gate that led to the footpath that made its way between the wood and the hedge next to the field. It was along this path that Melanie had been attacked, dragged into the wood, raped and strangled until she lost consciousness. Pepper had stayed with her until James and his friend Roger came along the path three-quarters of an hour later. The dog had alerted them and almost dragged James into the wood to rescue his mistress.

They passed through the gate, and after a few yards James stopped and made Melanie look around her. "Now just look at those trees, Mel. Look at all those different colours. Some leaves are already turning orange and red and before long we shall see the golden yellow of the field maples. There are many different species here, with quite a few silver birches. In about three weeks it will be a splendid kaleidoscope of colour, especially on a sunny day."

"It's beautiful," responded Melanie. "And look – there are sheep in the field. We must keep Pepper on the lead, although I don't think he would be able to get through the hedge."

They continued walking, and then James spoke, "In August, along this part of the path there were harebells flowering near the hedge. Do you know what harebells look like?"

"I'm not sure. Are they blue like bluebells?"

"They are blue, but smaller and much more delicate and a lighter blue. When we saw them they showed up well against the green of the grass through which they were growing. They like a chalky soil. It's many years since I last saw some, so I shall have to remember to look for them next summer. Just look how many sheep there are in that field. It certainly is a large flock and they all look quite content, don't they?"

While they walked she had linked her arm though his and looked at the things he pointed out to her. In this way they passed the spot where she had been dragged from the path, and they continued in a companionable silence for a few minutes before he spoke again, "How are you feeling, Melanie?"

"I am fine, thank you. I like walking with you, SG. Have we passed the ....?"

"We passed the place of your ordeal about six minutes ago and nothing nasty happened."

"Oh, I didn't notice and I don't think Pepper did. Thank you for guiding me past it."

"Pepper knew where we were. He stopped slightly, smelled the air and looked up at you and then carried on. His paw doesn't seem to be bothering him, does it? If we carry on this path, can we get back to the village?"

"Yes, we can. The path will turn to the right soon, and a bit later there is another path off to the right which will bring us eventually to the Coltsford Road. It's only about seven or eight minutes to home from there." She paused for a few seconds and then said, "I have read the story *Partly Old.* Is it all true or just a story? And if it is true, does the fact that they have sent Dad a copy mean you are in danger?"

"Now, you have asked several questions there. Just as the man in the story is partly old, so the story is partly true. I am not sure how it came about, but I think it was a combined effort of the police sergeant and two of my granddaughters after they met at the stables where they all have horses. I believe one of the criminals was overheard making a threat that they would get their revenge against the person who tipped off the police which led to their arrest. The three who were caught have been detained until their trial, but there may be other members of the gang who may try to exact that revenge. Although some of the story is accurate, some is not. You might think that I have been set up as a decoy, but I have protection. This little button in my lapel is a tracking device so the police – and possibly, by now, your dad – know where I am. Satisfied?"

"Yes, but I hope no one will try to hurt you. Please, be careful. How many grand kids have you got?"

"Five – three girls and two boys. My son has two girls, Carole and Lucy, and one boy, Robin, and my daughter has a boy, Phil and a girl, Holly. Their ages range from twenty-nine to twenty, and three have birthdays near Christmas. You can probably work out which were the Christmas babies." Then he added, with a smile, "I also have a surrogate granddaughter."

"That's me, yes? Do you think I could meet them and see the horses?"

"I think that might be arranged. I'll see what we can do."

By now Pepper had started to pull on his lead, because they were nearly home.

James was warmly welcomed by Melanie's parents, and the four of them were soon sitting down with warm mugs of coffee. Stuart and Becky Hardy asked how the walk had gone, and Melanie immediately responded by saying that she felt no concern or apprehension when they passed the place where she had been assaulted. In fact, she explained that SG had been busy talking to her and showing her things and they had passed the spot without her knowing where it was. She said she had felt quite safe all the time, but when SG had answered her question about issues around the *Partly Old* story she felt worried about his safety.

Before Stuart could say a word, James told Melanie that her dad had probably been monitoring their progress all the time. Melanie asked her dad if that was true.

He replied, "I looked for and saw the button in Mr Willoughby's lapel, and he knew that I had seen it. We didn't need to say anything."

The two men smiled at each other as though they knew things of which mother and daughter were ignorant.

Becky Hardy asked, "Have you two been in touch with each other before?"

"Yes and no," said James. "Let us say that we both have access to the same information, and perhaps our contact has been through telepathy rather than telephony."

"I think, though," said Stuart, "perhaps we do need to have a chat about procedures if they become necessary. Shall I give you a lift home? We can talk on the way."

"Can I come, Dad?" asked Melanie.

"There are matters your SG and I need to discuss that need not concern you, and you could be really helpful to your mother getting lunch ready. I think you are a very lucky girl to have a champion like James."

"I know," replied Melanie. "Thank you, dear SG." And she skipped across the room and placed a kiss on his cheek.

"You have my number – you can always phone me if you want to have a chat. Work hard at school next week. Let me know if you re-join the church choir." Then he turned to Becky Hardy and said, "Thank you very much for the coffee. I think Mel is going to be all right, she seems to be making an amazing recovery."

When they were in the car Stuart asked James if he had his panic button with him. James confirmed that it was in his pocket. Stuart informed him that the panic button also contained a radio transmitter so that sounds and voices could be heard by the police and at his own security base. He went on to say, "We have a new piece of kit which can be fixed to your headgear or placed in your lapel. It combines both a camera and a radio. Both means of communication can be received and recorded by those monitoring your movements. It sounds a bit invasive, but if you tap the device, the monitoring station will be alerted and, if necessary, help can be despatched immediately. We also have the facility of having covert observation located in your vicinity. I will bring you the equipment on Monday and show you how to use it."

"That all sounds a bit like cloak and dagger stuff. I hope it brings the required result. When do you think anyone might strike?"

"We don't expect any action for several days, but we need to be prepared. He, or they, will need to make enquiries and we hope to pick up that activity. We shall be checking CCTV installations in the area – including shops, pubs, eating places, the mobile library and newspaper offices. We shall be asking personnel in those places to inform us immediately if they are questioned about the location of Cloverhill Court or if they know of a Mr James Willoughby. Copies of *Partly Old* will also be visible in several outlets, and we shall want to know if anyone shows interest in it."

"I see. Have you considered that someone might pose as a reporter and visit Sam Small at Buckland's Farm, perhaps with a story about wanting to talk to the person who is to be given an award for his quick thinking?"

"No, I don't think we have. That's a very valid point. I'll follow it up. I'll call with the kit on Monday morning – will 10 o'clock be OK? Good, I'll see you then."

On the following Wednesday evening Melanie phoned.

"SG, how are you?" she said. "I want to ask you something. It's my eighteenth birthday on the 30th and Mum and Dad asked if I wanted a party, but I said I'd like to go out for a meal. Will you be one of my guests? It's a Saturday." She named a place and a time and said transport would be arranged.

He gave the impression of consulting a busy engagement diary and then said, "Melanie, my dear, I am greatly honoured to be invited. My diary says I can accept as I have no other engagements for that date. How lovely – a very special day!"

The copies of the story had been placed in the shops and most of the shopkeepers had read them, but no enquiries had been made that triggered an alert and James began to think that nothing would happen. When he went to the mobile library, on Wednesday 13 October, he saw a man sitting on 'his' bench reading *Partly Old*.

When he came out of the library, having changed his books, the man spoke to him. "Excuse me, mate – can you tell me where Cloverhill Court is?"

James pulled his anorak more tightly round him, touching the button in his lapel and said, "Cloverhill Court, did you say? I can't think of anywhere with that name, although I haven't lived here many months. There is a Cloverfield Road." And he gave the man some fairly vague directions. The man then walked across the square and got into a black Audi and James made a note of the number as he drove off. He noticed that a few seconds later another car passed him and followed the Audi.

As he was walking home, a car drew up alongside him and he was relieved to see that Stuart was the driver.

"Would you like a lift?" Stuart called. When they reached Clarence House, they spotted the Audi parked farther up the road. James noticed the man who had asked for directions walking along the road looking for names on the houses, some of which were quite large and set back from the road. He could see that there was another man sitting in the passenger seat of the car.

Stuart said, "I'll come in with you to make sure you are safely home."

On the way in James noticed that the list of residents was incomplete and his name had been removed while a different name was against his apartment number. Obviously, one of Stuart's team had been busy.

"Stairs or lift?" said Stuart.

"What do you advise?"

"If you can manage them, I suggest the stairs."

They climbed the stairs and James realised how much he had appreciated his car ride as he found himself getting short of breath. When they reached his flat Stuart asked him to check that nothing had been disturbed and then asked about his plans for the rest of the day and the next, suggesting he keep his surveillance device switched on night and day. As James's plan for the next day was a trip to the weekly market, Stuart wanted to know the time he would leave his apartment so that he could provide a 'tail' who would keep him in sight covertly.

James slept well, but woke with what he thought was a touch of indigestion. He decided on a small breakfast of cereals and a slice of toast. His other option was a boiled egg, but he remembered that he had used his last egg so needed to get some from the market.

He made his purchases at the market and then feeling a little tired, he sat down on a convenient seat for a rest before returning home. He had been there for only a minute when the man who asked him for Cloverhill Court appeared in front of him with another man.

He immediately pressed the button in his pocket and then said as coolly as he could manage, "Oh, good morning, did you find the place you were looking for yesterday."

"We think we have found what we were looking for. I think you are James Willoughby as we heard someone address you by that name. We aren't very happy with you as you interfered with our business in August by interrupting our supply chain."

His voice had been gradually getting more menacing, but James tried to remain calm and asked, "What business are you in and how did I inconvenience you?"

"We are wholesale meat suppliers to butchers, and a consignment did not reach us, because you decided to interfere. It has harmed our business, and we think you should be harmed as well."

"Right – I think I understand. You supply retailers such as butchers' shops, and someone supplies you with animals or carcasses that have been bought at market. The animals previously have been reared at considerable cost of time and expense by farmers, who in their turn may have bought young animals at market. So you must be talking about a break in the supply chain where your suppliers, instead of buying, stole the animals. Whether you knew about it or not, you received stolen goods which is, I believe, a criminal offence. And I suggest that you keep that knife in your pocket before you are seen to be carrying an offensive weapon which is another indictable offence."

"A pretty speech, my friend. You explain it so well, so it seems you knew what you were doing when you informed on us."

"So you admit it was your organisation."

'We have gone to considerable trouble to find you, and we are not going to be put off. I am just debating how we should teach you a lesson."

They had been so busy threatening James they had not realised that four of the people behind them had not just been passing by. So, they were surprised when their arms were suddenly pinned behind their backs and secured by handcuffs.

"Well done, Jim," said DC Robinson. "I think we have all that on video and it should be the evidence we need to dismantle this illegal operation."

As the two men were led away to a couple of police vans, Stuart appeared. He took James back to his apartment, where Sergeant Jane Cartwright met them. After a debriefing session they left James to rest, which he did while sitting in his chair gazing at the countryside.

During the next few days both of his families visited and heard about his experience. Adam, his son and Rachel had had an account from the Sergeant via their daughters who had discussed the case while seeing to their horses. His daughter, Ruth, with her husband, Michael Dawson, learned how the 'old geezer', as once Phil, their son, had unknowingly described his grandfather, had again helped the police with the arrest of criminals.

Late on Friday 29th October, Melanie answered the front doorbell and had a large bouquet of flowers thrust into her arms. The card simply said 'Happy 18th Birthday, Melanie. Much love, SG.'

Melanie took her time coming down to breakfast the next day, but was in time to hear her mother on the phone say, "I am so sorry to hear that. He will be missed, but hopefully he will recover. Thank you for letting me know."

"What was that about?" asked Melanie.

"That was Rachel Willoughby, SG's daughter-in-law. I'm afraid SG won't be with us this evening. He had a heart attack during the night. He managed to call the emergency services and has been taken to hospital.

His son is with him, and his daughter is on the way. He is conscious and sends you his love and hopes you will have a lovely day."

Melanie clapped her hands over her face and said in a small voice, "Oh no, he won't die, will he?"

OBSERVATION REWARDED

When the police decided to make a special award to an elderly citizen who had assisted them in solving crimes, they did not expect him to solve another case for them on the evening of the award ceremony.

When she woke on the Sunday morning, after the dinner the night before to celebrate her eighteenth birthday, Melanie Hardy considered how she would spend her day. She remembered that there were two things she had decided she must do. With her family and friends, she had enjoyed a lovely meal, but it was tinged with sadness because one person had been missing. This was her eighty-five-year-old friend SG, a short name for her surrogate grandad. He had suffered a heart attack during the previous night and had been admitted to hospital. She had met Mr James Willoughby after, at the prompting of her dog Pepper, he had rescued her when he had discovered her unconscious in the woods near her home. She had been subjected to a serious sexual attack. The attack had occurred about ten weeks earlier and they had since become good friends.

Melanie intended to phone SG's daughter-in-law Rachel, who had informed her of SG's heart attack. She wanted to find out if he was recovering and if she could visit him in the hospital. She also planned to attend the morning service at St Philip's church to pray for SG's recovery to full health. It was as a result of conversations she had enjoyed with SG that she had decided to start going to church again and to re-join the choir, which she had left in a fit of pique two years previously.

When she contacted Rachel she learned that James was making good progress, but that he was still under observation and visiting was restricted. However, if his improvement continued it may be possible for Melanie to visit him on Tuesday evening. Rachel thanked her for phoning and said she would pass on Melanie's good wishes. She knew he would appreciate her concern and would look forward to seeing her.

On Tuesday evening when Melanie found the correct hospital ward, she was pleased to see SG sitting in a chair in conversation with a younger man. It was his son Adam whom she had not met previously. She was greeted warmly by both men and told that SG should be able to leave hospital by the end of the week. The discussions taking place were about whether SG could continue to live in his apartment on his own. Adam lived 20 minutes from the apartment, but it took SG's daughter Ruth nearly an hour each way to see her father. They were considering whether it could be arranged for a carer to look in a couple of times a day, so Melanie offered to call on her way home from school. She was restricting the time she devoted to her own social life in order to concentrate on her A level studies, so she could easily spare an hour each afternoon. If she alighted from the bus one stop early she could be at SG's apartment in two minutes.

Adam thought he could see a way forward. He said, "If Ruth can phone you at breakfast time each morning, Dad, I will try to call in at some point during the day, when I can also check if you need any shopping and then Melanie can spend some social time with you on her way home from school."

"I could help get you a meal if you wish," offered Melanie.

"That all sounds very well," replied James, "but we probably won't need to do it for very long. I will soon be able to manage again, but Melanie, do you think your dad would be able to fetch you home? It might well be dark by the time you have spent an hour with me and, after your nasty experience, I would not be happy with you walking home alone. You won't even have Pepper to look after you."

"That's true. I'll talk to dad, I'm sure he will sort something out, especially as he holds you in high regard."

"If all else fails we'll order you a taxi," concluded James.

"I think we now have a good basic plan," said Adam. "You keep telling me about your girlfriends, Dad; no doubt one or more of them will want to come and fuss over you. I expect Ruth and Michael will try to visit as well. Should we tell the hospital staff that we have your post-hospital care sorted so they can discharge you when they think you have made sufficient progress and not worry about you bed blocking?"

"Bed blocking, what's that?" asked Melanie.

Adam explained, "That's what happens when a patient is well enough to leave the hospital, but they may not be able to manage on their own and there is no suitable care arrangement in place. So they remain occupying a bed that could be used by someone else."

They continued chatting until the bell signalled the end of visiting time. Adam discovered that Melanie had come by bus and was proposing to get a bus home or else ring her dad to fetch her, so he offered her a lift home. On the way he thanked her for taking an interest in his dad and she explained that both her grandfathers had died before she was four and she was just realising what she had missed without the relationship she was now establishing with SG. She said that he treated her as an adult, but also sometimes as a child when he shared his knowledge and wisdom. She had no-one outside the family that she could talk to as she did with SG. Somehow, she felt secure when she was with him. Perhaps it was because of the circumstances of their meeting that she felt a special bond existed between them.

Adam and his sister had been informed by James how he had met Melanie, but both had been circumspect in their conversations with friends and other members of the family about the developing relationship between their father and this lively young lady. The fact that James had come to Melanie's rescue after she had been the subject of a violent sexual attack that had left her close to death meant that their friendship was no ordinary relationship. Adam had not been aware that Melanie had missed out on being spoiled by a grandad and knowing the bonds that his father had with his own children he realised how beneficial to Melanie's recovery the relationship could be. He also considered that his father would benefit from time with Melanie for it would help him to focus on her development and not to dwell on his own health and aging.

On the first Monday of November Adam brought James home from hospital. As a self-employed accountant he was able to adjust his diary so that he could spend time each day with his father. He was grateful that this was November and not the busy month of January when many of his clients would need to have their tax returns submitted before the end of the month. It was also helpful that his twenty-nine-year-old daughter Carole, who was his assistant in the business, had decided that her wedding to Nicholas should be scheduled for the middle of February. This was the second marriage for both of them as both had lost their first partners to cancer. It was during their visits to the hospice that they had become acquainted.

James and Adam had not been in the apartment with its wonderful views for more than five minutes when there was a knock on the door. It was Elsie, one of the other residents of Clarence House, who had come to welcome him home and to see what help she could give. She had just made a cottage pie and there was enough for two. Would James like her to bring a portion up to him when it was cooked?

"Yes," Adam thought, "Dad's girlfriends will keep an eye on him. I just hope they don't tire him. It looks as though this Elsie has lots of news to share with him, and I bet she can talk."

When Adam arrived on Wednesday, he found his dad just finishing his meal having cooked himself a piece of gammon with potatoes, peas and broccoli. So he had been demonstrating his independence and was clearly feeling better. While they were talking for a few minutes and looking at the countryside through the balcony window there was a knock on the door. It was Elsie from downstairs. "I'm just about to go to the Wednesday Club meeting in the Church Hall. I don't expect you will be able to join us today, James, but I'm sure the members will want to know that you are 'on the mend'. I don't know if you are aware that the committee has fixed the Christmas Party for the 22nd of December. They are starting to collect numbers; shall I put your name down? I know you haven't been to one before, but it is usually a very happy occasion with tea and cakes, a quiz, some entertainment and carol singing." James opened his mouth to reply, but Elsie was in full flow and carried on. "Old Miss Greatrex usually plays the piano for the carols. I say 'old' but she must be younger than both of us. It's just the way she plays the carols that makes us think she is old."

When she took breath, James replied, "That sounds a fun afternoon. Yes please, sign me up and give them all my good wishes. I like singing carols. I'm sure Miss Greatrex plays very well, even if her style is, er, distinctive." As he said the last word he looked at Adam and raised his eyebrows.

Adam thought, "Dad's clearly regaining his form. I shall be interested to hear his account of the carol singing after the party."

Elsie left to go to the meeting, after which Adam said to his dad. "Do you miss your piano? I'll fetch you over to our house when nobody else is home and you can play our instrument. You could even practise some carols in case Old Miss G is older than Elsie thinks and doesn't make it."

"I should enjoy seeing if my fingers still work, but I'm not expecting to be asked to deputise – I have done my deputising for this year with my stint as a replacement umpire. I don't think anyone, other than my friend Ben, knows that I used to play. Now, what news of your girls? Are the plans for their weddings going ahead well?"

"Yes, I think things are fairly well advanced for Carole and Nicholas. They seem to be very happy with each other. It will be really good to see them settled after the traumas that they have both been through. Nick's daughter and Carole's son both have parts to play in the ceremony. As for Lucy and Tom, their wedding won't take place until Easter. I don't know much about their plans, but I have a feeling that horses might put in an appearance somewhere."

"I rather thought that the equine family members might be included somehow."

"I think it's a case of 'watch this space'. I wouldn't put it past Lucy to arrive at the church on horseback, riding side-saddle in her wedding dress. As long as she doesn't expect me to accompany her by horse."

"That reminds me. I promised Melanie that I would see if a suitable time can be arranged for her to meet your girls and their horses."

"I'm sure something could be arranged. She seems a lovely girl: we had a good chat when I took her home after the hospital visit. I'm glad you still have an eye for a pretty girl."

With that parting tease, Adam left.

The arrangement worked well whereby Ruth phoned in the morning, Adam called in at some point in the day and Melanie spent time with James on her way home from school. By the middle of the month James was able to collect his newspaper from downstairs without using the lift and had been for a stroll in the local park near his home. On Thursday morning 19 November after Ruth had phoned, he walked, accompanied by his friend Ben, to the market in the centre of the village of Compton St Philip and made a few purchases, including a box of locally made chocolates which he intended to give Melanie.

When Adam arrived at lunchtime, he found his father grilling sausages to accompany vegetables that were cooking in a saucepan on the hob. They shared the meal together and Adam realised that James was almost fully recovered, and he may be able to monitor his progress on some days just with a phone call.

After they had eaten Adam reported, "I have spoken to Ruth about arrangements for Christmas. We wondered if you would like to spend Christmas Day with Ruth and Michael, stay overnight with them and then one of them could bring you to us for Boxing Day."

"Goodness, yes, Christmas isn't far away now: what is it, about five weeks? I shall have to think about Christmas shopping. But that sounds like a lovely arrangement, Adam. Thank you very much. I accept, but how shall I get to Ruth's; I doubt if there will be any buses or taxis operating – it's a pity I haven't still got a car."

"Don't worry about that. Ruth will organise it, probably sending Michael or Phil to fetch you."

"Of course, I keep forgetting that my grandchildren are all adults. I'm sure Phil will be happy to collect 'the old geezer'."

"You're not going to let him forget that, are you?"

"I shall have a bit of fun at his expense, if I have a chance."

Melanie arrived shortly before 5 o'clock, rather damp after being caught in a rain shower between the bus stop and Clarence House. James welcomed her and told her, "Come in Mel, and take off those wet things and we'll put them to dry for when you go home. Have you had a good day?"

"Thank you, SG. I nearly missed my stop, because one of the boys from the lower sixth asked me why I get off the bus a stop early these days."

"A boyfriend?"

"No; he is rather silly and his conversation, at times, is almost infantile. I just said that I go to see my boyfriend who is a very clever detective." She had taken her coat off and nipped into the bathroom to remove her skirt and replace it with sports shorts she had in her bag. When she returned with the wet things she remarked, "I didn't think it was going to rain."

"It is a bit of a surprise. It was lovely this morning, quite warm when I went to the market, where…"

"You've been out and to the market!" exclaimed Melanie, "Well done, I hope you didn't get too tired. Did you go alone?"

"No, don't fret, love. I went with my friend Ben. And, while I was there ….. Oh, what have I done with it? I remember."

He got out of his chair and went into the kitchen.

When he returned, he explained, "One of the things grandads are expected to do is to spoil their grandchildren, so I bought you a little present." Thus saying, he gave her the box of chocolates.

"Thank you, what a lovely surprise." As he was still standing she stood up and gave him a big hug.

They could hear the rain hammering on the balcony just outside the window, which caused SG to enquire, "Is your dad coming to fetch you this evening?"

"No, but Mummy is. Dad has a meeting with some of the church people. Apparently, there have been some thefts of lead from churches in the north of the county and the Church Council have asked dad, with his security hat on, to advise them on any steps they should take to protect the lead on our church."

"I didn't know that lead thieves were active in this county. I shall have to get my field glasses out and keep an eye on the three village churches I can see from my window."

"Knowing how criminals manage to attract your attention, you are bound to spot something," laughed Melanie.

"I doubt I shall see anything. I may take a look before I go to bed, but they probably won't start their work that early. And anyway, I have other things to think about. Adam reminded me that Christmas is not far away and my neighbour Elsie was telling me about the old folks' Christmas Party and persuading me to let her sign me up to attend."

"What did Adam say? Is he arranging for you to go to his home for Christmas?"

"Yes. I am invited to Ruth's for Christmas Day, then stay overnight and they will take me to Adam's for Boxing Day."

"So you won't be at home for Christmas?"

"No, my dear, but I would like to stay at home for New Year and invite one or both families here, but I don't know whether I can get them all in and as for catering ...."

"I can help you with that. Oh, sorry, I shouldn't presume you would want me."

"If your family could spare you, I would be delighted. I'm sure we could arrange something suitably festive between us."

At that moment the phone rang. James stood up to fetch the phone, but Melanie beat him to it while he was saying, "I wonder who that could be at this hour?"

When Melanie had handed him the instrument, a voice said, "Hello James, Jane Cartwright here. I have only recently heard that you have been unwell. I hope you are recovered now."

"Thank you, Jane. I am making good progress. Members of the family have been keeping an eye on me and Melanie Hardy has been visiting me each afternoon and is here now."

"That's good. I have been asked to invite you to the County Police Awards' Evening on Friday 3 December. This is a ceremony when awards are given to police officers who have done something meritorious, such as this year acknowledging the bravery of an unarmed officer who disarmed and arrested a dangerous criminal, without any back up available."

"It sounds an interesting evening. Are you sure you want me there?"

"Oh yes; there is usually a good spread of refreshments and the Chief Constable and other senior people will be there. It is a time when the police thank members of the public and business associates who have helped them during the year. I understand that Mr Hardy is being invited in recognition of his assistance with security. There will be an official invitation in the post with all the details, but I wanted to forewarn you and to check that you are well."

"Well, thank you very much and it is good of you to check on an oldie like me."

When the call was ended Melanie could not contain herself any longer and burst out with, "Oh, how exciting, you see you are a celebrity now. I never thought I would know someone who was in the public eye. And Daddy is being invited as well. I wonder if he will let me go with him. Perhaps he will give you a lift. How wonderful!"

"Calm down, young lady, or you won't be able to concentrate on anything else this evening. Now, go and see if your clothes have dried and then we can continue our discussions of that book you have been reading."

A week later when Melanie arrived James told her that the New Year's Day gathering was feasible. Ruth and her family had arranged to go to see Michael's parents so it would be just Adam's family of nine, plus Melanie and himself to cater for. Rachel had suggested a finger buffet, and she would bring some party food.

He reported, "Ruth said her family would be sorry to miss this first gathering in my apartment but suggested that we should have another 'do' at the end of February to celebrate my birthday."

"Oh yes, SG, when is your birthday?"

"Well, Mel, you may find it difficult to believe this, but sometimes it is 28th February, or the 29th or even 1st March if that is a Saturday."

"I don't understand: you have a flexible birthday? .... Oh, of course, you must have been a leap day baby." Seeing him smiling she exclaimed, "That means you've only had about twenty-one birthdays and ..... and that means you are not too old to be my boyfriend."

"Yes, my dear, and if I were sixty years younger, I would be pursuing you and that silly boy on the bus wouldn't stand a chance."

At this she giggled and replied, "That boy has no chance while I can come and see you. But we shall have to start planning for NYD, that is New Year's Day."

"You're right, we shall have to start making plans. As to boyfriends, there will be other boys who will be interested in you and when you find one that suits you, I hope you will introduce me to him."

"I will, because I should like your approval. Now let's plan."

By the time she left that evening they had a clear plan and a timetable for making sure nothing was overlooked.

On the evening of Friday 3 December Stuart and Becky Hardy, Melanie's parents, with Melanie and James attended the Police Awards evening as guests. They had only been in the Hall a couple of minutes when Sergeant Jane Cartwright and DC 'Robbo' Robinson found them. Jane greeted James, "You are looking well."

"I am feeling well. I don't know if this is the right time, but I spotted something on the way here."

"You've not solved another crime for us?"

"I don't know, but Stuart had to stop in a line of traffic opposite a side road. A car went down the road, but had to wait for a cyclist to come from the opposite direction before it could proceed and pull round a parked lorry. The lorry had a tarpaulin on it, but highlighted in the car's headlights, some twisted metal that looked like lead was poking out."

"I expect you noticed the lorry's registration."

"I did, thanks to the strength of the car's headlights. Here, I've written it on my invitation and the name of the road."

"Brilliant, I will just disappear and make a call while Robbo finds your party your places."

The ceremony was soon underway, and five police officers were given awards for the special contributions they had made. When they had been applauded and sat down, the Chief Constable announced that a special award was to be made to a member of the public and he asked Sergeant Cartwright to provide the details.

HUMBERSIDE POLICE
Police Awards Ceremony
CERTIFICATE

Sergeant Cartwright stood up and addressed the audience. "This special award goes to someone who over the last six months has assisted the police by providing information from observations he has made that has enabled us to solve four crimes, some of which you will have become aware of through press reports. They include cattle stealing and selling unregistered meat products, drug smuggling, and sexual assault." Here she stopped and looked to the back of the Hall, then continued, "And I have just had confirmation that tonight he spotted something that has enabled officers, while we have been in this Hall, to arrest a gang who have been stealing lead from church roofs. Would Mr James Willoughby come forward to collect this special award. I am sure James will forgive me for telling you that he is eighty-five years old and a most remarkable and talented man."

The thunderous applause that followed this announcement made Melanie feel very proud of her SG and she felt quite emotional with tears of joy in her eyes. When they were served with refreshments people kept coming to their table to offer congratulations and then press reporters and cameramen appeared. As they took their pictures of James, Melanie held up the certificate and hid behind it. She wasn't sure whether she wanted her picture in the newspaper.

On the way home James invited Melanie, if she hadn't made other plans, to join him when Adam called for him the following afternoon. This would be an opportunity for her to visit his granddaughters' horses.

Her excited reply was, "I'd love that. I have a hair appointment in the morning, but the afternoon is free. What time shall I come to you?"

"We'll collect you just after two. Can you be ready then?"

At Adam's home, Melanie was introduced to Carole and Lucy who soon whisked her away in order to visit the Stables. Rachel and Robin were both out shopping independently. As Adam needed to spend a few minutes preparing some papers to take to a client he was due to see on the following Monday, he invited James to amuse himself at the piano. He found his fingers were still capable of playing carols and tried a movement from a Beethoven sonata, until Rachel returned. She made tea for James, Adam and herself and they chatted about the Christmas arrangements. They heard some lively chatter before the three girls put in an appearance. They had met Police Sergeant Jane at the Stables and she gave Melanie an update on the arrest of the lead thieves.

Carole and Lucy were delighted to relay to their parents the information they had gained about the Awards' Ceremony and particularly their grandfather's involvement.

After the excitement of the weekend James was pleased to have a few days to rest. On the Monday before the Wednesday Club Christmas Party, Elsie informed James that she had ordered a taxi and asked if he would like to travel with her. He was pleased to accept and when they arrived James's friend Ben, who was on the committee, came to him with a tale of woe. "Miss Greatrex is unwell, so we have no-one to play the piano for the carols. I remember you telling me you used to play. Do you ....'

"I think I know what's coming. Yes, I'll help. Have you a music copy of the carols you wish to sing?"

The refreshments had been prepared and served by some younger members of the W.I., including Melanie's mother, but they retired to the kitchen when the carol singing began. Melanie was helping with washing up, but after a short time everyone in the kitchen stopped to listen. One of the ladies remarked, "That's surely not Old Miss G playing. It is real quality playing and the singing is so much better than usual. I wonder who it is."

Melanie poked her head round the door and quickly shut it again. "Mum," she exclaimed, "it's SG. I didn't know he could play. Isn't he wonderful!"

"Who is SG?" several voices asked.

"Oh, I'm sorry, I should have said Mr James Willoughby."

Melanie and Becky were bombarded with questions and when they heard that James had helped to solve several crimes, some remembered reading about him in the paper.

Christmas came and went, church services were well attended and Christmas presents were given and received. Melanie was overjoyed and quite emotional when she opened her present from SG. Inside a small box was a dainty purple amethyst pendant on a silver chain. There was a note explaining that amethyst is considered to have powerful protective properties. It was given with his love and a wish that it would ensure that nothing and nobody would harm her again.

Melanie arrived early for the New Year's Day party to help James with preparations in readiness for Adam and Rachel and the rest of the family. She had put her coat in the bedroom and donned an apron while she was busy in the kitchen. Rachel took the party food she had brought with her into the kitchen and she and Melanie plated it ready for later. When they emerged from the kitchen everyone else, including the two young children, had arrived. Melanie went into the bedroom to remove her apron and then joined the company. James was waiting for her as she closed the bedroom door and, as some had not previously met her, he introduced her. "This is Melanie, my beautiful young lady friend, my Cinderella, who has been looking after me since I was ill and has helped with the planning and preparation of this party."

All eyes turned to look at her and without her apron she was transformed into a truly beautiful princess. At five foot, seven inches tall wearing a dress that suited her slim figure and complemented her amethyst pendant, her fair hair and blue eyes supported by subtle make-up that enhanced rather than obscured her natural colouring, her smile lit up the room as James introduced her to each member of his family. Nicholas and Tom welcomed her warmly, the children shyly came and held her hands, but twenty-one-year-old Robin stood open-mouthed, looking bewitched, before coming to his senses and greeting her with a bow.

The afternoon passed quickly. Inevitably, on New Year's Day, the conversation turned to future plans, chief among which were two weddings by Easter. When all had eaten Melanie began the task of clearing up and taking china and cutlery to the kitchen. As she did so she looked directly at Robin, who sprang to his feet saying, "May I help you after that lovely meal?"

As Melanie and Robin disappeared into the kitchen, Adam and Rachel looked at each other and exclaimed, "Would you believe it?" and his sisters cried, "Have you ever seen him help in the kitchen?", while someone else remarked, "Is it a New Year's Resolution or has he been dazzled by beauty?"

James left it ten minutes before he ventured into the kitchen to fetch a box of chocolate truffles. He left two for the 'kitchen staff' and then offered the box round to the rest of the family. "Are they getting on alright out there?" inquired Rachel.

James summarised the situation he had observed. "I think productivity is rather slow, but discovery is being given priority. It could be that the word 'surrogate' is time-limited and in two or three years' time we may be using the term 'grandad-in-law'."

"SAY CHEESE"

A fraudster makes a mistake when he selects an elderly man for a scam as the victim and his assistant plan a trap.

Tuesday 4 January dawned bright, clear and cold. James Willoughby could discern signs of frost when he looked through the window of his living room at the splendid view his south facing hillside apartment afforded him. The old year had departed quietly with mild, misty and mizzling weather as though it didn't have the energy to offer anything invigorating. Free from malevolent weather, Christmas and New Year festivities had been celebrated without undue interference from the elements.

The mild spell had enabled farmers to leave their livestock in the fields. James watched as a tractor drove into a field where cattle were standing waiting. As soon as the tractor stopped the beasts converged on it in expectation of the hay from the trailer being spread around for them to feed. His attention was then caught by movement in another field where two horses were seeking any fodder they could find. A footpath wound its way along the outside of the field hedge where a dog and its walker were taking their exercise along the path. The horses ambled over to the hedge in hope and were rewarded by being offered food, probably apple or carrot. The way this little scene was enacted suggested to James that it was probably a morning ritual.

Giving no heed to his eighty-five years and feeling the need for a walk, James decided to go to the village. The Country Trust Bank should be open today and possibly the Butchers: he would buy some fresh meat for his midday meal if the butcher had been able to replenish his stocks.

He left his apartment and maintained his regime of walking down the two flights of stairs to the ground floor. As he arrived at that level his neighbour Elsie, whose apartment was below his, emerged from the lift with handbag, stick and shopping trolley. They greeted each other and checked that they were both setting off for the same destination.

Considering she looked rather encumbered James offered to pull the shopping trolley. Keeping each other company, they walked to the village and spent the ten minutes talking about the weather, the festivities recently celebrated and prospects for the coming year. They were both members of the afternoon Wednesday Club and they speculated about the programme for the coming weeks of winter.

Entering the Bank, James and Elsie were still chatting when a voice called, "Hello Elsie, hello James, Happy New Year to you both." It was their friend Marjorie Webster who was already in the queue. They responded in like manner and the two ladies soon got into conversation. James looked round and noticed that Derrick the butcher was being served. He also noticed a man, in a rather expensive looking coat, sitting at a table in a corner with papers in front of him, possibly filling in a form. He hadn't seen the man before but then he himself had not been resident in the area for a year yet.

When Derrick left the counter, he spotted James and offered a loud greeting, "Good morning, Mr Willoughby, Happy New Year to you. You might like to know I've just taken delivery of some beautiful pork chops, just as you like them."

James replied, "Happy New Year to you as well, Derrick. I intend to call on you this morning when I have finished in here," and continued, teasing, "I shall be interested to see your special New Year bargains." Marjorie took Derrick's place at the counter and Elsie and James moved up which brought James level with the cash machine near to the table at which sat the stranger. James told Elsie that all he needed to do was to withdraw some cash.

"I've never used one of those machines, I'm not sure I could," remarked Elsie.

"It isn't difficult," replied James. "I'll show you." He went through the process with her, until he reached the screen that invited him to indicate how much he wished to withdraw. "You press which ever button is next to the amount you want. For £50, press that one, £100 that one and so on." He pressed a button and then said, "Next you take your card as it pops back out and wait for your cash." When his banknotes appeared, he took them and put them in his wallet.

"Oh, it's quite easy, isn't it? You just press the button and out comes £100 or whatever you want. And it looks as though Marjorie has finished. If you are going to the butchers I'll catch up with you there."

Elsie arrived at the butchers just in time to hear James say. "Thank you, Derrick. Now is Tuesday going to be your senior citizens' discount day?"

Derrick responded, "Not really, don't go telling everyone, it's only for my regular customers. I should be out of pocket if everyone came in asking for cheap rates."

When Elsie had made her purchase, they both visited one more shop and then met up to return home. As they passed the last shop, Marjorie emerged and joined them. Shortly after joining them, Marjorie posed a question. "Do you know who that man was in the Bank sitting at the table? I've not seen him before. He looked rather well to do with that coat. I looked round when you two were talking by the cash machine. He was obviously listening and then he started writing."

Elsie responded, "I saw him, but as I didn't recognise him, I didn't take much notice. Perhaps he is a businessman recently moved into the area opening a business account."

Just as they reached Waterfall Close where Marjorie and Roger lived, James enquired, "Is Roger still well since his heart surgery?"

"Oh yes, but he is immersed in one of his detective stories and can't put it down. It's not an Agatha Christie this time, but I can't remember the author's name. Bye now, see you both soon."

Later, when Elsie and James had returned to their respective apartments, the latter cooked himself one of his pork chops with a stuffing ball, vegetables and gravy. After his lunch, James sat down to look at the newspaper. When he woke up an hour later he retrieved the paper from the floor and began a further attempt to read it. He had done little more than scan the headlines on the first page when his doorbell rang to tell him that he had a visitor in the lobby on the ground floor wishing to see him. He was delighted to admit his eighteen-year-old friend Melanie who regarded him as her surrogate grandad and accordingly called him SG.

Melanie was now fully recovered from the nasty attack to which she had been subjected four months earlier. It was James and his friend Roger who had discovered her, unconscious and naked in a wood near a footpath. They had been alerted by her faithful cocker spaniel Pepper. When James himself had suffered a heart attack on the eve of Melanie's eighteenth birthday, Melanie began visiting him daily when he came home from hospital. As both her grandfathers had died before she was four a strong bond had developed between herself and her SG.

Their most recent meeting had been on New Year's Day when Melanie had helped James with the party he hosted for his son Adam and family. She was keen to share some news. "You remember, SG, that Mum and Dad gave me an iPhone for Christmas?"

"Why yes. I thought it was very generous of them and also very wise. I hope you take it with you when you go out so that you can summon help if necessary. Also, make sure you keep it safe and don't draw attention to the fact you have one by letting it create a bulge in the back pocket of your trousers."

"Oh, that's good advice: I'll remember that. But I want to show you some of the photos I took at the party."

"Well, let's have a look at them. We'll sit together on the sofa." They viewed the pictures she had taken; James noticed that his grandson Robin appeared in quite a few of them and could not resist the temptation to tease her. "I see that you have made sure that Robin features well in your selection. If you had asked me, I could have snapped the two of you together, perhaps in the kitchen when you were getting on so well. Has that young rascal contacted you since?"

"SG, it's not three days since the party, but yes he has," she replied, blushing slightly. "He was very pleasant and quite a gentleman like his grandad. He said that next time his old man comes to see you, he'll ask to come with him and he'll let me know, and if I come as well perhaps we can go for a walk together."

James thought he knew Robin well enough to consider that the two young people might be quite suitable for each other, but before he could say anything his phone rang.

An unknown and cultured voice spoke, "I hope I am speaking to Mr James Willoughby. Mr Willoughby, my name is Bryn Thorne and I am an inspector employed by the Country Trust Bank. I believe you visited our branch in Compton St Phillip this morning". At this point James interrupted him and said, "Sorry Mr Thorne, I am not hearing you very clearly. If you wait a moment, I'll move to a different position and see if that improves matters." He then signalled to Melanie by putting a finger on his mouth and cupping a hand behind his ear after which he pressed a button to open the phone so that she could hear. After this he spoke again, "Now, Mr Thorne let us see if that is better and if so you can tell me what you have to say."

"OK, Mr Willoughby, let's try and if you don't catch anything ask me to repeat it. I believe you used the cash machine at our branch today and I hope you withdrew £200." James denied withdrawing that much to which Mr Thorne continued, "That's what I am concerned about and hence the reason for this call. We are not sure whether there is a malfunction in the machine or if someone has somehow hacked into it, withdrawn cash and debited your account."

"That sounds very worrying. What can you do about it?"

"We are having the machine checked and we shall reimburse you for any loss. In the meantime, I have a suggestion which should safeguard you from any further attempt on your account."

"Have you? What does that involve?"

"Do you know roughly what the balance is in your current account? And you also have a deposit or savings account?"

"Yes. I do, but I couldn't say to the exact pound how much should be in the current account."

"My suggestion is this. If you can visit the bank in the next day or two, check your current account balance and if it is over £1000 say, withdraw £1000 in cash and transfer the rest into your savings account and close the current account. Bring the £1000 home with you, keep £200 for your immediate needs, put the £800 safely into a sealed envelope which can be used to open a new current account. I can assist you to open the new account at the main office in Molton, the county town."

"How do you do that? It's a long trip into Molton for me."

"Don't worry. I will arrange a courier to collect the envelope and give you a receipt. The courier will bring the envelope to me in Molton and I will open the new account which will then be secure and free from interference."

"I shall not be going into the village until Thursday morning when I visit the market."

"That's fine. If you visit the bank and do your shopping in the morning, I will phone you around midday to check that everything is OK and then I'll arrange for a courier to call on you by 2 pm so there is time to get the envelope to me for me to set up the new account before closing time. If you wish I can fill out the application form now so that the courier can have it ready for you to sign."

"OK. What do you need to know?"

"Well, I should have most of the information here, but the computer is being a little slow this afternoon, so perhaps you can tell me anything I don't have to hand."

Mr Thorne filled in name, then asked for date of birth and postcode, followed by house number. James explained that he lived in an apartment in Clarence House, but Mr Thorne seemed to know the name of his road. When he had finished, he bade James good-bye and reminded him he would phone on Thursday.

While the conversation had been progressing, Melanie sat beside James with her iPhone held close to his phone. James signalled her to be silent a little longer, then took his phone and put it in the kitchen.

James explained, "I didn't hear him shut his phone down, so he may have been waiting to see if I phoned anyone to check on him. Do you know what that was about?"

"I think so. You think that was a scam call and he is trying to steal money from you."

"Exactly, but we may be able to outsmart him. Would you like to phone Sergeant Jane Cartwright and tell her about the call? Here's her number."

They were lucky as the Sergeant was on duty when Melanie phoned and explained the situation. Jane listened carefully and then gave Melanie some instructions. Melanie explained to James, "She says that Robbo, that's DC Robinson, is on patrol in an unmarked car and is not far from here. She is going to ask him to call, but she wants me to check there isn't an unusual car parked out in the road with someone sitting in it. If there is I am to phone her again so that she can warn Robbo."

"I understand her thinking. Would you like to go to the pillar box down the road with this letter?"

When she returned, she reported, "When I went down the stairs I looked out of the window and there was a white VW Polo driven by a lady in a royal blue coat just pulling away from the kerb. I noted the number just in case it is significant."

"Well done! You'll make a detective yet. There's pad and pen on the surface there: write it down."

Fifteen minutes later while James and Melanie were sharing a pot of tea, DC Robinson arrived. He greeted them both, wished them both a happy New Year and said to Melanie, "You look well, so much better than when I first met you. That was just after you had been attacked. Jane has given me some information about a suspect fraud. Would you like to tell me more?"

Melanie responded by offering him her phone, saying, "You can listen for yourself." She pressed the button to play back the recording she had made.

When he had listened to the phone conversation DC Robinson agreed, "This sounds very much like an illegal activity and the sort we are trying to stop. Mr Willoughby, would you be willing to pursue this to try to help us bring these people to book? We would need to determine how we are going to catch them, but I think the first thing to do is to put some security on your phone." Looking at Melanie he continued, "I know just the right person to discuss this with."

Melanie immediately replied, "You mean my dad. I'm sure he would be delighted to do what he can for James. Do you want me to speak to him or will you contact him through official channels?"

"I think we had better speak to him, but you can tell him we will be in touch very soon. Now, I had better be away and I will check on that car number, for which many thanks, Melanie. It may not be of any relevance, but smart work all the same."

After he left Melanie and James looked at each other as if to say, 'Here we go again', but James gave their activity a name. "Well partner, perhaps we had better call ourselves 'Crime Busters United', especially if I am now to be called James."

"Oh, you noticed. It was a slip of the tongue. I'm sorry."

"You needn't apologise. I once gave you permission to call me James. I have no objection to being given the opportunity to feel younger."

They indulged in another cup of tea and then the phone rang again. "I wonder who that can be," said James as he went to fetch the phone from the kitchen.

As he returned Melanie heard him say in a teasing voice, "I'm not sure about that: you want me to be your messenger? I think you should speak to her yourself. I'm sure she won't bite you but be careful what you say as she is in a sleuthing mood. I'll pass the phone to her as she is with me now and you can ask her yourself." Then handing the phone to Melanie, "It's that young grandson of mine; says he wants to talk to you, I can't think why!"

As she took the phone Melanie remarked, "SG, you are a great tease!"

While Melanie and Robin were chatting, James took the tea things into the kitchen to wash up. He had finished washing and drying by the time Melanie joined him. "Robin is coming with his dad when they visit you tomorrow afternoon. He has asked me to go for a walk with him when he will tell me about his plans. He starts as a trainee solicitor on Monday and is not going back to the drive-through restaurant when they reopen next week. I didn't tell him about the suspected fraud."

"So, he has decided he needs to have a proper career. Good for him!" responded James. He forbore to say that he thought meeting Melanie probably had something to do with Robin's thinking. James had been wondering for some time how much longer his grandson would drift before deciding to try to make something positive of his life.

Melanie was putting on her coat ready to go home when the phone rang again. James picked it up and signalled her to wait. He listened for a short period and then put the phone down and said, "You can take your coat off. It's your dad and he is coming here in a few minutes and will take you home. He is coming to fit some device to my phone so that incoming calls can be monitored. It is so useful that you have a father who runs a security firm."

By Wednesday afternoon, under the gentle influence of the January sun, the air felt pleasantly warm, and Melanie and Robin went for their walk. It was never known by Robin's father and grandfather whether they roamed farther than a seat in the park about hundred yards from Clarence House. After the door closed behind the couple Adam looked at James and commented, "It looks as though Robin is really keen on your young lady and somehow, I don't think it is infatuation that will last just a matter of weeks. He has decided that he needs to have a profession that will convince her that he will be a responsible adult."

James replied, "I'm glad that he has found a firm with whom he can start his training. I think the attraction between them is mutual, judging by the number of times Melanie took Robin's picture at the party. I should be very happy if their relationship prospered." Adam agreed with his dad's assessment.

While the young people were out Adam told his father about the arrangements for Carole's wedding on 12 February and informed him that Carole had asked if her grandfather would be prepared to read a lesson during the ceremony. James responded, "Tell her I shall be delighted to do that for her."

James mentioned the incident of the suspected bogus bank phone call and the action that the police were taking. Adam's comment was quite revealing. "If you had told me that six months ago, I think I should have been very concerned, but your experiences since you moved here have shown me that you know perfectly well what you are doing and that you have some very able conspirators to support you. Nevertheless, please take care."

On Thursday morning James walked into Compton St. Philip and wandered around the market stalls where he bought vegetables, a small homemade cake, and a fishcake for his dinner. As he then made his way to the bank, he noticed a lady in a royal blue coat looking in the window of a shop near the bank. When he exited the bank with a bulky envelope, he saw the lady again making her way to the carpark, where she got into the passenger seat of a white car. However, he did not see either Melanie or her father in the village centre.

As he was leaving the shopping area, he was joined by his friend Ben who was also walking his way. They talked as they walked, but that did not distract James from noticing the white car drive past them and the car that he recognised as that of Stuart Hardy two cars behind.

As soon as he reached home James took the packet he had been given at the bank and placed it in a drawer in his bedroom. He then put the rest of his shopping away and made himself a drink. While he had his coffee, he read the headlines in the local paper and an article in which the reporter had interviewed a senior police officer about a spate of fraud cases. Two fraudsters had been apprehended and successfully prosecuted before being given substantial fines and custodial sentences. A third case was pending. James thought to himself that hopefully a fourth would not be far behind.

He had nearly finished preparing his dinner when the phone rang. "Mr Willoughby," said the voice he had heard before, "Brian Thorne here from Country Trust Bank. We spoke on Tuesday and made arrangements to safeguard the money you have in your current account. You said you would visit the branch this morning. I wonder if you have done so and if it is convenient for our courier to call on you this afternoon."

"I remember," replied James. "Yes, I visited the bank this morning and I have a packet containing cash waiting to be collected. What time can I expect the courier and how shall I know it is the right person? I believe you said I would be given a receipt and that there would be a form for me to sign. Presumably I also get a copy of that form."

"Absolutely. Will about 2pm be convenient?"

"That's fine: can you tell me the courier's name, and will he be wearing an ID badge with his name on it?"

"Oh, yes; it will be …. Miss …. Mary ….. Slade."

After he had rung off James said to himself, "Well Mr Bryn or Brian Thorne, you will have to get busy to produce an ID badge for your Miss Mary Slade who may well be wearing a blue coat. You will also have to tell her what her name is to be today. And I hope you will enjoy counting a lot of pieces of paper the shape of bank notes."

Half an hour later his apartment bell rang. DC Robinson was waiting to be admitted. Robbo explained that he had heard the telephone conversation, and everything was prepared. He reported that Melanie had done exceptionally well as a roving photographer and had really good photographic evidence. He was sending PC Porter within the hour, in plain clothes, ostensibly with a delivery of a part for a microwave which he would be fitting in the kitchen. He would remain out of sight but would be present if needed. The part would actually be a microphone and recorder.

Five hours later James, with Melanie's assistance, was providing cups of tea and biscuits for Sergeant Jane Cartwright, DC Robinson and Stuart Hardy. They were reviewing the afternoon's work and the detention of a Mr and Mrs Wayne Dale who had been caught red-handed. The police had further investigations to undertake, but they already had five other cases that might be the work of the arrested couple.

Robbo explained that as soon as the courier returned to the car in which her husband was waiting, they were boxed in by two police cars. Officers questioned the couple about the car which was neither taxed nor insured. Melanie's observation of the registration number had enabled the police to make their investigation in advance. The recorded phone calls and Melanie's photographs would also be excellent evidence. In one picture James recognised the man in the expensive looking coat he had seen in the bank two days earlier.

Stuart Hardy described what had occurred during the morning. While James was wandering around the market and visiting the bank, Melanie had been keeping him in sight and watching the white VW Polo she had seen previously. She was wearing a coat, hat and scarf that had belonged to her grandmother and carrying an old handbag and a shopping basket. She had snapped the lady in the blue coat observing James's movements, but she was most proud of the shot she got of the lady's accomplice who was sitting in the car. She had managed to creep up behind the car and while apparently rooting around in her basket had managed to get a close-up of the man's face reflected in the car's door mirror. As the lady returned to the car and her husband leaned across to open the door for her, they saw an old lady standing nearby and consulting her shopping list. As both looked towards her, she muttered, "Of course, Cheese" and pressed the button to take a clear close-up picture. Melanie then shuffled away towards a market stall.

Sergeant Cartwright congratulated Melanie and James for the contributions they had both made but pointed out that there would be a court case. The evidence was so strong that the defendants would probably plead guilty. If they decided to go for trial James and Melanie might be called as witnesses. Melanie responded, "If I am called can I come in my old lady's outfit? I would love to see their faces if I could stand in front of them with my phone and say, 'Say Cheese'. I think it would be another great picture for the album."

SECRETS DISCOVERED AT A WEDDING

At the wedding of his granddaughter a grandfather, his grandson and their girlfriend discover a centuries old secret.

Drip, drip, drip, was the sound as the snow on the roof above James Willoughby's apartment continued to thaw. Occasionally there was a swoosh as a lump of snow slid off the edge and landed on the balcony outside James' living room. It was now nearly a year since James, who would be 86 at the end of the next month, had moved into the apartment on the top floor of Clarence House. The snow that covered the surrounding countryside was the first fall since his arrival and the first time he had been able to enjoy the beautiful sight of the sunshine on snow that the splendid view from his south facing living room afforded him.

He could see that there were some hardy sheep in one of the fields: the farmer had provided fodder for them. He could also see two horses in another field. They were wearing winter rugs and before dusk would probably be taken in for the night, but for the time being they seemed to be enjoying the opportunity to have some exercise. In chasing each other they were making furrows in the smooth white surface that covered the grass. While he watched several birds flew past, mainly rooks and jackdaws: in the hedgerows there were many smaller birds flitting in and out, probably sorting out their roosts for the night.

With the year being nearly a month old, this being the last day of January, it was becoming noticeable that the days were getting longer. James anticipated that his young friend Melanie would arrive before the light began to fade. Despite the age difference James and Melanie had developed a strong friendship that had begun some six months earlier when Melanie's cocker spaniel Pepper had alerted James that Melanie had been attacked and left unconscious in woodland near a footpath. Both Melanie's grandfathers had died before she was four, so that the bond she had established with James was, for her, unique. She regarded him as a surrogate grandad and accordingly called him SG. She had been upset when a heart problem confined James to hospital for a few days in

November and had taken to calling on him on her way home from school to check that he was well.

The pair had enjoyed some special occasions together, most recently when they had combined to alert the police to a couple of fraudsters who were cheating vulnerable elderly people out of their savings. James found the company of the beautiful eighteen-year-old enlivening and they had many conversations about village matters and Melanie's A level studies. On New Year's Day Melanie had met James's twenty-two-year-old grandson Robin and a mutual attraction was developing. Although James could not resist a little gentle teasing, he hoped that the infant relationship would strengthen and was not averse to seeking opportunities for the pair to meet.

Melanie arrived in time to admire the splendid view and while they watched together the owner of the horses arrived to take them to their stable for the night. Although Melanie did not have her own horse she had been to the stables where Robin's two older sisters kept their own mounts.

When they were settled and enjoying a pot of tea together, Melanie turned to James and said, "SG I have been commissioned to ask you something."

James looked at her and replied, "Now what could that be and who might have done the commissioning? It's not some idea of my grandson's, is it?"

"No, it's not Robin, so you needn't get ready to tease me. Yesterday, after the service I was with the choir mistress when the vicar asked her if she knew anyone who might play a couple of hymns when he takes a short service at the Care Home. Apparently old Miss Greatrex has helped him for several years, but the stroke she had just before Christmas has paralysed her left arm. So I said ..."

"I can guess. That your friend James had played the carols when Miss G was indisposed. And they asked you to see if the old man would help out at the Care Home. Correct?"

"Correct, you got it in one. Could you? Would you like to? I didn't commit you, but it came as a shock to hear that Miss Greatrex is so ill."

"Yes, it is very sad when someone loses the use of a hand and fingers, particularly for someone who has played an instrument for years. Do you know when and how often these services take place?"

"I think it is three or four times a year and I think it is on a Friday morning. The Care Home is called 'Phillip's Rest' and is at the top end of your road."

"I know where it is. Melanie, if you would like to speak to the vicar, tell him I will help if he is in a fix until he can find someone younger."

"I will do that, but now let us talk about something more exciting." While she had been speaking, Melanie had been rummaging in her school bag. "I can see your wedding invitation over there: Look what I have received." And she held up another invitation. "Aren't I one lucky girl? I'm honoured and excited and it's only a few days away."

"I haven't seen the list of guests invited to Carole's wedding, but I'm pleased you have received one. I'm sure there will be at least three men who will be delighted to see you there, although the bride's dad will not be able to escort you."

"Three from different generations! That must be unusual." She put her arms round him and kissed him. While James was wondering whether she greeted his grandson in like manner, Melanie continued, "I don't know whether I should choose you or Robin as my escort. Would you be disappointed if Robin looked after me?"

James looked at her, tried to pull a long face while grinning at the same time and replied, "Terribly, I should be devastated." As Melanie giggled, James continued, "I suspect we shall all have allocated places at the reception meal, and I shouldn't be surprised if you are placed between us."

Except for a few icy patches in the shade nearly all the snow had gone by the following morning so James decided that he could take some exercise. Although he was not accustomed to burdening himself with a stick if he went for a walk, especially if shopping, he thought it would be wise to take the lovely walking cane he had been given at Christmas. The weather was quite mild, and a watery sun contrived to show its face from time to time. James was thankful that the biting wind of a few days earlier had introduced itself to a different community somewhere else.

After an invigorating twenty-minute walk, during which he stopped briefly outside 'Phillip's Rest', he returned to make himself a warm drink. As soon as he sat down, his telephone rang. When he answered a voice said, "Reverend Len Nesbit here. I believe young Melanie Hardy told you about our lack of someone to play the piano for the little service I hold at the Care Home every three months. I understand that you indicated that you might be able to help."

James replied that he knew the location of the Care Home but would like to know what would be involved. By the time the conversation was concluded James was aware what his role would be and that the next service was scheduled for ten-thirty on Friday the 18th, just over two weeks away. He was relieved to realise that the excitement of his granddaughter's wedding would have happened by then. Two days later he found in his pigeon-hole a note from Reverend Leonard E Nesbit with details of the Care Home service and a music copy of the hymn book used for the service.

The wedding, both ceremony and reception, proved to be a charming occasion. There were no hitches and the children, from the bride's and groom's first cancer terminated marriages, were very well behaved and played their supporting roles perfectly. James was thanked and congratulated for his sensitive rendition of the beautiful passage on love in Paul's first letter to the Corinthian church. The bride looked lovely and happy and her radiant smile captivated almost everyone. However, James noticed that Robin hardly seemed to notice his sister as his eyes were focussed almost entirely on Melanie for whom he was a most attentive escort. Whilst James was delighted that the two youngsters were so pleased to be in each other's company, he hoped that they would be sensible about pursuing their studies before allowing their relationship to become too much of a distraction. He decided that he might be in the best position, of all those who had the futures of the young couple in mind, to monitor, prompt and advise their progress. Perhaps words of caution or encouragement at the right times could be the appropriate way to foster and yet moderate their affections.

The reception was held at a hotel adjacent to the church in which the ceremony was conducted. Part of the hotel had been a manor house, but much new building had extended the premises considerably. With meal and speeches concluded, chief bridesmaid Lucy with her soon-to-be husband Tom drove the bride home to change, ready to depart on honeymoon with her new husband. While they were gone Melanie took the opportunity to visit the 'Ladies'.

Following what she thought was the correct direction she found herself in the old part of the hotel. Coming upon a door at the end of a corridor she tried the handle and found the door opened. Looking inside she realised she had strayed into the original Manor House kitchen, now obviously used for storage. Seeing a door in the opposite corner she could not resist the temptation to explore. The door was at right angles to the wall in which was a window through which she could see both the church and that the house wall turned through 90 degrees towards the church. Thinking there must be a sizeable room the other side of the door she opened it and was surprised only to find a small space, but there was another door which was locked. She wondered if the locked door might belong to another room providing access to the church.

Being an inquisitive girl Melanie returned to the corridor and found a door leading out of the building with a key to hand. Going outside she could see that the extra room was small and had no windows. Imagination took control of her, and she wondered if it could contain access to a secret underground passage to the church, maybe with a priest's hiding place.

Returning to the main hall and finding that the bride was not expected for half-an-hour, she claimed the attention of both her escorts and asked them discretely to follow her. She led them to the kitchen and to the locked door and told them her theory as to what could be behind it. Robin wondered where the key might be, but James felt above the door lintel and touched something cold and hard. It was the key, but whether it would open the lock was another matter. Robin had spotted an old oilcan amongst the junk in the kitchen and fetched it. The can wasn't completely empty and James was able to work some oil into the lock. He tried the key and after a couple of attempts it turned and the door was opened.

There was very little light and it was beginning to get dark outside. Robin ventured in very cautiously testing each step before proceeding. When a foot landed on nothing he bent his other knee so that he could feel down. He soon felt something. A step, possibly a staircase leading down and to where?

"We need a torch," cried Robin. "Dad has one in his car: I'll fetch it, shan't be long."

Melanie was getting excited. Not wanting her to be too disappointed James commented, "It could be a passage, but we don't know how old this house is or whether there had been another one before this. It could just lead to an ice-house which many of the big houses had before fridges." When Robin returned with a torch he went into the room, found a flight of steps and went down them.

He called back up, "There is a sort of storage space down here and I think there might be a passage."

Melanie, suddenly apprehensive called, "Be careful, darling: don't go too far."

He was not gone long, but when he returned, looking rather dusty, he was carrying an old bottle. "There is a room with a tiled floor and a recess in the left wall with bottles like this in it. In the far wall there is a wooden door with a trap door which I managed to open a little. Beyond is a passage. I don't know how far it goes, but it is straight and quite level. The sides are bricked and appear in pretty good condition, with recesses. I don't know how many recesses, but there are bottles like this in the first one."

James then took control. "Close everything up as it was. Robin, take the bottle and torch back to the car and clean yourself up as well as you are able. Don't say anything to anyone about our little adventure. Melanie, go to reception, say that you are studying history and see if you can find out dates for the hotel development and if they know anything about the old manor house, such as its date, ownership and whether there was a previous dwelling. See if they have a printed history. I am going to have a walk to the church to see if it is still open and if I can find any signs of a passage or if there is a guidebook."

James went to the church via the front door of the hotel. It was a walk of no more than 50 metres. When he arrived, the door was still unlocked and there was just sufficient light to look around. He discovered that at the west end of the church against the north wall was a vestry and in front of that a small chapel with an altar against the north wall. Behind the altar there was a reredos that was taller than himself. He peered behind the reredos, but he would have needed a torch to see clearly. However, he fancied he could see some form of framework which might have been for a door. As he left the church he found a fairly elderly copy of a church guide, cost 5 shillings. He bought it and put a £1 coin in the box. Outside the church there was a mausoleum-like structure against the north wall. He wondered about an access point and if it was no longer used. Could it also hide a staircase?

Feeling quite satisfied with his research he returned to the hotel and met Melanie waiting by the reception desk. She told him that the receptionist had been very helpful and had gone to find the manager who might be able to tell her more. When Javed Khan arrived, he was able to tell them that the hotel had been open ten years and, although some of the earlier building survived, much of it had to be pulled down. The site had come on the market nearly twenty years ago when the last member of the family, an old lady, had died. She had apparently lived alone for more than fifty years and for the last eight or nine in two rooms with daily visits by a carer. She was ninety-eight at her death. George Owen had sunk most of his own inheritance into the purchase and renovation. Mr Khan had been manager since the opening. They didn't have a history of the building. However, he thought Mr Owen might have some interesting documents, but he had taken a brief break and would not be back until Thursday.

Listening to this information James asked if Mr Owen was likely to be at the hotel the following Saturday morning and if so did Mr Khan think he might be able to spare them half-an-hour of his time. The most obliging manager reached behind the reception desk and found a diary. There were no appointments for Mr Owen in it for Saturday so he suggested he could book them in for ten-thirty. He asked for a name and when James gave his Mr Khan realised he must be related to the bride as a Mr Willoughby had booked the wedding reception. He then paused and thought before exclaiming, "Mr James Willoughby? Are you the person whose name has been in the press for solving several crimes?"

Before James could reply, Melanie responded, glowing with pride, "He is, and he is ever so clever and a lovely helpful man."

James then took up the reply, "Melanie is a good friend and has helped me in several endeavours and is also my grandson Robin's girlfriend," for Robin had just appeared looking rather smarter than when he emerged from the tunnel. James continued, "Melanie is studying History at A level and if, as I suspect, we can uncover some lost information she and I may be able to produce a little historical booklet for you. With a Manor House and a Church in close proximity there could well be some links between the two with which the Rector may be able to help. If you have no objection, I will contact the rector and invite him to join us next Saturday."

As they re-joined the other wedding guests James showed the other two the guidebook he had found in the church and told them what he had seen both inside and outside the building. He also said they would need to work out how they would travel to the hotel the next week, but Robin suggested that he would ask if he could borrow either his dad's car or the old banger that his sister Lucy used when she went to the stables. He told James that he had been contemplating buying a car, but that Melanie suggested he wait awhile as she thought it would be too expensive to run, like pouring money away in bills.

Carole returned to the hotel, ready to leave with Nicholas. Before everyone waved them off the rector, who had also come back, called them to him with their two children and gave the new family a blessing. As the guests waved the newly-weds away, James found himself next to the rector and took the opportunity, which he had created, to invite him to the meeting the following Saturday.

In a quiet corner of the hotel on 19 February, four men and a young lady were sitting round a table. They had been served with coffee and biscuits. George Owen, the hotel owner, welcomed them and James, Melanie, Robin and the Reverend Martin Pope introduced themselves. Then James began the proceedings by asking Robin to put the bottle on the table.

James explained, "This elderly bottle, which has not been opened, may be two or three hundred years old. We think that in most of those years, until last Saturday, it has been underground somewhere between the old Manor House and the Church next door." Looking at the hotel owner he said, "Now we need to confess how we have it. Melanie and Robin will you take up the story?"

First Melanie and then Robin explained their roles in the discovery. After watching the faces of the owner and the rector, James could tell that they knew nothing about a secret passage. He continued, 'When I looked in the church for anywhere that a passage might enter, I could not find anything like a crypt. I wondered if the entrance might be under a tomb and then I looked at the chapel in the north aisle. I peered behind the reredos. I think there might be a doorway hidden there, especially as there is a mausoleum like feature on the outside which could contain a staircase. During the week Melanie and I have done a little research. It seems that parts of the church date back to the early twelfth century and would have been standing during the reign of King Stephen when he and his cousin Maude, or Matilda, were contending for the throne of England. The church would have been closer to the coast at that time. The church's elderly guidebook suggests that at one time part of the church may have been used as a place to store smuggled contraband."

James could feel excitement levels rising so he continued, "One of Melanie's A level subjects is history and part of her course work is to undertake an investigation of a local historical event. This may provide a suitable subject, although it may turn out to be too big a project. There are several questions we would like to be able to pursue. Does the passage link the two buildings? What is its present state and is it safe to explore? When was the Manor House built and was there an earlier dwelling house? Was the passage used for any purpose other than storage of contraband, such as a hiding place for a priest in the sixteenth century? One of the vicars in first Elizabethan times was a de Courcey and there are several monuments to de Courceys. What were the names of the families that have owned the Manor House?"

His attentive audience was listening to every word and most were making notes. James continued, "One other question: what is in the bottle and what state is it in? The answer to that last question may have significance to the other bottles that are still down there, so we may be wise not to publicise yet what we have found. In due course there may be a fascinating story to tell, which if handled carefully could bring financial benefits to both the church and the hotel. Two final questions. First, do either George or Martin have any sources to help answer any of the questions? Secondly, would you be willing for Melanie and myself to organise an investigation and research? A final point: Robin would like to be involved, but he does not have the time to devote to research as he has recently started his training as a solicitor. Of course, he may be able to advise us if we need to undertake any legal investigation. Gentlemen, thank you for listening: your reactions, please."

Reactions of both the hotel owner and the rector were very similar. "Amazing. Extraordinary. I had no idea. This is exciting. I think we should try to find out more."

Seeing their enthusiasm James thanked them for their wish to proceed. He then outlined a possible initial strategy, "If we have time this morning we may be able to have a look at the tunnel a little more carefully, but we cannot rush down it until we have considered safety matters. Before we leave this table, firstly a question for you George. Have you any documents or even anecdotal knowledge about the Manor House, such as occupants, building adaptations in the past, dates, any historical evidence?"

George replied, "I do have some papers, including, I believe, some deeds of the property. I can certainly peruse those. We also have a few regular clients who have lived in the area a good many years: I might be able to get them talking about the old days. I am with you all the way and I'll help you in any way I can. Certainly, I can grant you access when you want it."

"Many thanks, George. Now Martin, do you think there are any church records that could help us to unearth, sorry that wasn't intended as a pun, any history of the church and possible links with the Manor."

"I can certainly do some research. Although my personal knowledge only goes back 6 years, I do have access to church registers. The county records office might be a source of information and the diocese may have records, particularly in relation to any building work. I don't know if the churchwardens will have had to obtain a faculty from the diocese to erect the reredos, but we can enquire. I have always had an interest in church history and I had already determined that we need a new guidebook."

"Melanie, as the hound that started this chase, do you want to add anything at this stage?"

"I think I am as excited as everyone else, or even more so. Part of the investigation would make a wonderful A level history project, but the whole exercise would be far too big to complete in a few weeks. I would like to be involved initially in the research, particularly the processes for searching information from records and other sources such as past copies of local newspapers. From the way you have heard him conduct this meeting I am sure you will agree that James would make a very good project manager. He is remarkable for his age. I have been privileged to see the calm and methodical way he works."

There was no dissension to Melanie's proposal, so James spoke again. "I will make some notes of this meeting and send them to you with an outline suggestion as to how we should proceed with possible dates for future meetings. George, do you happen to have any hard hats in this establishment?"

"I have been thinking about that. I am sure there are some the builders left behind and they may even be in the old kitchen."

"OK," cried James. "Shall we go and have a look at what we have been talking about?"

The five of them made their way to the old kitchen and to the door of the small room, which at one time was possibly used for storage. James felt for and found the key, opened the door and nominated Robin and George to explore very carefully. Both had torches, but before they went down James advised them not to shout or make any unnecessary noise. The three at ground level remained in silence listening for any sound that emanated from the passage. It was nearly ten minutes before the explorers returned.

They reported that they had been able to open the door and gained access to the passage which was dry, with brick walls and roof, and generally appeared to be in good order. For most of its length the tunnel was straight but there was a slight kink about half-way along, suggesting that it may have been dug from both ends. By torchlight they could see a staircase at the other end, but they had not ventured up it. Robin had been busy with his phone taking pictures. They found five niches in the wall which contained bottles and chests. They left everything in place, but they were intrigued by what appeared to be another opening that had been bricked up, but possibly at a later date. Could this be another tunnel, another storage space or a priest's hole? They did not have the knowledge to be able to estimate the date of the bricks, but by this larger bricked-up opening they found some marks that might be initials or a date. They looked like MDL.

Hearing this Melanie exclaimed, "1550 in Roman. The reign of Edward the sixth, when Catholics were being persecuted, although three or four years later it was the Protestants that were in danger under Bloody Mary. How exciting!"

"Absolutely right," responded Martin. "I wonder who the vicars were at the time and who was living in the Manor House and of which persuasion they were. And I wonder why they had this tunnel. I doubt if it was just so they didn't get wet going to church when it rained."

Having locked the door and left the kitchen Melanie led them outside and showed them what she had noticed. There was no visible sign of the tunnel from above where there was a lawned area free of trees and their roots. They continued to the church and James pointed out the possible mausoleum or burial chamber and inside the reredos. With a torch it was just possible to see what looked like a door frame behind. Looking under the altar table Robin noticed a strange pattern in the wooden floor and wondered whether there might at one time have been access to a chamber below.

All five members sat in church for a few minutes with their own thoughts before James allocated tasks. George and Martin were asked to research the history of the house and the church respectively. He also suggested to George that he might like to ascertain the nature and the quality of the contents of the bottle. Robin was asked to send copies of his photos to each of the others and to try to find out how to locate any relevant legal documents relating to church or manor house. Melanie and James agreed to conduct on-line searches including local newspapers and relevant historical publications.

During the next week Melanie called on James each evening after school when they spent the best part of an hour searching websites and in discussing reports from George and Martin. On Friday Robin joined them and both he and Melanie read the summary of initial findings that James had compiled. When they had agreed to the summary James emailed the document to the other two with suggestions for further meeting dates.

James then spoke to the two young people, "This is an exciting project, but it could be time consuming. You both have studies that require your attention and must be given priority. Be careful how you allocate your time. We may have discovered something that could put the Village of Cricken on the map, but after five centuries or more it can quite easily wait another two years for its moments of glory. In the meantime, my dears, we can enjoy being researchers visiting bygone ages and allow our imaginations to think what it would have been like to live without all the conveniences and trappings of the present day. If we can produce a history of the site, it could make interesting reading for the general public and be a source of finance for both church and hotel. We can look forward to fun and excitement."

WHERE HAS THE FLOWER GONE?

A surprise birthday party and exceptions to the normal routines in a Care Home.

After the excitement of his granddaughter's wedding and the discovery made by his grandson Robin, their girlfriend Melanie and himself James Willoughby, he needed a few quiet days. The three of them were due to return to the hotel on Saturday 19 February, a week after the wedding and discuss their discovery with the hotel owner and the rector of the neighbouring church. For the day prior to that he had accepted an invitation to play a couple of hymns at the small service the vicar held at the local Care Home 'Phillip's Rest'. Although living now in an apartment with a wonderful view he no longer had his own piano or regular access to one. In the week before Christmas, he had substituted at very short notice to play carols when the pianist was suddenly taken ill. He found that his fingers were still sufficiently supple and for this facility at the age of nearly eighty-six he was extremely grateful.

On Friday 18 February James left his apartment at ten-fifteen to make the 5-minute walk to 'Phillip's Rest'. He was welcomed by the Registered Manager Cedric Field and the Lead Carer Barbara Pollard. Barbara took him into the residents' lounge where all was almost ready for the service. On the way he passed some pigeon-holes and noticed that one was labelled QQ. He asked if the QQ was the initials of one of the residents. "Oh yes; unusual isn't it? That's our Quentin."

"I have only come upon one person with those initials and his name was Quentin. We were in the same class at primary school. He was Quentin Quinn."

"Extraordinary! I wonder if it is the same person for our resident is Quentin Quinn, but he is eighty-six."

"The age I shall be at the end of this month."

James and Barbara were not expected to enter the lounge with their mouths wide open looking as though they had just seen something astonishing, and the vicar was very surprised to see his new pianist looking as though he had witnessed a miracle as that was to be the topic of his little homily. The first hymn the vicar had chosen was 'God moves in a mysterious way'.

At the end of the little service it was time for the residents to have a drink and Vicar Len and James were invited to join them. They moved round the room talking to those who were able to hold a conversation. James had a short chat with Gertrude Greatrex who was able to speak a few words but only with difficulty as a result of her stroke. She was able to thank him for playing and regretted that her playing days were probably at an end. When he reached Quentin Quinn he discovered that it was his old school acquaintance and that he remembered him. He was physically rather frail, but his mind was still sound.

After they had expressed their joint surprise at discovering that they lived so close to each other, more than two hundred miles from where they had last met, Quentin looked at James and challenged, in a peeved voice but with a smile, "I remember you. You tried to steal my painting."

"I did and I doubt if you ever knew why. As I remember, we all had to draw or paint an animal for a competition. You did a wonderful picture of a horse. We had to put our entries on a table with a card with our name on. You had already put yours on the table when I brought mine along. I knew it was yours but the card beside it had a different name. I was sure two names had been interchanged, so I picked up the name by your picture and was just going to look for your name card when Miss Oliver came into the room. I hastily replaced the card, but put mine there instead. Then you came in and spotted the wrong name. You know what happened next and my entry was disqualified."

"Which was a pity because you had drawn a fine leopard up a tree. But whose name was on the card you removed and why didn't you reveal it?"

"It was a boy with whom you were particularly friendly. You would be described as 'best mates'. I didn't want to see your friendship broken so I said nothing and then you and he went to a different school to me at the end of the term. I don't think we met again after that."

"I wonder if I can guess. Was it Roger Silk?"

"Yes, it was. Did your friendship last?"

"It lasted until Roger killed himself at the age of twenty-six, driving far too fast in France. He never married but he used to come to see me after I married. We lived at the end of a L-shaped cul-de-sac and when he came to visit us you could hear him coming on the main road and he took the bend in our close on two wheels. He was obsessed with fast cars and ultimately it was his undoing. I suppose you could say he died doing what he loved best.

"Now, will you be coming to play for us in future?"

"I will if the vicar asks me again, but I can come and visit you at other times if you wish."

"Yes please, Jim; I have been in here nearly two years and have only had two visits by relatives. Since my wife died, my sons, both of whom live on the continent, pay the fees for me to live here. I am quite content, but it would be lovely to have someone to chat to about our childhoods and since."

"I must go now, Quinney, but I'll try to call in for half-an-hour or so each week."

Before James left, he exchanged good wishes with some of the other residents and chatted with Barbara for a few minutes about Quentin. While he was chatting with Barbara the vicar paused on his way out. He stopped to thank James and said that he would be in touch, then bade them both good-bye. James noticed that as the vicar left one of the residents tried to slip out of the door behind him, but a carer was alert and took her back into the lounge. 'An escapologist', thought James.

When Melanie called in the afternoon, she wanted to know how the session had gone at the Care Home. She was amazed to hear that James had met an old school friend he had not seen for three quarters of a century. He told her that he had been asked if he would be able to play the piano occasionally to entertain the residents and he had wondered if she would like to go with him and bring her cello to play, or failing that, to sing.

Although hesitant initially Melanie gave the idea a cautious approval, but insisted that they would need to practise together, especially if James was prepared to accompany her. "The week after next is half-term and if you were to come to our house we could practise with our piano. As my brothers will be at uni. they won't be able to tease me."

"I shall certainly need to practise as well. I don't know whether I have any music at home or whether it all went to Adam or Ruth when they moved me here. I shall need to have access to a piano. Maybe there are times when the Church Hall is not booked."

"I'll find out for you. Mum knows the Hall secretary who does all the bookings. Now I want to talk to you about a most important matter. I remember that it is your birthday during half-term: are you going to celebrate it on Monday 28th February or Tuesday 1st March?"

"Has it to be just one of them? I thought I might make it a two-day event."

"You can't do that! I don't want you overdoing it and becoming ill again. Too much excitement at your age……"

"Just a moment, young lady. Who was it, a few weeks ago, said that I wasn't too old to be your boyfriend because I had only had about twenty-one birthdays?"

"Oh yes, that was me, wasn't it? Dear SG, I do love you when you tease me, but have any arrangements been made?"

"I'm not sure, but I think Ruth may be planning something, although I don't know when, what or where."

"I think I will phone her and see if she would like any help. I have her phone number. We had a good chat at Carole's wedding, when I escaped from my two admirers. Well, that's how she described you and Robin."

"And do you think, my cheeky girlfriend, that you deserve to be admired?" responded James with a grin.

"Probably not, but I do think you deserve to have a fuss made of you and I would like to be involved in some way."

"Find out what Ruth is planning and if it doesn't satisfy you, we'll have a little party of our own."

Melanie nodded her agreement, but James had a feeling that she knew what she wanted and had some scheme of her own in mind. For the rest of the hour the two of them gave their attention to Melanie's English A level studies and discussed the characters of King Lear's daughters. They agreed that Regan and Goneril were selfish, scheming and two-faced, but found it difficult to understand why their father was taken in by them. They felt sorry for Cordelia and would have liked to find someone to make Lear realise that he had a real gem alongside the counterfeit jewellery portrayed by the older girls.

On Tuesday of the next week James made time to visit Quentin in 'Phillip's Rest'. They spent most of that first visit talking about their experiences and other pupils at the primary school they both attended. Quentin returned to the matter of his painting and thanked James for his kindness and sacrifice and explained that his thanks were sincere even if they were seventy-five years late. He then asked, "Have you lived in this area very long?"

James explained, "I have been here less time than you. My wife and I retired to the neighbouring village of Compton St. Mary about eighteen years ago as both son and daughter lived in the county. Within a year of moving into our bungalow, Anne was diagnosed with Parkinson's disease. We coped with that for two years and then she suffered a stroke and although she seemed to be making a good recovery she had a second stroke and died three days later. I continued to live in the bungalow with very good support from neighbours and friends from the church, where for a few years I sang in the choir and occasionally helped out as a relief organist. Then my daughter spotted an advert for an apartment just along the road from here. She talked to her brother and subsequently the two families organised the sale of one property, purchase of the other and all the removal arrangements. I took up residence last March, shortly after my eighty-fifth birthday. Since then, I have had an enjoyable few months exploring this village and getting to know people."

As he was leaving the Home, James encountered the lady he had nicknamed 'The Escapologist' hovering by the front door. Two carers appeared and one guided the lady to the lounge saying, "Come along Rosie, it's time for your coffee." The other carer explained to James, "That is Rose Bloom; we have to keep a careful watch on her as she would be out of the front door if she had a chance. She would wander away and have no idea where she was."

On Wednesday Adam called to see his father and brought with him a parcel of piano music and a book of songs for soprano with piano accompaniment. When he apologised for not being able to include any pieces for cello and piano James realised that Melanie was involved somewhere, and he wondered what else she had been organising. He was given another clue when Melanie arrived in the afternoon and told him that she had managed to book the Church Hall for an hour on the Saturday morning so that they could practise together. She was pleased, but not surprised, that Adam had sought out some music for James and she herself produced three duets for cello and piano. James perceived that Melanie had 'got the bit between her teeth' and to use another metaphor intended 'to strike while the iron was hot'. When she told him that her mother had invited him to Sunday lunch after church he wondered if she was hoping that they would be sufficiently rehearsed to be able to provide some entertainment at the Care Home at the end of her half-term week.

The two musicians spent the remainder of the afternoon deciding which pieces they would practise first and which would be suitable for a short recital programme for the Care Home.

On Saturday in the Church Hall and then on Sunday after lunch at the Hardys' home the pair rehearsed the pieces they had chosen. Melanie's mother Becky provided a trial audience, and both encouraged and advised them. They had a very enjoyable time practising together with plenty of laughs when one or both made mistakes, especially when one observed the repeats, and the other didn't.

During the meal Melanie's parents told James that they had heard that he was about to celebrate his birthday and asked on which day he would be doing so. James was about to repeat his previous remark to Melanie and suggest Monday and Tuesday, when Melanie chimed in with, "He can't have Monday because that is before his birthday, so it has to be Tuesday 1st March." Then addressing herself directly to James she said, "SG, you told me you hadn't made any plans, so you can do what you like tomorrow, but please will you play with me again on Tuesday as I have booked the Church Hall for the afternoon?" and, turning to her father, "Daddy, will you fetch James and bring him to the Hall for 3 o'clock?"

Stuart and James looked at each other and Stuart commented with a grin, "It sounds as though we have been given our instructions, and woe betide us if we don't obey" at the same time circling his little finger with the index finger of his other hand.

When it was time for James to go home, Stuart insisted on taking him by car. On the way Stuart reminded James that sentencing was to take place for Melanie's attacker the next day. He was hopeful that the music practice might help Melanie to put her ordeal of last September to the back of her mind.

When he reflected later on the events of 1 March James realised that his birthday had arrived at just the right time for Melanie and enabled her healing progress to continue while protecting her from any chance of a relapse.

On Monday James spent the day quietly, reading and watching a little television. He also spent some time reviewing the exciting visit he and Melanie, with his grandson Robin, had made two days earlier to the hotel that had staged his granddaughter's wedding reception. Melanie was able to visit him for a few minutes at coffee time in the morning as it was half-term. Noticing that she seemed to be a little withdrawn, he asked if she felt alright. She came and sat by him. "Do you know what is happening in London today?"

"Yes, I do. Does it worry you? Are you being reminded of the whole experience?" As he said this he put his arm round her, which caused her to bury her head in his jumper and shed a few tears. It reminded him of the times when he had needed to comfort his daughter after she had experienced something that upset her.

"Do you think they will lock him away for life? He is only young and it is such a long time. In a way I feel sorry for him."

"It may not be for life, but it may be for twenty years or more. Remember that he attacked seven women and although he did not kill anyone, he came very close to it in your case."

"If he hadn't attacked me, you wouldn't have rescued me and come into my life and I wouldn't have met Robin. I do have much for which to be grateful."

"Mel, dear, I am greatly heartened that you can look at positives and that you have compassion in your make-up. You are quite special to me too."

Feeling better Melanie left saying she had many jobs to do, leaving James pondering what those jobs might be.

On Tuesday morning James fetched his post from downstairs. It consisted of six birthday cards from family members as well as two requests from charities asking for donations. He also collected his national newspaper. On an inside page of the paper he found a headline 'Sex Attacker Sentenced'. He had been sent down for twenty years, but he had not been denied the opportunity to appeal for early release if the parole board should deem him no longer a threat.

In the afternoon, as it was his birthday, James decided to put on a smart shirt and jacket, even though he was only going to rehearse some music. Stuart came for him at the appointed time and checked that James had his music with him. On the way to the Church Hall Stuart told him that Melanie had been rather low in spirits the previous day, but had bounced back when she heard the sentence given to her attacker. She was pleased that he could look forward to a life after prison and hoped he would be able to become a better person.

On reaching the Church Hall all was very quiet and James wondered if Melanie was still to arrive. However, when they opened the door all the lights were switched on and he was greeted with clapping and a rousing rendering of Happy Birthday from about twenty friends and family. Nearly all his family were there, only Carole and her new family were missing. His neighbour Elsie, his friends Marjorie and Roger as well as Ben Foster and Melanie's parents were present as was QQ. Adam had been detailed by Melanie to fetch Quentin from the Care Home. Following hard on the heels of James and Stuart as they entered the Hall was Sergeant Jane Cartwright in uniform, who caused a gale of laughter as she put a hand on James's arm while producing handcuffs and saying "James Willoughby, I hope you have not been involved in any more crimes as we have difficulty keeping up with your sleuthing." With that she put away the handcuffs, gave him a kiss, wished him a Happy Birthday and produced a large card signed by many of her colleagues.

The next hour was filled with chatter, cups of tea, sandwiches and cakes. It was evident to James that the event had been arranged as a joint exercise by his daughter Ruth and his surrogate granddaughter Melanie with help from his real granddaughter Holly. As James moved round the room he came upon Quentin and Jane in conversation. Quentin turned to him and shook his hand, "I have just been hearing about all the crimes you have helped solve. Congratulations. I reckon we shall have plenty to talk about in our future meetings."

Proceedings were interrupted when a spoon was banged on a table. Stuart Hardy addressed the gathering. "Please excuse me for interrupting your conversations, but today seems an appropriate time for me to say a huge personal thank you to James. It was he who came to the rescue with his friend Roger and later another friend Ben, when Melanie was attacked and nearly lost her life. Yesterday the attacker was sentenced to twenty years. By showing continuing friendship to Melanie, James has greatly assisted her healing, particularly of her mental health. As part of her thankyou Melanie has, with James's daughter Ruth, organised this party. Recently James and Melanie have been practising some duets and it was under the pretext of a rehearsal that James came here today knowing nothing of what was planned. I think as both have their music with them we should ask them to provide some entertainment."

James and Melanie responded by playing some of the pieces with which they felt sufficiently competent. James noted with interest that Robin, his grandson, who had given up playing the piano when he was fourteen, offered his services as a page turner for his grandad.

At the end of the party Ruth and her husband Michael took James home together with three pot plants, two bunches of flowers and boxes of chocolates and biscuits. When inside his apartment he needed several minutes to find homes for all his presents.

Early on Friday afternoon, the last day of her half-term Melanie visited James. James thanked her for the party but chided her that he hoped she had not spent too much time on the arrangements to the detriment of her studies. They quickly, with mutual consent, turned their conversation to the item that was providing them both with great excitement. This was the discovery of a secret passage leading from the fairly new hotel where the wedding reception had been held. The hotel incorporated the remains of an old manor house and the pair, with Robin, were keen to investigate whether the passage linked to the nearby church. They had been given permission to research the tunnel to see if it connected the two buildings. They were busy considering how they were to proceed with their investigations when they were interrupted.

They were sitting facing the view from the window when they heard a helicopter very close. It seemed to be almost next to the apartment. It flew backwards and forwards quite low as though searching. From time to time it would hover, spinning round slowly. What were they looking for? A criminal on the run, someone hurt and in need of immediate medical attention, perhaps someone lost or even seeking a suitable landing site? James was quick to point out that it was a police helicopter and not the air ambulance. He feared that the thought of the latter could cause Melanie some distress. They stood up, went close to the window to see if they could spot anyone who might be hiding or in trouble. James, whose eyesight had been so good since he had had cataracts removed, thought he noticed something moving. "Mel, please fetch me my field glasses." He had seen something. There was a person without a jumper or coat walking alongside a hedge and making towards a shed or shepherd's hut in the corner of a field. "I wonder if Rosie Bloom, from the Care Home, has spotted an opportunity to abscond. Would you like to phone the police? We might be able to get a message to the helicopter to tell them where to search."

While James kept the person in view Melanie managed to contact the police. He heard her say, "I am Melanie Hardy. My friend and I can see the police helicopter scanning the Coltsbrook Valley. We have seen someone in the fields without suitable clothing and wonder if he or she is lost and being sought." There was a pause then Melanie continued, "My friend James is watching with his field glasses and if it is possible with technology to put us in touch with the crew, we could direct them. ..... OK, I'll wait." In a few seconds she came and stood next to James, put the phone to his ear and he heard the pilot's voice.

James reported, "I can see both you and the person on the ground. If you turn and travel west, ... that's right. I think you should be above a large field with sheep. ...... Good, keep moving forward until you are above the next field. ..... That's it. Now turn to your left, over the hedge and you come to a smaller field. ..... To your left now, in the far southeast corner, there is a shed or a shepherd's hut. The person has just gone into that shed. ...... OK, while you land, I'll keep a watch on the shed."

James and Melanie watched and waited as the helicopter landed and an officer got out and went towards the shed. After two or three minutes a voice came on the line again. "We have her. It is the right person, Rose Bloom from 'Phillip's Rest' Care Home. She is quite distressed, cold and completely disorientated. We have a blanket to keep her warm, but we need a ground vehicle to fetch her."

James provided further advice, "Next to the opposite hedge to the west there is a track used by tractors. My friend Melanie, standing beside me has just spotted a police Range Rover on the road to which that track leads. If they can hear our conversation they are perfectly placed." Watching the Range Rover he continued, "Yes, that's the track." A policeman alighted from the vehicle to open the gate, then turned and looked at the buildings in which James's apartment was situated, spotted them as they had moved onto the balcony and gave them a wave and a thumbs up.

While the Range Rover was proceeding up the bumpy track, the officer from the chopper was guiding Rose to a gate in the hedge. Meanwhile the two watchers on the balcony spotted an ambulance making its way along the road to rendezvous with the Range Rover when it returned. In a few minutes Rose had been transferred to the ambulance where a check was made to see if she had come to any harm. The helicopter took off, turned towards James and Melanie and made a little bow before returning to base. Next the police Range Rover departed to continue its patrol. Ten minutes later the ambulance turned round and was soon lost to sight of Melanie and James as they left the balcony.

After such excitement they felt that they needed to steady their nerves with a cup of tea. While they had their tea, and a slice of birthday cake left over from the party, they wondered if they could pick up their discussions that had been interrupted and whether they would be able to concentrate. But a further interruption came in the form of a telephone call. It was Cedric Field at 'Phillip's Rest', wanting to thank them for the part they had played in Rosie Bloom's rescue. She had slipped out when the door was opened to receive a delivery. Between one parcel and the next she was gone. The staff looked for her as soon as the door was closed and soon realised she had used the distraction of a delivery to good use. By the time they looked outside she had disappeared and although staff went looking Cedric decided to phone for help.

Rosie was now back in the Home and in her room resting after her adventure. After James had put the phone down Melanie looked at him and inquired, "What are you grinning about?"

James replied, "I have just remembered what I heard the helicopter officer say to Rosie when he found her, 'Come along, flower, you're safe now, we'll look after you'. Then he called across to his colleague, 'Success, the flower can go back in its pot'."

HISTORY OF ST STEPHEN'S CHURCH, CRICKEN AND THE MANOR HOUSE HOTEL, CRICKEN

By Melanie Hardy and James Willoughby

A commentary on discoveries made initially during a wedding.

Cricken is not mentioned in the Doomsday Book, although two neighbouring villages are listed. The first recorded mention of the village appears in the twelfth century as Creek End. When the Empress Matilda, also sometimes called Empress Maude, invaded England from Normandy in 1139 intent on snatching the throne from her cousin King Stephen, she was supported, amongst others, by Henri Dacours. When Henri Dacours arrived in England, he switched sides and promised fealty to the king. In recognition of his support King Stephen granted Henri and his Saxon wife a parcel of land. This estate lay about five miles inland and in 1140 was located at the end of a creek that had access to the sea. In the intervening centuries the creek has silted up and laxity of speech and illegible writing has modified the name of the village.

Having taken possession of the land Henri Dacours first built a modest manor house with stables and outbuildings. His next project was to build a small church adjacent to the house. This church was consecrated by the King's brother, Henry of Blois, Bishop of Winchester, on his return journey after spending Christmas Day with the monarch. The consecration took place on the day following Christmas 1145, that is the feast day of St Stephen, the first Christian martyr. Henri's land proved fertile, and he was very satisfied that the farm next to his estate belonged to a Benedictine monastery, some twelve miles inland.

By the time Henry II, the son of the Empress Matilda, had succeeded to the English throne and peace had replaced the anarchy stemming from the civil war, Henri Dacours was prospering. He was able to establish a viable import and export business with his native Normandy as a result of the opportunity afforded by the access he had to the sea via the creek that reached his property.

Some three hundred years after Henri Dacours had settled in England, his descendants were well established. The wars between England and France and the battles between rivals for the English throne made little impact on the Lord of the Manor of Creeken and the villagers. Not only had the name of the village been modified, but so had the name of the family changed and they were known as Lord de Courcey and his Lady. The relationship with the Benedictine neighbours had also strengthened and the church had been enlarged.

When the first Tudor king, King Henry VII seized the crown, Thomas de Courcey believing that the country could look forward to a period of peace and prosperity, decided that the time had come for him to build a grander Manor House. He strengthened the current house and built another storey above it and then embarked on building a new wing each end. The project was nearly complete when the first rumblings of religious unrest in the land became apparent.

It was at about this time that a tunnel was dug to connect the church and the Manor house. The tunnel appears to have been dug from each end, but it is not clear if both parts were commenced simultaneously. Nor is it clear what was the original purpose of the tunnel. One theory is that the excavation at the house end was for the purpose of providing an ice-house. It is doubtful if the tunnel was intended to provide a dry passageway for the family to make an inconspicuous entry to the church.

Some considerable thought, effort and expense went into the construction of this passageway as the walls and ceiling are lined with brick. This construction has been effective for there is no evidence of any collapse. There are seven full height niches in the wall that provide good sized storage spaces. Somewhere near the midpoint of the passageway there is evidence of another tunnel, a sort of spur, leading off the first at right angles. The purpose and intended destination of this spur is open to speculation as no documentation has so far been discovered in which it is mentioned. It was probably abandoned soon after it was begun as it is no more than three metres in length and was bricked up many years ago. There is an indication of a possible date for some activity related to it as the letters MDL are scratched on the brickwork. These letters may relate to the initials of one of the tunnellers or could refer to the date 1550, which falls in the period when priest holes or hiding places were in active use. In the reign of King Edward VI catholic priests often needed to disappear from view at short notice, but during the reign of his successor Queen Mary I (often called 'Bloody Mary') it was the turn of protestants to make themselves scarce.

Both ends of the tunnel were sealed up many years ago, perhaps as many as one hundred and fifty years. The passageway was discovered by accident recently when a hotel guest lost her way and spotted a disused door. Investigation by a small group of researchers failed to find anyone with any knowledge of the tunnel. Such knowledge that is now available has come from old records that have been archived for at least a century. Some further information has been acquired through careful examination of the tunnel and possible access points at both ends.

During examination of the spur tunnel human remains were discovered. The wall was not dismantled but a camera was inserted through a small aperture. On the other side of the wall the body of a man was found laid out respectfully as though he had been given a Christian burial. The clothing that was found with him suggest that he was a priest. It is not possible to tell whether he lies where he died or if his body was brought in after death.

It maybe that the dead priest is the Rev Pierre de Courcey who was the incumbent of the parish from 1536 until 1550. He may have been hiding in the chamber in the tunnel and expired before he could be released. A decision may have been made to make the place where he died his burial chamber with the tomb sealed at that time, hence the date letters MDL scratched on the wall. If any identification plate was fixed to the tomb it has since disappeared, because the tunnel was not abandoned at that date, but could still have been used for as many as three hundred years.

Even before the tunnel was re-discovered there was knowledge amongst the local population of rumours of smuggling in the area. A few elderly residents who have spent their whole lives in Cricken believe that the smuggling of liquor (in bottles and tubs or small barrels), perfume and silks was a regular night-time activity in which many of the parish participated in the eighteenth century and perhaps the first part of the nineteenth. Although the creek had been dried up well before that time there was still a very easy passage to the shore, and it was possible for those who carried the contraband to move very quickly. There may have been other places in the village in which to hide goods on which duty had not been paid, but there is sufficient evidence to suggest that the tunnel was in regular use as a repository.

It appears that the use of the tunnel must have come to an abrupt halt as, when it was recently re-discovered, there was a significant quantity of booty still stored in it. Records of the proceedings of the county assizes for 1787 contain a list of five men and two women who were apprehended by excise men near the village of Creeken smuggling items of contraband ashore from a ship in the bay. All seven were sentenced to transportation for seven years to Sidney Cove in Australia. This may have resulted in a cessation in smuggling activity. It seems possible that the tunnel was boarded up at this time with an intention to resume activity at a future date and in order to protect previous hoards for later distribution. It is probable that changes in circumstances delayed the resumption, memories faded to be replaced with rumour. The discovery of the tunnel and its contents now gives credence to the rumours of smuggling.

The de Courcey family remained in the Manor House until the male line came to an end with the death in a riding accident of Albert de Courcey in 1807. His brother Edward, a sea captain, who would have inherited the estate, had died the previous year of wounds received at the Battle of Trafalgar. Their sister Amelia moved back to the house which had been her childhood home with her husband Hubert Deacon, whom she had married in 1796, and their two children. The children were a boy, also named William, then aged eight and a daughter, aged three, who died of consumption in 1809.

The Deacons lived quietly in Cricken for the next hundred years. Generation succeeded generation, but all families were small in number and the staff consisted of no more than a housekeeper, a maid and an estate manager. The estate during the Victorian years consisted of three small farms in the charge of tenant farmers. The first forty years of the twentieth century were not kind to the family. War and illness contributed to a reduction in their numbers, so that by the outbreak of the Second World War the house was inhabited only by the Reverend Francis Deacon and his sister Emma. It had been necessary to sell most of the estate land to pay death duties. Much of the village of Cricken, which had expanded during the interwar years, was built on land that had been part of the Manor House estate.

As Francis and his father before him were incumbents of the parish, the Manor House, for several years, doubled as the Rectory. In 1930, when his father died, Francis was thirty-six and unmarried; his sister Emma was twenty-nine and their two siblings who were born between them were both buried in the churchyard between house and church. While Emma supported her older brother in his work, she had plans to live her own life as she was engaged to a handsome airman, a test pilot named Rupert Fellowes.

Tragedy did not leave the members of the Manor House unscathed during the 1930s. In January 1931 Captain Rupert Fellowes's plane suffered serious engine failure while over the English Channel. He tried to restart the engine but failed and crashed into the sea. The pilot did not survive, although his body was recovered, and he was buried at Cricken two months before he was due to be married there. Francis, like many men of his age, had been a heavy smoker in his early adult life and by 1936 his lungs were not functioning as well as they should. He continued his ministry, but by the time war was declared he was a sick man. He died in April 1940 at the age of just forty-six, leaving Emma as the only surviving member of the Deacon family. She never married and lived almost as a recluse but continued tending the graves of her siblings and her fiancé until she was well into her nineties. Except for the last ten years when she had some help from visiting carers she lived alone in two rooms of the house. She was ninety-eight when she died three days into the new millennium.

In 2003 the Manor House and the remaining two acres of the original estate was acquired by a new owner. Part of the house was still habitable, but the rest was in a poor state of repair. The new owner demolished much of the building and replaced it with a modern hotel, while retaining one wing of the original for offices and storage.

*

The earliest part of the church is the north aisle built by Henri Dacours. Two major extensions have been added, expanding the church to the south and east. A bell tower was added at the west end in the reign of James I.

It now contains six bells. A form of minstrels' gallery was added in the south-west corner for the choir and an assortment of instrumentalists who accompanied the congregational singing.

Towards the end of the eighteenth century a partition was constructed in the north-western corner as a preparation area for the musicians before they ascended to the gallery. Probably at the same time a small area was devised next to this vestry for private prayer and an altar placed there against the north wall of the church. It is assumed that it was at this time that the mausoleum of the de Courceys, located behind the altar, was sealed up.

During the reign of Queen Victoria most new church buildings were built to gothic designs and many others underwent restorations or modifications. Following a visit by the architect Sir George Gilbert Scott in 1855, the gallery was removed, choir stalls were installed in the chancel and an organ was introduced. This work had been completed when another younger architect visited the church to view the alterations that had been made following the visit of a master church renovator. The young architect, who visited in 1867, was twenty-eight years-old Thomas Hardy who later turned to writing poems and novels, most of which were based in his Wessex.

No date has been determined for the insertion of the reredos behind the altar of the chapel in the north aisle, but it may have been included in the works undertaken following the visit of Gilbert Scott. It is believed that the font dates from the time of the building of the first church, but it was probably moved to its present position during the first expansion of the church, at which time seating, in the form of pews, was introduced. The present pulpit and lectern date from about 1800 and a small plate indicates that they were purchased by public subscription in memory of the seven villagers who were transported and never heard of again.

The three windows at the East End contain some fine stained glass. The side panels, which may be more recent than the central window, consist of coloured patterns designed to enhance that of St Stephen. As the first Christian martyr he is depicted being stoned. It is thought that this panel may date from the first expansion of the church, or it may be even older and originally located in the first building. Clearly evident is the use of yellow for the halo recognising sainthood, red for the blood of a martyr and blue, a colour used to depict sincerity and piety.

With the agreement of the Parish Church Council, the Diocese and the owner of the Manor House Hotel it is planned that, when finance is available, work will begin to make the passageway connecting church and manor house safe for limited viewing by the public. Proceeds from the sale of this booklet will be donated to the fund to allow this work to commence and, once completed and safety certificates obtained, to pay for its maintenance.

REVELATIONS AND DISTURBANCES

An unexpected meeting results in the revelation of past experiences and leads to the possible disturbance to the status quo of an elderly man.

The second Sunday in Lent was a bright clear day in March. James Willoughby stood on the balcony of his south-facing top floor apartment and observed the splendid view of the Coltsbrook Valley below him. There were so many signs that Spring was anxious to take over from Winter. In a field over to his left, next to the dual carriageway that connected the county town to the coast, he could see some of the first lambs of the year. Even at this distance he could see their tails sweeping a wide arc of excitement as they bonded with the ewes that had given them birth. As his gaze swept across the valley, he noticed that several of the hawthorn hedges were showing substantial patches of green as the season's new leaf-buds were opening. There were further signs that plants were awaking from sleep. He could see two, no three, places where the blackthorn was thrusting forth white blossom.

James was too far away to be able to distinguish wildflowers that had begun to make their appearances in verges bordering the hedges, but he knew that snowdrops and primroses had made their presence known. He knew a spot where he had caught sight of winter aconites flourishing last year and he determined to see if they were showing their yellow flowers yet. It was now almost a year since his family had helped him move into his current abode and he was looking forward to revisiting some of the exciting features he had noticed when he first arrived. Many of the hedgerow birds had built their nests when he arrived on the scene last year, but now he could see that nest building was a major occupation as nesting materials were being carried to chosen sites.

He did not know how long he might have stood there watching the activities of flora and fauna, had not a gust of cold air blown his dressing gown aside and rushed round his body. It reminded him that under his dressing gown he was naked, and he had only intended to take a quick glance outside while he was on his way from the kitchen, where he had had his breakfast, to the bedroom to get dressed for the day.

When he was dressed, he went down to the vestibule to collect his Sunday paper. He avoided the lift, nobly he thought, ensuring that he achieved some exercise. As he returned with the paper and its supplements, he wondered how much of it he would throw away without reading. On regaining his rooms, he prepared some vegetables to go with the portion of cottage pie his young friend Melanie had cooked for him. It only needed warming through. While he was cutting a serving of broccoli, he reflected on the way his friendship with Melanie had developed over the past nine months.,

He had met Melanie when she urgently needed help after being attacked and left unconscious. Although there was an age difference between them of nearly seventy years they had shared many happy times. Melanie regarded him as a surrogate grandad and called him her SG. Her original grandfathers had both died before she reached the age of four so James filled a void in her life. He had suffered a heart problem in the previous November and when he returned home from hospital, she had made a point of visiting him regularly on her way home from school. On many of her visits they would talk about her A level studies, discussing her English texts and talking about the historical context of them. As history was another of her subjects they were currently working together on a guidebook, which would explain the connection between a twelfth century church and the adjacent manor house. This exciting project had provided them with many hours of absorbing study as they researched old records.

His clock striking ten prompted James to make himself ready to walk to St Philip's Church to attend the ten-thirty holy communion service. He anticipated a pleasurable ten-minute walk on this beautiful morning with the sun providing early Spring warmth. As he reached the end of Waterfall Close, he met his friends Marjorie and Roger as they joined his route, making for the same destination. He was pleased to see how well Roger looked following the heart bypass operation that he had undergone in the summer.

On reaching the church some twelve minutes prior to the starting time for the service he found his favourite seat at the end of a pew immediately in front of the Crossing. When he sat up after a short time of private prayer, he discovered that a lady he had not seen before was occupying the other end of the pew. They had just introduced themselves when the vicar, Rev Len Nesbit, and Melanie demanded his attention. The husband of the organist and choir mistress had arrived at the church in a state of agitation to say that his wife had phoned him from A and E to say that she had broken a bone in her wrist. Apparently, she had tripped and fallen when she took her dog out first thing in the morning and as her wrist hurt, she thought she should have it checked. James had previously responded to pleas for help with providing an accompaniment for carol singing and the occasional service the vicar conducted at the local care home. This time he was asked if he could play the organ for the hymns during the service due to start in about eight minutes.

It was seven years since he had last played an organ, and he had never seen the one in this church. Ideally, he would have liked at least an hour to explore the instrument and familiarise himself with it. Melanie, who was a passable pianist offered to help him. There was just sufficient room for them both in the organ loft and all five hymns were fairly straightforward. He had played them all at some stage in his long life. He was pleased to find he had two manuals as well as a full pedal board at his disposal. In the five minutes left to him before the start of the service he extemporised, both with the introductory music he played, and in acquainting himself with the different stops and combinations that the organ contained.

With Melanie's help he provided the accompaniment needed. He was experimenting with some of the sounds the organ could produce and when he didn't like what he heard Melanie was quick to respond when he called "put the oboe in" or "cut out the swell to pedal". She nearly collapsed with suppressed laughter when he joined in with his own words with one hymn. He followed 'forty days and forty nights' with 'but only eight minutes for me'.

James admitted afterwards that he was thankful for a longish sermon, but as he hadn't listened very carefully, he wasn't sure whether it was boring or inspirational. It's length had allowed him time to study the variety of stops on the organ and consider which he might try for the remaining

hymns. He found sympathetic sounds to accompany the choir during the hymns while communion was being distributed. The final hymn was 'To God be the glory'. By then he had become much more confident of what the instrument was capable and for the last verse he pulled out most of the stops. As he had no organ music for a concluding voluntary, he enjoyed himself improvising on the tune of that last hymn by experimenting with some variations, changing the time, playing sometimes in the minor key and finishing with a final run through in which he increased the volume to a final flourish of the chorus with the full organ.

Some of the congregation were on their way home by the time he had locked the organ and made his way down the nave, but a sizeable proportion were chatting over coffee. Melanie, who had processed out with the choir before he started his voluntary, spotted him and rushed over to him, threw her arms round him, kissed him and exclaimed that he had done splendidly. He returned her kiss, thanked her for her help and turned to meet a beaming Revd Len who was coming towards him with the lady James had met very briefly before the service started. The vicar was effusive in his thanks and congratulations and then introduced the lady. Her name was Sylvia Marchant and although she had lived in the village for over a year this was only the second time she had been able to attend a service. She was now hoping to attend regularly as her mother, who had been bedridden and for whom she had been a full-time carer, had recently passed away at the age of ninety-five. The funeral was arranged for the Monday afternoon of the following week, but if Mrs Byrd was still incapacitated, they would need a replacement organist.

James looked at the vicar, then at Mrs Marchant and then caught sight of Melanie who had taken a step back. She was grinning as if encouraging him to respond positively to a question which had not yet been asked. He looked again at Mrs Marchant, caught her eye, smiled and she immediately asked, "Please, Mr Willoughby, would you be willing to play for mother's funeral? You played so beautifully today. I know you are now retired, but I would so love to hear you play again."

James replied, "If Mrs Byrd is unable to play and the vicar is happy for me to substitute, I should be pleased to offer my services. I do appreciate having eight days' rather than eight minutes' notice."

Seeing everyone smiling, Melanie interrupted, "SG, erm sorry, James, Mr Willoughby, would you like a cup of coffee?"

They all moved to a table to discuss the arrangements and to get to know each other. The vicar soon left them to speak to others of his flock. James soon discovered that Sylvia's mother had been taken ill soon after they arrived in Compton St Philip, so she had had little opportunity to get to know people. James asked, "Does her death mean that you are now on your own?"

Her reply was the start to another conversation, "My husband Kenneth had a stroke and died within two days, a month before we were due to move house."

"What a terrible shock and presumably a most difficult time for you. You said your husband's name was Kenneth. I knew a Ken Marchant several years ago. I don't suppose it could be the same person. Your husband wasn't a diplomat, was he?"

"Yes, he was. We spent about five years in Russia and ..."

James continued, "And how long in Hong Kong?"

"That's right, it must have been about eight years. Did you meet him there? Were you a diplomat, as well?"

"No. I wasn't in the diplomatic service, but I did have contact with your husband quite often. Shall we say that I was a dealer in antiques and erm, collectables. Ken and I had many very brief conversations in strange places as he was most interested in some of the 'exhibits' I discovered on my travels."

"Mr Willoughby?" she mused. "Oh! I think I know. Were you known as 'W'?"

"Well, we always thought Willoughby was a bit of a mouthful, although I suppose 'double U' isn't much shorter."

Melanie, with eyes nearly popping out of her head and her imagination running riot, exclaimed, "SG, does that mean you were a SPY?"

"My dear girl. Spy is not a very nice word, you know. Agent is much better, more refined. Don't you agree, Sylvia?"

"Oh, it's so lovely to meet someone who knew Ken, even if some of your contacts might be regarded as state secrets. And you will play for mother's funeral. It is many days since I enjoyed a day as much as I am enjoying this one." Turning to Melanie, she inquired, "May I ask you: why do you call Mr Willoughby SG? Is he still known by codenames?"

Melanie laughed and explained, "I suppose it is a codename that I invented for him. It stands for Surrogate Grandad. Both my real grandfathers died before I was four and last summer SG rescued me after I had been attacked and left for dead. Since I recovered we have done lots of things together and I love him to bits. He is so much the grandad I never had."

"That's lovely," responded Sylvia, "but I don't mean it's lovely that you were attacked, that sounds terrible, but that you have such a relationship with your SG. Was the attacker caught?"

'Yes, and SG was partly responsible for his apprehension. He was sentenced to twenty years last month. In a way I feel sorry for him; it's such a long time."

James had been quietly listening to this exchange, but then commented, "I love having Melanie around, she keeps me young. Now, Sylvia, we shall need to talk about the plans for next week and perhaps also how we can help you to be integrated into the community of this village. Here is my card with address and phone number. If you would like to give me a call in the next couple of days, we can meet to discuss the funeral arrangements and any other matters with which I may be able to help."

While James was having his mid-morning coffee the next day Sylvia phoned to say that she would be meeting the vicar during the morning the following day and asked if she could call to see him in the afternoon. Shortly after she had phoned the vicar rang to inform him that Mrs Byrd would have difficulty using her hand for three or four weeks. After some discussion he agreed to play for one service each Sunday until she could return and to rehearse the choir on Friday evenings.

Precisely on time on Tuesday the buzzer sounded in his apartment and when he had checked via the intercom, he went down the stairs to meet Sylvia and accompany her to his home. They did not take long to agree the music she would like him to play, leaving the choice of pieces before the funeral party arrived in church for him to select but she would like him to include something by Bach. Once the matters relating to the funeral were settled, they continued to chat about shared experiences. It was James who moved the conversation on to recent times.

"Where did you live before you came to this village, Sylvia?"

"London, or to be more precise, North London, Southgate. We were there 24 years from the time Ken's overseas service ceased, but we had always promised ourselves we would seek a village life when Ken retired. It took a long time before we finally made the decision to put that plan into practice. Firstly, there was mother's illness and we felt we couldn't leave her. She had been a widow since she was forty and she lived five minutes from us. Then there was our son, Matt, to consider, until three years ago when he fell for an Australian girl and decided to make his home in Brisbane. We looked at several places and had a shortlist of about four, but the house in this village settled it as there was suitable accommodation for mother. Then Ken had his stroke and now mother has gone, and I have this big house to myself."

"Does being alone concern you? There are ways of dealing with loneliness. I am well into my second decade of living by myself, but I do have the advantage of having family not too far away. They have been good to me, but they have their own lives to live. We keep in touch, but mostly by phone. I moved here just under a year ago, but I have made several friends. I suppose my best friend is young Melanie. We must appear a very odd pair, but I don't feel the age difference hampers our relationship."

"I have been wondering about her. You rescued her when she had been attacked, I believe. Would you tell me about it?"

James then described the incident when Melanie's dog had sought his help when he had taken his friend Roger out in his wheelchair. *[see 'The Dog Rescuer']* He then explained that after he had a week in hospital with a heart problem Melanie had offered to help with his aftercare when he returned home.

"She has been calling here for an hour most evenings on her way home from school for about four months. I have to admit my life has been enlivened since she came into it, although she has another admirer now, my grandson. I suppose it is nearly time for her visit."

"Then I should go."

"Please stay, if you can. I should like you to get to know her better and she can tell you about the project we are currently working on."

"That sounds interesting. Yes, I should like to know her better. In fact, I should like to know you both better as I need to shake off the image, if I have it, of being a recluse."

"You can also ask her to tell you about my birthday party. Oh, here she is. Time to put the kettle on again."

Talk of birthday parties had to take a back seat when Melanie arrived as she had news of her own to impart. "I'm sorry I am a few minutes late, but I stayed on the school bus and went home first, then Mum lent me her car. I had to promise to be very careful as I only passed my test this morning."

"Congratulations!" cried both James and Sylvia at the same time. James continued, "You kept very quiet about learning. I knew you could keep secrets. Does Robin know you have been taking lessons and have you told him your news, but I suppose he won't be home yet?"

"Yes, he wormed it out of me, or rather he guessed. When he borrowed Lucy's car to come over to see me, he noticed the L plates on Mum's car. Now I shall be able to take you out SG and we can go for picnics."

Sylvia chimed in at that point, "You might have to fight me for that privilege as I was thinking the best way for me to explore the area is to take a real-life guide with me. Perhaps we can share if I have school days, and you have weekends and holidays."

"That might work" agreed Melanie.

"Just a moment," interrupted James. "Am I allowed a say in these arrangements? Why can't I go out with both my girlfriends on the same outing?"

Melanie was quick to respond, "James Willoughby, you are becoming too greedy. First you want your birthday to last two days, now you want two girlfriends at the same time. And I still have to have words with you for not telling me you could speak Russian and that you have visited several different countries."

"Melanie, I know you can now drive a car, but that doesn't mean you have to get on your high horse as well. Would you both like a cup of tea?"

"You always find a way of teasing me, don't you? I'll make the tea and then you can tell us about your Russian experiences. Robin didn't know much about your early life, and he had never thought to ask his dad."

While she was in the kitchen Sylvia enquired, "I assume Robin is her boy-friend and your grandson?"

"She and Robin met here at a party on New Year's Day and what happened between them is the clearest manifestation I have witnessed of 'love at first sight'. Robin changed from being a useless layabout to becoming a responsible adult. Within two days he had decided on a career and got himself a position with a firm of solicitors, so that he could start his training. Within a few days he had engineered an invitation for Melanie to attend his sister's wedding. It was while we were at the wedding that Melanie discovered the entrance to a closed-up tunnel connecting the hotel and the nearby church."

Melanie emerged from the kitchen with a tea-tray and took up the story. "It's ever so exciting, and SG and I are now writing a history of the church and manor house that has been turned into the hotel. But I want to hear the Russian spy story. How did you get involved SG?"

"Do you want to hear this as well, Sylvia?" inquired James, and receiving a nod he commenced his story. "At school I did well in languages and history. Unusually we had a teacher who was fluent in Russian – I think his family may have been Jewish-Russian emigrees who had fled from the pogroms. He taught mainly French, but also Russian to sixth formers. I continued to study Russian at university as well as history. I was more interested in social rather than political history, including the way the use of artefacts had assisted civilisation. One day I was scrutinising some jewellery in an antique shop when the owner noted my interest and we got talking. I mentioned the works of Karl Fabergé and wondered how you could tell the genuine article from a fake. Out of that conversation came a job with a world-renowned auction house and a trip to Russia to try to get an answer to my question."

"When did you go to Russia and were you there during the cold war?" asked Sylvia.

"I had worked with the auction house for several years and built up a long list of contacts in many parts of the world before I made my first trip to Russia at the beginning of 1964, by which time there was a hint that there might be some thawing of the cold war."

"Was Khrushchev still in charge then?" inquired Melanie.

"Yes, he was although he was deposed by Brezhnev later in the year. When I met him he seemed to have mellowed, but that may have been because he had no need to demonstrate his power."

"You met Khrushchev! Really? How did that happen?"

"Purely by accident. I visited an ex-employee of the Fabergé company in Moscow. He had retired but was still an eminent jeweller. During our conversation, his wife, who also acted as his secretary, buzzed him to say that Mr K with two men was downstairs and would like to see the expert as he had a jewel on which he would like an opinion. Mr K and his bodyguard were shown in before I had a chance to say goodbye and leave. Mr K was happy for me to remain, realised that I was English and asked me why I was visiting Russia and how long I had been in the country. I explained that I was an antique dealer and worked with a London auction house and that I had come to Russia to learn more about the fine art works that Russians had produced. I told him that I had visited the famous Hermitage Museum in Leningrad, as St Petersburg was then named. He asked me if I had met many English in Moscow and mentioned Kim Philby. I replied that I had not met him in Russia as he wasn't a friend of mine, although I was acquainted with him. He wanted to know how much longer I would be in his country, and I told him that sadly I only had two days left and I hoped to be able to get a ticket to see Swan Lake at the Bolshoi before I left. He commended me for that wish, but remarked that it was a pity I would not be able to see Galina Ulanova dance, to which I replied that I had been fortunate to have seen her when she visited London and danced at Covent Garden before she retired. As I withdrew, having thanked my host, I realised that I had previously met one of the bodyguards and I was permitted to tell him that I had located a client who had some fine Tonbridge Ware to sell. The bodyguard indicated that he would contact me later. When he did so he presented me with a ticket for the ballet sent by the compliments of his boss."

"Kim Philby?" questioned Sylvia. "Wasn't he a double agent? How did you become acquainted?"

"He was revealed the previous year and lived the rest of his life in Russia. I rather stretched a point when I said I was acquainted with him. A few years earlier in London on a tube train I noticed that name on the briefcase of a man sitting opposite me. As we both got off at the same station he said, 'after you'."

"It's a wonder you didn't get into trouble. What if your questioner had known the truth?"

James continued, "I think that's enough about me for one session."

Sylvia decided it was time to take her leave. Turning to James, she thanked him for his hospitality for a most agreeable afternoon and for agreeing to play for the funeral. "I shall see you on Sunday with my sister who is staying with me from Thursday until Tuesday. James, there won't be a wake for there will be so few of us, so please come back to the house for some refreshment after the funeral." As she left, she turned and gave James a resounding kiss.

When she had gone Melanie remarked, "There you are, now you have two girlfriends, so you can't complain about me having two boyfriends. She is nice, though, isn't she? I could tell you liked her from the way you looked at her."

"Your observational skills are improving all the time, but you're right. Sylvia is very pleasant, and I should be quite happy to get to know her better. She will need some time to get used to living alone. It occurs to me that when we have finished the first draft of the Cricken history we might ask her to read it critically."

"That's a good idea as she is detached from the whole episode of discovery. Now I must be going."

"Be careful how you drive, my darling. Once again, my congratulations and I hope to say that again when you get your A level results in the summer. Now I must say goodbye to both my girlfriends in the same way." So another kiss and then he was left alone.

He sat for a while and reviewed the afternoon. "Melanie was right," he thought. "I do like Sylvia and she is a little nearer my age than Mel. She must be around seventy, but still very trim and upright, looking younger. What colour are her eyes? Perhaps a sort of ash blue. Her hair is cut fairly short, now grey but just sufficient hint of colour to suggest it was originally fair or perhaps a light auburn. She has a gorgeous smile and I love the way her top lip crinkles on one side when she says something a little saucy."

He continued to sit and think. After a while he thought, "I wonder what has attracted me to Sylvia. It is not as though I have not been in contact with other ladies since Anne died. Is there something about her that I have not seen in anyone else? I certainly like the idea of being with her and I feel that I want to know her better. At the moment I feel that I want to share much more time with her and explore places with her. This really is quite disturbing, as I had determined that I would live out the rest of my days alone or in residential care. I feel that I am facing a battle between my head that tells me that I should not enter into anything more than a platonic friendship and my heart that is inclining me towards a much deeper relationship. I wonder if Sylvia has similar feelings or am I just being a silly old man?"

Two hours later he woke up to the phone ringing. He wondered if, or perhaps hoped that, it would be Sylvia phoning. Someone had dialled the wrong number. No solution to his dilemma and certainly no calming the disturbance to his equanimity. Maybe he would have to resort to the advice he had been given as a young man by his mother, that if he had a problem he couldn't solve, he should sleep on it.

CONFESSIONS OF A SERIAL ATTACKER

A sex attacker repents in prison.

Sylvia Marchant and James Willoughby were taking advantage of some warm spring sunshine to sit on the veranda of a hotel restaurant overlooking the sea while they enjoyed afternoon tea. This was the second excursion they had undertaken since they had become acquainted. Their friendship had begun in a somewhat unusual manner.

On a Sunday in March James had settled himself in his favourite pew in church waiting for the service to begin. He had just greeted a lady, whom he not met previously and who had sat in the same pew when he was tapped on the shoulder by a worried vicar. The vicar had just received news that the organist had fallen and broken her wrist. Although eighty-six years old and with what he considered were dormant organ playing skills he had agreed to help. He managed to acquit himself well and received many thanks and congratulations at the end of the service including from the stranger he had met briefly before the service. It was Sylvia who was introduced to him as a lady whose mother had recently died at the age of ninety-five. He agreed to play for the funeral and discovered that he had known Sylvia's husband Ken whom he had met in Russia and Hong Kong when he had contact with British diplomats. Sylvia and her mother had moved from London to the village of Compton St Philip just over a year ago, a few days after Ken had died unexpectedly.

Having cared for and nursed her bed-ridden mother almost from the day she arrived in the village Sylvia had made very few contacts, but she found that James and she had much in common and a friendship rapidly developed. The fifteen-year age gap was no barrier to their enjoyment of each-other's company.

Where they were sitting they were well placed above the beach to be able to see a fishing boat at work. "What do you think they are fishing for?" questioned Sylvia.

"I was wondering that," replied James. "I wonder if they are after mackerel or possibly sea bass. They are bringing something on board now. Where are my glasses?" He located his field glasses and continued. "I think it is mackerel. I wonder where they take them for sale."

"We could take a tour along the coast and see if there are any stalls with freshly caught seafood."

"What a splendid idea. Perhaps someone will also have a facility for smoking mackerel. That reminds me of your sister. Is she well?"

"Yes, she is well, thank you. I spoke to her last night. But why does mackerel remind you of my sister? What a funny thing!"

"I suppose it does sound a bit odd. When we had refreshments after your mother's funeral Norma offered me smoked mackerel pieces on biscuits. And at the same time she told me that she thought you and I would get on well together."

"She said something similar to me. In fact she came on quite strongly and said that I needed to get to know you so that I wouldn't just stay in the house all the time. But then Norma has never been slow to offer advice, which sometimes is close to telling me what to do."

"Have you told her about our plans for our next excursion?"

"Oh, you mean the visit to the Cricken tunnel. No, that is something I am keeping quiet about. By the way, is the guidebook back from the printers yet?"

"I'm expecting it tomorrow, but I shall wait until Melanie calls after school before opening the package."

Sylvia was silent for a few moments before she inquired, "How is Melanie? I thought she was rather quiet when I saw her last Sunday."

"I am a little concerned about her. I know her A levels are only two or three weeks away, but I don't think they are worrying her. I am afraid the attack that nearly killed her has been on her mind rather too much recently."

"Does she fear another attack? You said it was a very nasty experience and she has told me that it was a good thing you found her when you did."

"No, it is not fear that is bothering her. I think she received a shock when she heard the length of the sentence handed down to the attacker. She would like to know if he has repented and if he has, whether his time in prison might be reduced. Since she has become so attached to my grandson Robin and dreams of a happy future with him, she realises that the young offender will be forty-six before he is released and his chances of meeting a wife and raising a family might be for ever denied him."

"I think I can understand that. Is there anything we can do to help her?"

"I have been considering whether there is a way to help. We may be able to find out something about the young man, but I don't think the court records will be much help even if we can have access to them. He pleaded guilty, so a psychiatrist's report, if there was one, may not have been read out in court. There was certainly none in the press coverage. I think I shall have a word with the police sergeant I have met several times: she even came to my surprise birthday party."

"Yes, see what you can find out and what you are allowed to know. But talking of birthday parties it will be my seventieth next month and I should like you and Melanie to come to tea."

"I shall look forward to that. Why don't you call tomorrow afternoon when Melanie and I unwrap the guidebook and then you can invite her yourself? The guidebook and the party might give her new matters on which to focus her thoughts."

The following morning James phoned the local police station and asked if Sergeant Jane Cartwright was available. He discovered that she would not start her duty until 1400, but that a message would be left for her to phone him when she could.

James had the kettle on when first Sylvia and then Melanie arrived shortly after 4 pm. When everyone had had a cup of tea James opened the package that had arrived earlier, and they all received a first sight of the guidebook that Melanie and James had co-authored. The authors had been admiring it when Sylvia remarked, "You realise that there will need to be a second edition when the tunnel has been made safe and available for public inspection. That will be the ideal time to include some photographs."

"Of course," Melanie responded, "and perhaps we should launch the book at a special first viewing to which distinguished and knowledgeable guests could be invited."

James was about to comment when his phone rang. He picked it up and heard Jane Cartwright's voice, so he slipped into the kitchen and closed the door. After brief checks on each other's health James explained his concern about Melanie's state of mind in relation to her attacker's imprisonment. He asked if it was possible to find out about the man's background and whether he had shown any remorse since he had been in prison. Jane promised to make some enquiries, but it might take her a couple of days.

Sylvia looked up when he returned. He was able to give her nod and a thumbs up while Melanie was not looking his way. Melanie then turned to him and informed him that Sylvia had invited her to her birthday party, to which Sylvia said, "It won't be a big affair as I don't know many people yet, but I have some very helpful and friendly neighbours who I hope will join us. I have begun to get to know a few people at church and your parents have been very friendly, Melanie."

James did not have an opportunity to tell Sylvia about his phone conversation with the police sergeant as she offered Melanie a lift and they left together, but he did invite her to meet him in the village for coffee the following morning. He also noticed Melanie's reaction to his invitation and wondered what she was reading into him meeting Sylvia. He thought there was a suggestion of approval that he should spend time with Sylvia.

Over coffee the following morning James explained that Sergeant Cartwright had agreed to make some enquiries and report back to him in a couple of days or so. James also remarked that Sylvia's birthday being on a Saturday and planned in advance would mean that Melanie would not have an exam on that day, and she would not be involved in planning a surprise party as she did for him.

Early on Friday morning James received a phone call from Jane Cartwright with some information. James was in his sitting room looking out at the valley and watching the traffic on the dual carriageway from the coast, as Jane started to tell him that she had some interesting news about the young man who attacked Melanie. James interrupted her saying, "Jane, I am sorry to interrupt but I am just looking at something on the dual carriageway that you and your officers may need to be aware of. From my window I can see a lay-by on the north facing carriageway which is well back and screened from the road as it was a bend in the old road. A lorry has just pulled in, the driver has left his cab, gone to the back of the lorry, opened the doors and several people have just got out and are now standing around. And two minibuses are just pulling in. I don't know if the lorry has come from a port and if the people are illegal immigrants. Most, if not all, are men. Perhaps they are a sports team, although they don't look very athletic."

"It sounds as though you may have happened upon a crime again, James," replied Jane. "Now, just a moment ...... I am sending out an alert and hope to be able to get officers to the scene as soon as possible. Please keep watching....... Good, we have an unmarked car and a patrol car about a mile south. Are the people getting into the buses?"

"Not yet, they are just standing around. There is some discussion going on between the drivers. I think there could be about twenty of them, mainly men, and they have been given bottles of water. A few seem to have disappeared into the bushes, probably to relieve themselves. Nothing much happening at the moment..... Oh! that's clever. I think it is probably your unmarked car that has pulled into the lay-by and the patrol car has gone past and is reversing into the other end to block the exit. And I can see a chopper coming from the east – it's quick work if it is a police one. I'll keep observing. ...... I am mightily impressed at the speed with which the operation is being conducted as a police van is just arriving as well. I am looking at the drivers now and there are two of the visitors talking to them. By the amount of arm waving I think the discussion could be quite heated. .... One of the drivers and one of the men have gone into the lorry. Now most of the others are crowding round the back of the lorry, ... but they are now moving back and .... Oh..... they are carrying someone out. It looks like a child. I notice that some of the passengers are sitting down or lying down. I don't think they look very well. A second police van is on its way. The helicopter is hovering overhead – I think it is probably checking that no one is making a run for it. I think you might now say that the situation is contained."

Jane then spoke up, "James, thank you so much for being so observant. I think I had better give my attention to this little matter and ring you back in an hour or so with the information I was about to give you."

It was three hours before Jane rang again. She began by reporting on the morning's exercise, 'Twenty-two immigrants have been detained including a boy who is very ill and several others are receiving medical treatment. The three drivers have been arrested and Border Force officers are currently questioning them. The operation is on-going and the BF are very interested in mobile phones, laptops and satnavs they have seized, not to mention a significant quantity of drugs and other contraband discovered hidden in a secret compartment in the lorry. I believe the sniffer dogs had a lovely time. I have been asked to express very grateful thanks to our unofficial detective."

"Thank you, Jane, and many thanks for giving me an update. Perhaps you will have more news later and maybe there will be a press release sometime in the future."

"If, as I suspect it will, this turns out to be a major coup, I am sure it will be reported in the press and probably on television news. Now, let's rewind about three hours and I'll tell you what I have found out about Mr Dean Savage. He is in prison in Exeter and still has more than nineteen years of his sentence remaining. Initial reports of his attitude are favourable and he has been open in his discussions with prison staff, counsellors and visitors. Importantly, he has recognised that what he did was wrong and that he deserves the punishment meted out to him. It seems that his upbringing and home circumstances during which he was sexually abused gave him a very warped view of relationships. He has expressed a wish to apologise to the women he assaulted. From what I have learned I feel that he is making the sort of progress that might lead to a reduction in his sentence. At the point of release, he will need to be given a supportive environment to develop his future life. I hope this information will help you to reassure Melanie."

"That is very helpful, but can you tell me if the visitors he has spoken to have been prison visitors or family members."

"Oh yes, that is a significant point. Neither his mother nor any family member has been near him, either by visit, letter or telephone enquiry.

He thinks his mother has a brother in Australia or New Zealand, but he has never met him. It is just possible that the omission of family visits is a good thing."

James did not meet Sylvia for the next four days to discuss the information he had received about the young man in prison, there being no opportunity for such a conversation when they met in church on Sunday. By the time they had a chance to chat James had further information to impart.

"Well James, tell me what you have found out," demanded Sylvia, almost before they had sat down.

"Quite a lot has happened since we last had a chat. I told Jane about our concern over Melanie's state of mind when I disappeared into the kitchen while you were both looking at the guidebooks, so Jane had agreed to find out what she could about the attacker's progress in prison. Jane phoned on Friday morning and after we had disposed of a little matter relating to the apprehension of a score of immigrants and the arrest of traffickers, she was able to give me some positive news of the attitude and progress of Dean Savage in Exeter prison. I have made some further telephone calls and spoken to both the prison Governor and the Chaplain. I had a long chat with the Chaplain, who has apparently had a series of lengthy discussions with Dean. I had explained that as an elderly friend of one of the ladies who had been attacked, I wanted to be able to provide some good news to set the young lady's mind at rest. That statement prompted the response, 'Is your name Mr James Willoughby, by any chance?'"

"I am not sure how he had heard about me, but he seemed relaxed about discussing the prisoner's attitude. It seems that the lad is quite bright but hasn't achieved what he is capable of. That underachievement is not surprising given his home background. The Chaplain felt he could give me some information without going into great detail. As a child Dean was abused and there seems to have been an absence of any real love in his home relationships. Apparently, the lad has no idea who his father is and the only men he saw in his home were his mother's clients. Do you understand what I mean by that description, Sylvia?"

Seeing her nod James continued, "His early life seems to have been almost devoid of contact with any individual who offered him any warmth or care. Some of his teachers seemed to have recognised his need and he is thankful for the attention and encouragement they gave him. There was also a neighbour who would take him into her home after school and give him a drink and something to eat on occasions when she found him sitting on the front door-step waiting for his mother to return.

"Again, not surprisingly, he became a loner at school having no firm friends as he could not join in with other children who talked about their home lives with two parents, grandparents and siblings. He had no experience he could share and he had no knowledge of going on holiday or of trips out. He admits he just drifted aimlessly. When he discovered that he could join the junior library he borrowed story books and would sit in his room during school holidays reading. Later, when he became a teenager he was able to borrow books from the senior library.

"He had a reasonable school attendance record and managed to achieve a few GCSE's, albeit with rather low grades. He seems to have been quite competent in mathematics and found history interesting. He read historical novels, detective stories and a range of fiction, so that when he left school he had difficulty relating the real world to the fictional one that he had inhabited in his mind.

"The Chaplain told me that Dean found a job with a car dealership when he left school. He admits that he would have been one of the unemployed but for the fact that when he was admiring the cars on the forecourt he was asked if he was looking for a job. He was taken on initially to wash the cars before they went on display. Having employment probably kept him out of trouble with the law, although he admits to some petty theft such as shoplifting sweets and biscuits. As soon as he had a regular wage packet he left home and rented his own rooms.

"He seems to have had very little contact with girls and admits that he didn't know how to talk to them. He met a couple of girls in his twenties, but the relationships never developed. He seems to have regarded them more as objects rather than people. His attitude towards them was that if he fancied them he could make free with them without considering their feelings. So when he progressed in his workplace to more responsible roles and was asked to drive cars from one branch of the dealership to another elsewhere in the country he found that he had the opportunity to look for females walking alone that took his fancy.

"It was clear to me that a vital element of his education had been missed. His social and moral development had been totally neglected. The Chaplain repeated what he had implied earlier that Dean had realised that his behaviour was totally unacceptable and that he deserved to be removed from society. He now thinks that he was not a fit person to be a member of society. He actually described himself as evil.

"Then the Chaplain played me part of a recording of a session he had had with Dean. I was so impressed that I asked to hear it again. I think I can repeat it fairly accurately. This is what Dean said:

'Do you know I feel much more confident in here, because I don't feel an outcast, but I have learned a lot? I realise that I never used to think about others and how they felt. I certainly didn't think I could help someone else by doing something for them or just sitting talking to them. You *(that's the Chaplain)* have really encouraged me to come to terms with my past life and plan how I can live a better one. As you know there are several of us prisoners that go to chapel regularly. When we are challenged to think about our sins I just wish I could blot out my past. You say that when I confess those sins to Jesus and say I am sorry he will wipe the record clean. But I still feel I need forgiveness from those I harmed. I would like to be able to write to each of them and express my regrets for what I did to them and ask them if they could ever think of forgiving me.'

"Before we finished our conversation," James reported, "I told the Chaplain that I would tell Melanie of Dean's confession and repentance as she has expressed concern about the impact that his long sentence could have on his future life and, if I thought it appropriate, I would ask her how she would feel if she received a letter asking forgiveness from the man who attacked her.

"We agreed to keep in touch and exchange information about how the two young people progress in their different forms of rehabilitation. Now, dear, you have been very quiet. Did I do the right thing?"

"I think you have done well and that you have gleaned enough information to be able to settle Melanie's concerns. Are you going to tell her or would you like me to talk to her?"

"Although Mel seems to be willing to discuss potentially quite difficult matters with me I think she might appreciate it if you talk to her woman to woman. But, perhaps, it would be best if I report to her parents before anything is said to the girl. They knew that I had spoken to Jane Cartwright and they were happy for me to contact the prison. I'll let you know when I have spoken to Becky and Stuart."

"Fine; I'll wait for the signal. In the meantime, what's this little matter of immigrants that you mentioned in passing?"

"Oh yes. That was fun, but I haven't told Melanie about that. Can you wait until I can tell you both at the same time. You probably know some of it already."

"OK, but you are a tease, aren't you?"

When Melanie arrived at her usual time the next day, she found James and Sylvia looking very serious and the teapot and cups already waiting to be served. Sylvia spoke first. "Melanie, please sit down and listen carefully because we have something to tell you."

Looking at James, Melanie whispered, "You're not going to tell me you have a serious illness, are you?"

"No, my dear," replied James. "I am tired, but that's because I have been making some investigations that Sylvia will tell you about."

Sylvia took up the tale. "Mel, we both felt that you seemed to be not quite yourself as though you have been worrying about something. We may be wrong, but from comments you have made we thought that someone has been on your mind. James has been making some enquiries and has had a long conversation by phone with a prison Chaplain about an inmate named Dean Savage."

"Is that the man who attacked me?"

"That is correct. He learned a lot about Dean's upbringing. I don't think I have ever heard such a terrible story, and we do not know all that he went through during his childhood. Enough to say that he had a very warped view of life and what is acceptable behaviour. What he has been through does not excuse his actions, but it does go some way to explain why he behaved as he did. It seems that he has had many conversations with the Chaplain who has worked wonders with him. It sounds as though he is a changed man. Dean has expressed remorse and wishes he had not behaved, as he said, wickedly towards the ladies he attacked. He says that prison has been the right place for him. He even thinks he has been happier there than at any other stage of his life. He has talked to the Chaplain about his wish to write personally to all the ladies to apologise and to ask if they can forgive him. It is far too early in his sentence to talk about reducing it, but when the time comes for review the Governor thinks that if he continues to make progress he would have every chance of being successful.

"James and the Chaplain are going to keep in touch, so that we can learn if Dean's rehabilitation is maintained. You may be interested to know that his best subjects are mathematics and history. Your parents knew that James was going to phone the prison and they now know what I have told you."

Melanie sat still and silent for two or three minutes, before speaking in a small voice full of emotion. "You undertook all that enquiry for me, so that you could help me to understand why he attacked and why he had such a long punishment? Thank you, thank you, I feel so loved, my dear SG." She came and sat beside him, put her arms round him, kissed him and then the tears flowed. After a short period, she dried her eyes, got up and went and kissed Sylvia and thanked her for the help she had given.

Melanie continued thoughtfully, "So he never had the sort of home life that I had. He must have felt that everyone rejected him, and life was against him. His attacks must have been his way of getting his own back and the only way he could stick up for himself. What a mess! But I am so glad to hear that he has realised that he needs to change and is making an effort to do so. Although it might upset me, I would be willing to receive a letter from him."

After a further pause James dealt with practical matters by saying, "Now shall we have that cup of tea? And there may be some biscuits as well and then I will tell you about the immigrants."

"The immigrants!" cried Melanie. "The ones that were in the national papers? Don't tell me you were involved in their arrest!"

"That's right and I did it all from my balcony." He then told them the story and concluded, "They thought they had found a secluded spot away from the road to make the exchange, but they hadn't looked my way. I had a wonderful view and I was already talking to the police when it all started. Unfortunately, I was too far away to see the expressions on the faces of the drivers when the police turned up. It's a pity you weren't here, Melanie, with your camera."

THE CASE OF THE AERIAL PHOTOGRAPHS

Examination of aerial photographs taken in preparation for an archaeological dig leads to the discovery of a forty-year-old crime.

By rising early on a pleasant June morning and having done all he needed to indoors, James Willoughby decided that he could spend a few minutes in the local park before reading his morning newspaper. Although now eighty-six and living alone in an apartment in Clarence House with a splendid view over the Coltsbrook Valley, he was still active, both mentally and physically.

Accordingly, he walked down the two flights of stairs to reach the ground floor, through the front door, turned right and came to the park. It was not a large park and it was not enclosed by fences or railings, but it contained a small lake that was home to several water birds. The flower beds and lawns were well tended and the roses were just beginning to provide a wonderful show of colour and fragrance. After having walked round the park James parked himself on a seat facing the road where he could watch the world go by.

He was thinking about the time about a year before when he had sat on the same seat and a decrepit van pulled up and the driver asked for directions. That inquiry was the start of the capture of sheep stealers for he had been able to provide information to the police at the right time. Sitting still in the pleasantly warm sunshine he was daydreaming, as he had been on that other occasion, when a car stopped and hooted. This time it was his friend Sylvia Marchant.

"Good morning, Jim. I thought you must be out as I could not get a reply when I phoned."

"Hello, Sylvia. You're another early bird today."

"That's right, I have just been up to Bate's farm for some eggs. How about coming back with me for coffee, followed by a short walk up the track that leads to Compton St Mary and then back for soup and a roll?"

"That sounds splendid. Thank you, I'm not at a loose end, but I have nothing that I must do today. I accept."

Whereas James lived a gentle ten-minute walk east of the centre of Compton St Philip, Sylvia lived about the same distance to the west. After coffee they set out along the road in which Sylvia's house was situated. At the end of it they reached a junction where Sylvia's road met three others. One was the main road from Compton St Philip which then branched into two: one branch went to Coltsford village and the other by a rather circuitous route to Compton St Mary. Opposite the end of Sylvia's road was a track and bridleway to Compton St Mary. It set out between two of three properties that had been extended from detached farm cottages. The single one on the right was set in over two acres of field in which there was stabling for horses.

As they followed the track up a steady gradual incline between hedges with wild flowers at the border, it turned slightly to the right. Once round the bend they saw a stand of trees in a field that was accessible through a field gate. They stopped to look at the trees and realised that the trees were growing around a small lake. Their attention was caught by a slight movement. They noticed that there was a man sat at an easel painting. Curious to see his work they went through the gate. He saw them coming and waited to speak to them.

The painter greeted them, "Good morning, you have caught me at my hobby. I just had to take the opportunity of painting the lake in this morning light. I have painted it several times but have never been fortunate to see it as it is this morning. Do either of you paint?"

James replied, "I'm afraid I don't, but that does not stop me admiring the skill of others. I have had contact with many fine works of art in the past. May we look at your creation?"

"Be my guest, but there is still much more to do. I shall continue to work on it when I get it back to my studio."

As they looked, Sylvia noticed a name. "Tobias Schiller! Is that your name?"

"That's me, but most people call me Toby."

James and Sylvia introduced themselves. James was looking not just at the picture but at the lake and trees generally. "This place makes me think of a place I visited in my youth in Surrey. Do you know it – the Silent Pool at Shere near Newlands Corner?"

"I have heard of it. Isn't there some legend attached to it?"

"That's right. The legend dates from the time of King John. Some nobleman riding past on his horse spotted a woodcutter's daughter bathing naked in the lake. He tried to lure her out of the lake, but she went further in, so he rode into the lake on his horse. She went into the deepest part and drowned."

"How terrible!" exclaimed Sylvia. "But Newlands Corner? Isn't that where Agatha Christie's car was found when she disappeared for a few days?"

"Absolutely right," replied James. "It is also near where we lost my grandfather."

"You lost your grandfather!" cried Sylvia and Toby in unison. "How did you do that?"

"Well, my parents, my grandfather, my brother and I were going out for the day. I must have been fourteen or fifteen. I think we had a planned a picnic, but our route took us over the North Downs at Newlands Corner. As we approached the top of the hill there was a common on the right-hand side of the road with lots of blackberries ripe for picking. So we stopped and started picking and gradually wandered apart. After half-an-hour or so my father called to us to return to the car. Four of us did so, but grandfather didn't. We searched and searched. There was no sign of him. Eventually we contacted the police, who came and joined the search. It must have been nearly three hours before my dad thought he should find a phone box and phone a neighbour in case grandfather had found his way home. And he had. He had come out of the common land on to a road but couldn't find our car. He walked along the road and eventually found a railway station, caught a train and made his way home. We found out later that there were two roads that met in a fork about half a mile farther on from where we had parked. He had come out on the other road."

Sylvia commented, "What a worrying time that must have been. Isn't there a village somewhere near there with a famous clock?"

"Oh yes. That's Abinger Hammer. I can remember driving along that road with my future wife and managing to arrive opposite the clock a few minutes before noon. Of course we stopped and waited for the clock to strike and to see the little man come out with his hammer and hit the bell twelve times. It wouldn't have been nearly as much fun an hour later."

Toby, now standing – a tall, refined and handsome man probably in his early seventies – looked at James and remarked, "James, you look as though you are wondering about this lake."

"Yes, I am. Do you think it's natural or man-made? I seem to remember that the Silent Pool was originally an old quarry that filled with water from natural springs in the North Downs. I wonder if there was a water course here fed by springs and someone created this lake as a water supply. There are several lost villages in this county."

"Now that is a thought," responded Toby with excitement in his voice. "The field up the hill is full of undulations. I thought they may have been made by cattle grazing here for centuries, but that might not be the reason."

Sylvia considered, "I wonder if anyone has done an aerial archaeological survey of this area. Viewed from a helicopter it might be possible to identify patterns that we can't see from the ground."

"Hey, what a splendid idea," enthused Toby. "And I have a friend with a small chopper who owes me a favour. He has also offered to take me up with him. He is the grandson of a Polish Jew who came to Britain in 1930-something, trained as a pilot and flew in Wellington bombers, I think, during World War 2. If he is willing to fly over the area with his cameras, I'll have a word with the farmer who is a great chap."

James turned to Sylvia and said, "This has turned out to be a most exciting walk. Thank you for inviting me."

Sylvia was about to reply when she heard the sound of horses on the bridleway. Toby heard them as well and remarked, "That will be the two A's returning."

James and Sylvia turned to look at him with questioning expressions. Toby continued. "Anna my wife and Alex her friend decided early this morning to give their mounts some exercise. I had better pack up my gear and go and get them some lunch. We live in the cottage at end of this lane."

He had soon collected everything together and said, "Let me introduce you to the two ladies."

They met at the field gate and introductions were made, where upon Alex cried, "Willoughby! Are you Lucy's grandad?" Seeing him nod she continued, "You have helped the police solve several crimes, haven't you? And you helped research the history of Cricken."

Toby, looking as though he had just discovered a £20 note for which he had been searching, commented, "When you told me your name I knew that I had heard it before but I couldn't work out the context. If there is anything interesting in that field you would be just the person to investigate it." Turning to his wife he explained. "We have had an exciting few minutes speculating that there may be a buried village in the field up there, or at least its remains. I am going to ask Roddy Walenza if he will take some aerial pictures."

Anna leaned over to Sylvia and said, "You must realise that Toby is an eternal enthusiast. He loves the thought of a new adventure."

Sylvia replied, "Don't worry about his enthusiasm, we are just as excited." Turning to James she asked, "Have you got one of your cards with you so that Toby can let you know if there are any developments?"

James duly produced one and then commented, "We haven't got very far with our walk, should we go a little farther?"

With a 'until we meet again!' the new friends parted company.

On their return James and Sylvia noticed the two horses, Sammy and Robbie, having been rubbed down after their exercise, contentedly grazing on freshly grown grass in the field with the stables.

When James's young friend Melanie called on him after school later in the day, James asked her about her A levels. She was pleased to tell him that she had one more exam to do on the next day.

"I thought that was the case. What happens after that? Do you still have to go to school?"

"No, I will have finished with school, except for the leavers' assembly and, if I am selected, there are still two cricket matches against other schools. But, except for those, I shall be free to take you out if Mum will lend me her car."

"Another question, my dear. Do you know anything about archaeological digs?"

"No, not really, but my history teacher, Mr Clifton, does and I think he is a big buddy of the 'digs man' at Exeter Uni. Why?"

"Now, don't get excited, but I had a very interesting morning. There is a faint, perhaps a very faint, possibility that there could be the buried remains of a village in a field outside our village."

James then told her about his meeting with Toby Schiller, but did not divulge where he had met him. He also told her about the possibility of being able to get some aerial pictures and she immediately wanted to know if she could be involved if the site was explored.

A week later an excited Toby phoned James, "James my friend, I've got something to show you. Roddy took me up in his chopper and we went backwards and forwards over the fields, lake and wood. We have some great pictures. I think you could be right about a village. You must see them."

"Toby, you sound really excited. Would you and Anna like to come for tea this afternoon when Sylvia and Melanie will be with me? Melanie is the young lady who worked on the history of Cricken with me."

Later that day five heads peered over photographs of the field behind the pool and trees. They could see what looked like two parallel rows of rectangles, which they considered might be the outlines of buildings either side of a street. As they looked more closely, Sylvia commented, "That shape in the form of a cross at the end of the street, could that be a church?"

The others agreed with her, until James remarked, "It seems very large for such a small village, unless there was further habitation that is not shown. Would an early church have been cruciform?"

Melanie agreed, "You remember, SG, that the first Cricken church was a very simple structure and that dated from the middle of the twelfth century. Surely, what we are looking at is not likely to be much younger?"

"I wonder when it was abandoned and why," mused Anna. "Could this be a development that was never finished when the plague ravaged the country?"

"That's an interesting thought," responded James. "I wonder if this was just a village. With a church that size, could it have been a monastery in construction?"

James looked at Melanie who cried, "Yes, I think I know what you are thinking. We know there was monastic activity in the area by the thirteenth century, because much of the land near Cricken was farmed by Benedictines. I wondered when we researched Cricken church, why the abbey to which those farms belonged was so far away, more than twenty miles. Had they originally belonged to a nearer abbey from which the monks departed?"

Toby had been listening to the debate and commented, "We seem to have identified several questions which we may not be able to answer without digging. There may be some old records about the area, but I don't know where we will find them. The farmer is prepared, if there is a very good case for doing so, to allow a team to conduct an archaeological survey, but we want to be assured they know what they are doing. That means professional and not just amateurs. Do we know anyone?"

James replied, "I told Melanie about our discussion of a week ago and asked her if she knew anything about archaeological digs. She said that she thinks her history teacher has a pal at Exeter University who is an archaeologist."

Melanie took up the story, "I had a chat with Mr Clifton, the teacher who took us for A level history, and he said that he thinks his friend is looking for a new site to explore."

"Do you think he would meet us?" asked Toby.

"I will go into school and see Mr Clifton tomorrow. Can I take a couple of photos to show him? Just a thought; what's the time? He might still be in school. I'll try phoning him."

Melanie went into the kitchen while the others continued to peruse the pictures alongside the OS map that James placed on the table. "Success," yelled Melanie as she joined them again. "Mr Clifton is going to phone his friend, Dr Ditchburn tonight. I think he is as excited as we are. I gave Mr C your number, SG, so he might call you back. I thought you were most likely to be available."

They all applauded Melanie and then Toby looked at James and asked him. "Why have you got your finger on that spot on the photo? Have you seen something else?"

"I'm not sure. There seems to be what the archaeologists might call an anomaly here. You see this small rectangle – Mel, second drawer right hand side there is a magnifying glass, could you pass it to me – ah, that's better. It is much closer to the lake, and it doesn't look the same as the other covered shapes. I wonder if it is more recent and what it could be."

Several suggestions were offered: some mechanism to do with waterflow to or from the lake, an ancient piece of farm machinery, a log that had been covered over or the remains of a bird hide, a grave, even buried treasure.

It was Toby who suggested that amateurs might be allowed to investigate the anomaly, but they would have to wait until they heard from Dr Ditchburn about the village.

Sylvia and Melanie took the empty teacups into the kitchen to wash them, which provided Anna with the opportunity to ask James why Melanie called him SG.

"It stands for Surrogate Grandad. Melanie never really knew her grandfathers, but about a year ago I came upon her after she had been the victim of a very nasty attack and left unconscious. Since then we have become very good friends and been involved in several adventures together, not least of which has been the researching and writing of the history of Cricken church and manor house. It is possible that in a year or two she might drop the word surrogate as she has become my grandson Robin's girlfriend."

The fine day turned into a glorious evening. James sat with his balcony door open through which he could hear the birds rehearsing their bedtime chorus. He was reading and had become absorbed in his book when he realised that the birdsong was being augmented by his phone ringing. When he answered the phone, a deep cultured man's voice said, "Is that James Willoughby? I am Archie Ditchburn. My friend Trevor Clifton tells me that you may have discovered the remains of a buried village."

Ten minutes later James finished the phone call having made arrangements to meet Dr Ditchburn at the field in two days' time. He spent the next ten minutes contacting Melanie, Sylvia and Anna to give them date and time for the meeting and was pleased to find that all could be there. Anna reported that Toby said he would inform the farmer and ask him if he wished to join them.

Having finished his phone calls James sat down to continue reading, but found himself thinking about the last person he had spoken to. Anna was a very attractive lady. He supposed she must be in her mid-sixties but she didn't look more than fifty. He thought she must have been an absolute stunner in her twenties. When his book slipped off his lap he came to his senses and said to himself, "Now James, you should be ashamed of yourself – you already have two girlfriends. At your age you should control your roving eye."

Two days later, a Saturday, with the weather continuing balmy, a group of eight people and Melanie's dog Pepper stood in the field with the lake and scrutinised the aerial photos. In addition to the five who met in James's apartment were the farmer Joel Small, Dr Ditchburn and Mr Clifton, the history teacher. Having determined the layout of the possible village most of them, led by Archie Ditchburn went to try to identify features that they had noticed in the photos. Melanie talked to Trevor Clifton about the theories that had been suggested by the group for the abandonment of the site. Meanwhile James and Sylvia looked for the anomaly nearer the lake. The anomaly seemed to be a raised rectangle of ground covered in grass with two saplings that looked to be struggling to survive. James grasped one of the saplings to try to make it lean so that he could get a better view and it almost came out of the soil.

Toby and Archie came over to join James and Sylvia to see what they had found. James suggested that the mound probably had no link to the main site and may be much more recent. Archie agreed with James. He said it would be worth excavating it as it would be a fairly quick exercise. However, he thought the main site had possibilities for archaeological investigation and he was also puzzled by the apparent size of the church, if church it was.

Having obtained permission of Joel to draw up a plan for a dig Archie suggested that he could select a team for the work to start in about three weeks. Melanie asked if she could join the team, as did Trevor as it would be starting just before the school summer holidays. Archie also suggested that, in the meantime, James and Toby might like to investigate the mound.

On the following Monday, James, Melanie and Toby visited the field again with a variety of garden implements to dismantle the mound close to the trees. After little more than thirty minutes they had removed the turf, mainly by the efforts of Melanie and Toby. They went more carefully as they dug deeper starting at one end of the mound. After no more than another ten minutes Melanie spotted what appeared to be a bone, so she continued with trowel and brush and soon exposed the bones of a human foot. Another two hours and they had exposed a complete human skeleton. James told Melanie to use her smartphone to alert the police as he guessed the body had not been in the ground for hundreds of years.

Before the police arrived Sylvia came with some refreshments. Based on her experience as an operating theatre nurse she suggested that the body was that of a young woman. While they waited for the police Melanie spotted something sticking out from under a shoulder blade. Very carefully, so as not to disturb the bones she withdrew a spectacle case.

By the time the police arrived she had cleaned the case and managed to open it. A pair of glasses were inside and there was a label on which it was still possible to read the name and address of the optician and the name P Green, although that might not be the complete name. Surely the glasses could not belong to the body as there was no sign of any clothes: could it have belonged to the person who buried the body?

The police cordoned off the area and erected a tent over the grave. Melanie handed over the glasses and case, showing the names inside. While this initial police activity was in progress Sylvia had been looking at the lake and the trees around most of it. As her gaze lighted on an ancient oak she saw a squirrel run along a branch then down the trunk before disappearing inside only to emerge through a hole near the bottom. She wandered over to have a closer look and discovered that the inside of the trunk was hollow. She peered inside, then called to Melanie, "Has your phone got a torch on it?" Receiving an affirmative nod, she continued, 'Could you bring it over here." The light displayed some clothing, to which they drew the attention of one of the police officers.

A detective arrived to take charge of the investigation. He arranged for the clothing, which seemed to consist of a miniskirt, top, underclothes, trainers and a small handbag to be put into an evidence bag. One of the trainers fell out of the bag. Sylvia picked it up with the tea towel in which she had wrapped the refreshments she had brought and noticed the letters FW inside the shoe. The detective informed them that the police would need to carefully lift the skeleton and take it with the clothing for forensic investigation and then follow up the leads they had to see if they could identify the body and the means of death.

Toby offered his observation. "I have seen skeletons of people who have been hanged and thereby have died of suffocation and the angle of this victim's head suggests that she may have been strangled."

The detective agreed and commented, "We will be able to search the lists of missing persons and also follow up the lead provided by the glasses case as there was an indistinct date on it that might be 1981. The letters FW might be the victim's initials and we shall also be following up the name of P Green or similar names."

A week later James had a visitor. It was Sergeant Jane Cartwright whom he had met on several occasions in recent months. After greeting each other Jane commented, "Detective James, I take my hat off to you. You have set us off to solving a crime that we didn't know had been committed. We have discovered that in 1983 a twenty-two year-old girl from Compton St Mary by the name of Felicity Waynewright went missing. A search was made and it was assumed that she had run away, either to elope or to go abroad. She had often talked about wanting to go to Australia. Her passport was not with the things she had left at home. She had been described as a 'free spirit' and she was known to visit nudist beaches. We don't yet know where her parents are or whether they are still alive. We believe they moved soon after their daughter disappeared."

"How is the surname spelled?" When Jane told him James said, "I may be able to give you a lead. When my wife and I moved into a bungalow in Compton St Mary I noticed on the deeds that the name of the first owner of the property, built in 1981, was Waynewright. I noticed the spelling as unusual. We were the third owners, but there may be some living in the Close who knew them and may be able to tell you what became of them."

"That is worth following up. But we have had some success on the glasses. We think they probably fell out of the pocket of the murderer when he was burying the body, possibly in the dark. The optician in Molton is no longer practising, but his successor still has some records. We have been able to find details of a Percival Greening. He is no longer at the address the optician had for him, but a neighbour remembers him and thinks he may have joined the Merchant Navy about twenty-five years ago. We are following up that lead."

"Jane, thank you for that feedback. May I tell the others?"

"I don't see any reason why you can't. But I would like to know how you found the body."

James told the story of meeting Toby and their speculation about the bumps in the field that are leading them towards an exploratory dig. "It was just good fortune that we spotted the grave. The helicopter pilot took one photograph at just the right angle when the sun accentuated the shape of the mound. He was also just in the right position for the trees not to obscure that particular spot."

Two weeks later most of the preparations for the dig had been completed, so the original five, together with Archie and Trevor planned to meet in James's apartment in the evening. During the afternoon Sergeant Jane rang with news. James suggested that rather than just tell him, she should come and tell the whole group in the evening.

When Jane arrived and they were all assembled she gave them news of the first dig. "Firstly, I want to thank you for helping us to close a cold case. The name of the girl who had been strangled was Felicity Waynewright. We could not tell whether she had been sexually abused or what the murderer's motive was. However, we have been able to follow up the P Green written in the glasses case. He was Percival Greening. I say 'was', because he is now dead. He left the area to join the Merchant Navy in 1992 and served on an oil tanker for five years before there was a fire on board. The fire was brought under control but not before Percy and two others had suffered injuries from which they died. We have also been able to locate Felicity's parents who are still alive, in their mid to late eighties and living near Plymouth. We are pleased that after forty years of not knowing what became of their daughter, we have been able to tell them and that she can now have a proper funeral and burial. They want the funeral to take place in Compton St Mary."

"Jane, thank you for telling us. Do you think Mr and Mrs Waynewright would object if some of us attended the funeral? For them it will be the end of a vigil that they must have thought they would be unable to complete. For us it will bring closure of a different kind knowing that the mystery of that mound has been resolved."

Toby provided a final summary, "We had been talking about The Silent Pool where another young girl died. This is more recent history. Perhaps we can now think of it as The Peaceful Lake."

GARDEN CENTRE REVELATIONS

An eighteen-year-old girl's wish to discover how her relationship with her boyfriend should be allowed to develop results in her observing an act of dishonesty.

Sitting on the balcony of his south facing second floor apartment eighty-six years-old James Willoughby and his eighteen years-old friend Melanie Hardy were observing the early morning activities of the birds in the trees, hedges and fields. It was that time of year, early July, when many fledglings had recently left the nest, while others had yet to fledge. It was a beautiful clear morning although there had been a freshening shower of rain during the night.

The watchers were able to identify many of the birds they spotted though their binoculars. In the hedges they saw house sparrows, dunnocks, robins, finches and several LBJs (little brown jobbies that they were not able to identify accurately). They spotted several titmice flitting about in the trees, as well as blackbirds and starlings. In the fields and on the ground they could see members of the crow family and wood pigeons and a song thrush. As he trained his glasses on a denser area of trees James saw something to which he drew Melanie's attention.

"What is it?" asked Melanie.

"It looks like a sparrow hawk. It is quite still at present, but if it is ready to hunt it can fly very quickly and low. It is perfect at ambushing its prey. Those birds in the hedges will need to be alert. Look, there she goes, so swift. She may have babies to feed or if they haven't hatched her mate will be keeping the eggs warm. Did you see that? She has made a catch and I think it is one of those wood pigeons. There will be several meals out of that."

"But the wood pigeon is such a big bird."

"True, but also rather slow, especially when taken by surprise by something flying so low at speed. That pigeon was too close to the hedge. It is surprising that they will catch a prey that size."

"So will she share that meal with her mate or will it just be for her young."

"With a catch that size I expect they will all have some."

"Do birds mate for life?"

"I'm not sure whether all birds do, but I rather think that Sparrow Hawks will."

Melanie had called on James early in the day, before joining an archaeological dig in a field on the opposite side of the village of Compton St Philip. Their, perhaps unlikely, friendship had begun about a year earlier when James had come to Melanie's rescue when she had been attacked and left close to death. Before joining the team on the archaeological site Melanie wanted to give SG, short for Surrogate Grandad, the name she had given James, an update on the dig. Melanie had been allowed to join the excavation team as she had been instrumental in bringing the site, of a possible buried village, to the attention of the dig leader. However, the original interest in the possibility had emanated from a conversation that James and his friend Sylvia had when they encountered Tobias Schiller at his easel painting a pool in the field. It was pictures taken by Toby's friend Roddy from his helicopter that initiated the desire to undertake the exploration. The excavation was being led by Dr Archie Ditchburn, a friend of Melanie's history teacher, with students and colleagues from Exeter University.

After a day spent mostly on her knees Melanie visited James again in the evening to report on her day. After telling him how many trenches had been opened up and where they were, she turned to him and said, "Could I ask you something else, not connected with the dig?"

"Fire away, tell me what's on your mind."

"Well, I've been thinking all day about the birds we were watching this morning and how some pairs mate for life. I think that mating for life is an ideal situation for humans, but it doesn't always seem to work out that way. And then I thought about a suggestion one of the girls from school put to me. Her idea is that she and her boyfriend, and Robin and I should all go on holiday together. She said we could book a room for the boys and one for the girls which would satisfy our parents and when we were there we could change our room partners. I said that I didn't know whether Robin and I would be free to go on holiday. I'm not sure that I am ready to sleep with Robin and I don't know how he feels. What do you think?"

"That is not a question that has an easy answer, but I think you are right to seek advice. I could just answer 'don't do it, unless you are absolutely sure', but it would not be fair to you without an explanation. Are you ready for something like a sermon?"

When she indicated that she really wanted his views and that the matter was bothering her, he continued, "Much of what I am going to say has something of a historical context, but as a history student that should not present a difficulty for you.

"When I was your age people started to use the phrase 'sex before marriage' and whereas the liberally minded suggested that it was a way of finding out if you were suited to each other, the more conservative frowned on the practice and suggested that each partner should keep themselves pure before they shared the marriage bed. In more recent years many couples have engaged in sex without any consideration of it being a prelude to marriage. Some partnerships remain for years, children are born and brought up and later the couple decide to formalise the relationship with a wedding. Sometimes the wedding is delayed for years because weddings have become big business and can be very expensive.

"Now the desire that a couple have for each other is natural and healthy and can be the start of a beautiful relationship. Unfortunately, that desire can become almost irresistible and does not wait for a convenient date. I remember a colleague who had four daughters telling me that he had given them this simple advice, 'if you can, don't; if you can't, take precautions'. If you have watched the TV programme 'Long lost families', you will know that thirty or forty years ago many illegitimate children were taken from their mothers as soon as they were born and given up for adoption. Less than a hundred years ago there was a stigma attached to mothers who produced children out of wedlock. Fortunately, for one-parent families, society is much more tolerant nowadays, but that doesn't make the life of the single parent easy.

"You have read books set in Victorian England at a time when young ladies had far less freedom for meeting young men unless they were in the company of a chaperone. Several authors have written about mothers taking their daughters to Bath for the season where the young ladies may have the opportunity to attract the attention of eligible bachelors. The nearest a young couple might get to spending time together was on the dance floor where protective eyes kept a careful watch on them. How different to today, and yet unplanned pregnancies still occurred. The girls from poor families, however, were not so well protected and needed to keep their own wits about them if they were not to find themselves in trouble.

"As a Christian I have my own view of marriage and I am not certain that every other Christian has the same view and views may have changed during my long life. I can only tell you what I believe and that is that sexual activity between a man and a woman should ideally only exist as a part of a marriage relationship. I have always understood that in marriage a man and woman leave their parents and become one. If you look in the Bible in Mark's gospel you will find that Jesus pronounced this in the early part of chapter 10. Also, it is in the marriage service that both bride and groom promise to be faithful to the other.

"If you and Robin become seriously attached to one another and you think that your love will stand the test of time, you will know when you need to discuss your relationship and whether you will wish to follow the example of Robin's sisters and formalise that relationship by entering into the holy estate of matrimony as it says in the marriage service."

"Thank you, SG. I think the degree of freedom we have nowadays gives us much more to think about than was the case for couples eighty or a hundred years ago."

"That's true. When Anne and I were courting more than sixty years ago, everyone assumed that we would get engaged and, when we could afford to do so, we would get married and that the marriage would last. In our case, even though I was sometimes away for a week or more, our love for each other held strong until Anne sadly died."

They sat quietly for a few minutes with their own thoughts until James said, "If either you or Robin is able to persuade a parent to lend you a car, I would like to take the two of you on a little afternoon excursion. There is a couple of places I would like you to see."

"I'm sure I can speak for Robin as well as myself and say that we should like that very much. But if neither of us can borrow a car do you think your friend Sylvia would take us in her car?"

"I think she would be pleased to join us, but she has her sister staying with her for a few days, so I am keeping out of the way."

"Why are making yourself scarce: don't you like her sister?"

"Well, it's not that I don't like her, but she is rather domineering and inclined to bully Sylvia. If I appear in the frame too much while she is around, she might make assumptions about our relationship and put two and two together and make ten."

Melanie thought about what James had said and then replied, "I think I understand. If anyone is going to put two and two together you want to do the addition. But I thought you were fond of Sylvia or, ... now what is the expression? .... that you were romantically inclined. I have seen you holding hands. Admittedly, you were helping her out of the car, but neither of you seemed too keen to let go. And, Sylvia has kissed you during the Peace in church."

James looked at her and then laughed saying, "You know, my dear girl, all this detective work you have been involved in is turning you into a young Miss Marple. Nevertheless, I might ring her this evening and pass on your information about the dig and at the same time inquire when her sister leaves. If she is not staying too long, I might follow up your suggestion and ask Sylvia to join our excursion. And, yes, I do enjoy Sylvia's company."

An hour or so after Melanie had left Toby Schiller rang in a state of excitement. "James, I expect Melanie has told you about the dig, but she probably doesn't know that in a trench she hasn't been involved with they found, just before the close, some dressed stones. I think it could be their first wall. I am really hopeful that our guess of abandoned habitation might be true and dressed stone might indicate a high-status building. I went up there at the end of the day because I couldn't contain my curiosity any longer."

"That's great news, Toby. Thanks for telling me. I plan to phone Sylvia this evening as I promised Mel that I would give her an update and now I can add your news as well."

When James rang Sylvia her sister Norma had just gone to wash her hair so they were able to have a conversation without interruption. He told her about the progress on the dig; and then said he had had a conversation with Melanie about her relationship with Robin, but didn't go into any detail. He also found out that Norma had three more days before she went home, so told Sylvia of his wish to take Melanie and Robin out for an afternoon. Sylvia indicated that she would be happy to take them all in her car. After the phone call was finished Norma reappeared and wanted to know what it was about. Sylvia explained about the dig which started a different conversation and deflected Norma from asking questions about who had phoned and whether anything else had been said.

At 2 o'clock on a Saturday afternoon just over a week later James, Melanie and Robin were settled in Sylvia's car ready for the proposed excursion. After some twenty minutes of driving James asked Sylvia to turn off the main road down a country lane. About three-quarters of a mile later he invited her to pull into a gateway and a further hundred yards on to stop beside a small church. James explained, "I hope this church is open. It is small and very old and used to belong to a village that no longer exists. It has been de-consecrated but is still maintained by a body called, I think, something like The Historic Churches Trust or perhaps Church Conservation Trust. I won't say any more until we get inside."

When they entered the building through a door set back slightly in the south wall they realised that it contained just a nave with no side aisles. Immediately, Melanie exclaimed, "I suppose Cricken was this shape originally, but that was enlarged later."

"Could well be," responded James, "but look around and see what else you notice."

Robin was first to comment, "No pews or chairs and benches along the walls."

"Do you know why?"

Melanie replied, "Didn't the congregation have to stand, but the benches were for those who were elderly or infirm?"

"That's correct, anything more?"

"Wall paintings. These are good and quite well preserved," commented Sylvia. "I seem to remember that when many could not read, bible stories were illustrated with paintings and also stained-glass windows, but didn't the Puritans cover up many of the wall paintings?"

James replied, "I am not sure if these escaped Cromwell's men or whether they have been carefully restored."

"Then why," asked Melanie, "did they write the Ten Commandments and the Lord's Prayer on the walls at the front if people could not read?"

"A good question and well spotted. I think that these were two passages of scripture that everyone was expected to learn and remember. But there is something else we can learn from the inclusion of these two passages. Any suggestions?"

After a pause Sylvia ventured a thought. "I have seen these two important biblical references in other churches, but I have only just realised that one is from the Old Testament and the other from the New. Only that from the New Testament are words of Jesus, so I wonder why they didn't use Jesus's summary of the ten commandments which is recorded in the New Testament."

"It is a good question. Any suggestions?" James asked, but when the others shook their heads, he continued. "I will offer this thought. When Jesus replied to the Pharisees, he was talking to people who would have been able to quote all ten commandments. He quoted the first and then summarised all the rest simply as 'love your neighbour as you love yourself'. When this list was written up many would have needed to be reminded what 'love your neighbour' meant in terms of their behaviour. Amongst other requirements they would have wanted to stress that murder, stealing and adultery was sinful and, in many instances, illegal. Church attendance when this building flourished was probably much higher than it is in present times and immoral behaviour was strongly discouraged and sometimes denounced publicly."

Robin was prompted to make a contribution to the debate. "Melanie told me about the conversation she had with you the other day about sex and marriage. The people who attended this church would have been encouraged to be faithful to their spouses."

When they came out of the church, James made them stand still and watch a female blackbird feeding a newly hatched chick. As they watched the male bird appeared with food. The mother bird flew into a nearby hedge. James suggested, "I expect she has a nest in the hedge with more chicks in it."

Melanie commented, "So the pair are working together as one to feed the babies. It reminds me of when we talking about some birds mating for life."

James replied, "Let me ask you a question. They are raising a family now, but which do you think came first, mating or nest building?"

Robin and Melanie looked at each other, clearly understanding the relevance of James's question and Robin spoke for both when he said, "They will have become acquainted first, then they will have built the nest, possibly together, and then mated. They will probably have taken it in turns to keep the eggs warm so that when the eggs hatched the chicks would have been given the best possible start in life. I think the birds can teach humans a thing or two."

James suggested they walk round the church which still had evidence outside of a graveyard. As the ground was rather uneven James offered Sylvia his arm. By the time Robin and Melanie came round the corner of the church behind them the elderly couple were arm in arm. Melanie whispered to Robin, "See that, I told you that I suspected they were fond of each other."

After walking round the church James asked, "Have you seen any signs of habitation that this church would have served?"

Melanie responded, "There only seems to be that big house over there: that may be a farm-house. Oh, I think I know. That house may have replaced the original manor house, but the village has been lost when the land was cleared. It's like Cricken, but there the village survived and expanded. Do you think the squire or Lord of the Manor who lived in the original house built the church?"

"It could well be. There was much more land available then and important people often acquired large estates from the monarch. They first built a house, then started to farm the land, provided houses, perhaps in some cases little more than hovels, for farm workers and then built a church."

James continued, "It's such a pity that so many of these rural villages have disappeared, but the population of England decreased dramatically in the fourteenth century, during which it almost halved. The cause of the depopulation and the disappearances of villages, amongst other reasons, is a mixture of disease including plague, war including civil war, and starvation with poor harvests. It is really difficult to imagine what it would have been like to live in England in 1400 when the population was less than 3 million, a twentieth of what it is today.

"Now let us leave here as I would like to take you to a Garden Centre where they used to serve rather special cream teas. Anne and I used to be regular visitors, but it must be six or seven years since I last called in. However, the lovely couple that own and run it are still in charge and I would love you to meet them. I am certainly looking forward to seeing them again."

They returned to Sylvia's car and twenty-five minutes later arrived at the Garden Centre. "Let's have some refreshment first and then we can have a look around," suggested James.

They found a table and James went to order four cream teas. When he returned, he had a man and lady with him, the owners of the Garden Centre. Introductions were made and then the lady exclaimed, "James, it is lovely to see you and you look well. You know we still miss the regular visits you and Anne used to make. Anne was always keen to find out if we had any new and exotic plants. I used to feel sorry for you when she had made her selection, knowing that you would have to plant them when you arrived home. But what brings you this way?"

James explained that he had wanted to show his grandson and his girlfriend an abandoned, but conserved, Norman church, because they had been involved in an investigation of the church and manor house at

Cricken. His friend, Sylvia, had kindly offered to drive them. The mention of Cricken prompted Geoff, the Garden Centre owner to comment, "Now why have I heard about Cricken recently? I know, there was something in the press about a tunnel linking the church and the adjacent hotel that no one knew was there."

Sylvia responded, "That's absolutely correct. It was this trio that investigated it after Melanie discovered the entrance to the tunnel from the old Manor House that had been extended to form the hotel. Melanie and James have written the guidebook that includes the history that the three of them and two others have researched."

Denise, Geoff's wife, asked Sylvia if she had been involved. Sylvia explained that she had not met James until the work on the guidebook had begun, but she had been invited to read the proof copy and to offer comments. As Sylvia turned to speak to Denise, she noticed the pendant she was wearing with a cross on it. "That's a lovely cross you are wearing, the enamelling looks very fine."

"Yes, I love this cross. Geoff gave it to me a couple of years ago. It replaces the first one he gave me before we were married. He gave me the original after we had started walking out as they used to say. He said at the time that it was a sign of faith and also as it could been seen as a capital 'I' crossed out, he wanted me to know that while we were together he promised always to be faithful. Later we became engaged and a year after that we married. But because of what he had said when he gave me the cross I ensured that I kept myself pure, as I know he did, until our wedding night. I can honestly say that our love has remained steadfast through forty-two years of marriage."

Melanie had been listening very carefully to Denise and then, glancing at Robin, but still addressing Denise she said, "Thank you for telling us about the cross and its meaning for you. I can see why you are attached to it. Do you wear it all the time?" Gaining an affirmative she turned to Robin commenting, "That's something special, isn't it, Robin dear?"

At that moment the cream teas arrived and Denise and Geoff said they would leave them to enjoy their refreshment in peace. James said that after tea they would look round the Centre, so Melanie asked for permission to take photographs with her phone.

They enjoyed their cream teas and talked generally about the rural location of the Garden Centre that was surrounded by countryside and beside a minor road. Although it might have appeared to be somewhat off the beaten track, it was clearly well-known judging by the number of customers. The tearoom was situated close to one edge of the site, with hedges and shrubs marking the boundary. Melanie had been gazing at the hedge and saw something which caught her attention, "SG, what is that small bird on top of the hedge just in front of that tree that I think is a young chestnut?"

"I think I can see what you have spotted. I think it is possibly the prettiest of the birds that frequent the hedges. It is a goldfinch. There may be others not far away. Yes, there you are – five or six of them. Oh, and look, just to the right of the first bird you saw are a couple of linnets. They are all seed eaters. Are we ready to walk round and look at the plants: they usually have a very good selection of container plants here, but they may still have a few bedding plants. The rest of you have gardens, but I have a gap on my balcony. However, we must be careful how much we try to get into Sylvia's car."

Because they had been talking about birds it transpired that to start with Melanie and James walked together while Robin and Sylvia followed. As they walked between the rows of containers, James spotted an agapanthus that had buds forming and would probably flower next month. The picture on the label suggested that it would have bright blue flowers. He put it in a basket and looked for a suitable pot to put it in for it to stand on his balcony. Melanie took a photo of James selecting the plant and then noticed a wonderful display of roses and determined to get some close-ups as well as a long shot of the display.

As it was now about 4 o'clock the sun was no longer overhead but behind Melanie so that it highlighted the roses but also lit up the covered area beyond where there were racks with seed packets and pouches with late-flowering summer bulbs. When she found the right position for her picture she noticed an activity in the covered area. For some reason she did not at the time appreciate she decided not to take a still picture but to video as she moved towards the roses. When she had her picture, she put her phone away and guided James round a corner out of sight of the covered area. Checking that there were few people near her, she showed

James the scene she had videoed. She told him not to look at the roses but to observe what was going on in the background. What he saw was a lady in a bright purple top and an orange cap with a trolley with several container plants and some trays of bedding plants. He noticed that she had several packets of seeds in her hand and about six pouches of bulbs. The lady looked around and then opened the very large handbag she had on her shoulder and slipped the seeds and bulbs into it.

James decided on action. "Mel, I think you should find Geoff or Denise while I go to the check-out with my basket. I will observe our 'friend' to see what she pays for. Watch to see I if give you a signal. If I take my sun hat off let the owners see your video and keep an eye on me."

"OK, sleuthing partner," replied the excited girl and off she went.

James reached the check-out just ahead of the possible shoplifter and then turned, having made his purchase, to assist the lady as she presented each of her containers and then returned them to the trolley before paying for them. He raised his arm, took off his sunhat and put it back on and followed the lady out of the shop as she wheeled her trolley to the carpark. As with many Garden Centre trolleys, it seemed to have a mind of its own so James offered to steady it while the lady transferred the containers and the bedding plants to her car. He was holding a tray of asters when Geoff walked up with Melanie. James looked at the asters and said to the lady and to Geoff, "One of these asters looks a bit sickly, was this the best tray?"

Geoff took the tray and said, "I'll replace that for you or give you a rebate. Do you have your receipt?" When the lady produced the receipt Geoff scrutinised it, looked closely at the lady with the purple top and remarked, "The seed packets and the bulbs you selected aren't on this receipt. Are they still in your handbag?"

The lady opened her mouth, but no sound came out as her face turned bright red. Then she managed to splutter, "I don't know what you mean."

Geoff continued, "Madam, I think you know perfectly well or would you like to see yourself shoplifting. The proof is on this lady's mobile phone as I expect it is also on our CCTV."

She looked at Melanie and said in a spiteful voice, "You were spying on me."

Melanie calmly replied, "I had no reason to spy on you, as you put it. I was taking pictures of the roses, with permission, and you were in the background putting items in your bag." The lady was persuaded to return to the checkout in Geoff's company, where she paid for all the items in her handbag.

Geoff then accompanied her to her car and as a parting shot, he warned, "The elderly gentleman who assisted you has undertaken much detective work for the county police and has an exceptional memory. I would advise you not to attempt anything dishonest again."

VILLAGE TREASURE

A plea for forgiveness by a prisoner starts a trail that leads to the discovery of treasure that had lain buried for several centuries.

"Sylvia, I'm .... sorry .... I'm late ...... but I had........ to deal with ..... an emergency .... Oh dear!"

"James dear, sit down and get your breath back. Have you been running all the way from your apartment? Do take your time, I don't want you having another heart attack. Eighty-six-year-olds shouldn't be trying to run a four-minute mile."

James Willoughby usually met his seventy-year-old friend Sylvia Marchant for coffee in the village bakers-cum-tea shop on a Thursday morning when they had completed their market shopping.

While James recovered his breath and composure Sylvia caught the eye of Maisie, the waitress, who came to their table to take her order. "Is Mr Willoughby all right? He looks a bit flushed."

"I think he just needs time to recover from his training run. I would like to order two coffees and two of your cheese scones with butter, please Maisie."

James recovering added, "And could you bring me ..... a glass of water, Maisie? Thank you."

"Certainly, Mr W. I guess you were running to make sure nobody snatched your girlfriend away," said Maisie grinning.

"Now that's being cheeky, young Maisie," replied James smiling, "but you are absolutely right." Young Maisie was not young, except compared with James, as she must have been on the upper side of sixty.

"Now, what's this about an emergency?" asked Sylvia after Maisie had taken the order.

"It's Elsie, who lives in the apartment below mine. She has not been quite her usual lively self lately, so I have been fetching her morning paper with mine. Today she had a magazine as well so, rather than leaving it on the floor outside her door, I knocked, but I received no reply and there was no sound coming from inside. We have each other's door keys in case of emergency, so I decided to investigate. I opened her door and called, again received no reply so went in and found her unconscious on the floor. She had a bruise on the side of her head where she must have banged it when she fell, but she was breathing and had a pulse. I phoned 999 and after I had been assured that help was on the way, I contacted her daughter. A paramedic soon came and decided an ambulance was needed, but I waited until Laura, Elsie's daughter, arrived. Elsie had begun to come round before I left, but I don't know whether it was a heart attack or a stroke, but Laura has been worrying for some time how much longer her mother could continue living on her own."

"I hope she'll be OK, but I suppose that might mean that there could be a vacancy for a new neighbour for you," replied Sylvia thoughtfully. "If the apartment does come on the market, please will you let me know?"

"Do you think you would be interested? Are you thinking of moving?"

"Well, now that Mother has passed away the house is bigger than I need, although ideally I would need two bedrooms for when Norma comes to stay."

"Elsie's apartment is larger than mine and has two bedrooms."

"Well now, that is interesting. How would you feel if I were your neighbour?"

"Ooh! I would have to think about that," teased James. "I think we would need a thorough vetting procedure. We have to maintain standards you know. No pottery amongst the china. And there is another problem, I would have to behave myself."

"You certainly would, you big tease."

"Seriously, I would love to have you next door. I suppose it could happen. It would be like finding buried treasure." James reached across the table and took Sylvia's hand in his as he said, "Now the thought of you living next door is something worth living for."

They were holding hands when the door opened and in walked beautiful blue-eyed blonde Melanie and her mother Becky. James had discovered eighteen-year-old Melanie unconscious after she had been subjected to a nasty attack about a year ago and since then the two had become firm friends, so that Melanie had named James, 'SG' standing for Surrogate Grandad. "SG and Sylvia," exclaimed Melanie, "Oh, I'm sorry, have we interrupted a proposal?"

"Not yet," responded Sylvia, winking at Melanie.

"No," said James at the same time, and he continued, "We were enjoying a delicious speculation. Please join us and we'll explain, or Sylvia will as I continue to recover. Perhaps I can just enjoy being in the company of three lovely girlfriends!"

"Thank you," replied Becky as she put her shopping bags on the floor and sat down. "Will you give Maisie our order, Mel? Now, James, from what do you need to recover?"

Sylvia took up the tale. "James gave me a fright a few minutes ago. He came in here panting and snorting like an old carthorse. I think he had run all the way from his apartment. He needed several breaths to apologise for being late because he had been dealing with an emergency." Mel returned at that point, sat down and reported that Maisie told her that James had been very red in the face when he arrived and she was afraid he would collapse. She looked at him with clear concern on her face. Sylvia continued, "He had found his downstairs neighbour unconscious on the floor of her apartment and had to phone 999 and call her daughter. It was after he told me that the daughter had implied that Elsie might not be able to continue to live alone that we started 'building castles in the sky' as the saying is, thinking that I might be able to move to Elsie's apartment if it came on the market."

Becky asked James, "Did the ambulance men give any indication of what had caused Elsie to fall?"

"Not by the time I left. When Laura arrived I decided it might better if I wasn't there. I said I would contact her later."

Becky turned to Sylvia asking if she would miss her garden, while James spoke to Melanie, "How is the dig going?"

"Well, we have most of the church walls identified and some of the other buildings suggest that it could have been a monastery, although it is too soon to say if it was completed before it was abandoned. Now, have you completed your shopping, or did you come straight here?"

"I haven't started yet, but I have only a few things to buy today," replied James while he studied his list.

'Would you like me to get them for you, while you finish your refreshment here?"

"That's very kind of you. I can get my bread here, and then I need a couple of things from the fish stall and the greengrocery stall, if they still have fresh strawberries. Last week the greengrocer had some new season's leeks. I could do with a couple of those. I had also intended to visit the butcher, Derrick Lamb, who should have a pork chop and some sausages for me. He knows me and he may already have my order set aside."

"I know he knows you and I know you tease him, although I think he gives as good as he gets. I'll tell him you prefer to spend time with your girlfriend rather than talk to him."

"Yes, you cheeky monkey, I can imagine you would. But thank you for sparing my legs. Here is my list, my shopping bag and some money."

"Do you need any of the items for lunch time or shall I bring them with me when I call this afternoon I'll put the fish and meat in the fridge until later."

"That will be fine. I think Adam and possibly Robin may call this afternoon. I see that has put a smile on your face."

Adam, an accountant, lived about twenty minutes from James and called to see his father once a week and sometimes Robin, Adam's son, training to be a solicitor, accompanied his father, especially if there was a chance of spending some time with Melanie. The two young people had met at a party on New Year's Day and since then had spent as much time together as they could.

After a pleasant afternoon during which Adam updated his dad on family news and Robin and Melanie went for a country walk, it was well into the evening before James had an opportunity to contact Laura and to ask about Elsie. The news was not as bad as he had feared. Elsie was in hospital and undergoing tests. It was believed that she had had a blackout and suffered a fall and that the fainting may have been caused by a slight stroke. Laura commented, "It was a good thing you thought to go into her apartment when you did. She seems to be comfortable, but quite shocked. We shall know more when the tests are complete, but she was inclined to agree with me that her days of independent living may be over. That will mean finding somewhere else for her, either with me, but I would need to have some modifications made to our house, or in a care home. Either way it looks like an upheaval with the need to sell her apartment."

James decided to put down a marker, "When I left you this morning I had to hurry as I was due to meet a friend in the village. I apologised for being late and explained why and I said that it might mean that I would lose a good neighbour, and I would have to get used to someone else living below me. My friend surprised me by asking me to let her know if the apartment came on the market. She feels her house is too big for her as both her husband and her bedridden mother have passed away since they bought the house."

Laura replied, "I will certainly let you know. That could ease one part of the relocation process."

"Thank you. Please give my good wishes to your mother and keep in touch. When she is able to receive visitors, I should like to visit her if that is acceptable."

After such a busy day James decided he would leave it until the morning before telling Sylvia about his conversation with Laura. He thought it might be a little early to start getting her excited.

The following morning brought new matters with which he would need to deal. First, he realised that he needed to contact the shop to stop Elsie's papers while she was in hospital. That was a small matter compared to what the post brought.

A bank statement and two charity requests presented no problems, but an A4 envelope was a surprise. It was marked Exeter Prison on the outside and in it were three letters labelled 1, 2 and 3. He realised that he was required to read them in the order specified.

Letter 1 was typed and from the Prison Chaplain.

Dear Mr Willoughby

Further to our conversation a few weeks ago, I felt I should update you on the progress of the prisoner Dean Savage about whom you enquired. His desire to change has continued and he has made considerable improvements. Not only is he a different person in his attitude and concern for others, but his moral compass has undertaken a complete reversal. He visits the chapel daily and spends as much time as he can studying in the library. He reads his Bible regularly and at some length and his study of the Acts of the Apostles has led him on to research the growth of the Christian Church. Recently he has spent time reading about church buildings and has been explaining to me the reasons behind the construction and layout of monasteries and abbeys.

I told Dean about our conversation and mentioned that you had collaborated on the history of a parish church and the neighbouring manor house-cum-hotel. He asked if it was possible to see a copy of the guidebook. I also mentioned that you know one of the ladies he assaulted. He asked if he could write to you and the young lady. I enclose the letters he has written and will leave it to your discretion whether you pass on letter number 3, say nothing about it or read those parts that you feel would not cause distress.

Perhaps you would let me know your reactions to what you read.

Paul Divine

Letter 2

Dear Sir

My name is Dean Savage and I am writing from Exeter Prison with the help of the Chaplain Mr Paul Divine. I am sorry I do not know your name, but Mr Divine tells me that you know one of the ladies I attacked. The attacks I subjected those ladies to were terrible and evil things that I should never have committed. I feel dreadful about what I did and there can be no excuse for my behaviour.

I know I can never put right the wrong that I did, but I wish to apologise to each of the ladies from the bottom of my heart and ask them to try to forgive me. I can honestly say that sending me to prison was the right thing for the court to do to me. I have learnt a great deal about behaviour and attitudes to other people. I hope that when I am eventually released, I shall be able to show that I am a much better person.

I have written a letter of apology to the lady I assaulted. I don't know her name as in court she was just referred to as Miss X where X was an initial. Please read the letter and if you think it would not distress her, pass it to her or read as much of it to her as you think is appropriate. Don't tell her about it if you think it would upset her too much.

I have been using my time here to read and study. I read the Bible regularly and the Chaplain helps me to understand those parts I find difficult. He also guides my reading and has helped me to discover how to pray regularly. One of the subjects I enjoyed at school was history and I have enjoyed finding out how the Christian church grew after the resurrection of Jesus. That study has led me on to find out about the architecture and fittings of church buildings. The Chaplain has told me that you have done some historical research into a church near you and have helped to write a guidebook. I would love to read it if it is possible for me to see a copy.

Thank you for reading my letter. From a very repentant Dean.

Letter 3

Dear Miss X

I am sorry to have to address you in this way, but I don't know your name. To my everlasting shame I have to tell you that I am the rotter who attacked you a year ago. You probably know that I am in prison as I was deservedly given a 20-year sentence for assaulting you and six other ladies. I now know that what I did was wicked, and I am ashamed of my behaviour and the harm I did to you all. I am writing to ask you if you could find it in your heart to forgive me.

You may find it difficult to believe but I think that being sent to prison has given me an opportunity to turn my life around. I have been doing a lot of reading and learning about history. I have also spent hours reading the Bible and I keep returning to Psalm 51 where there are verses that apply so strongly to me. The following verses, in particular, are my prayer because they speak for me.

'Be merciful to me, O God, because of your constant love. Because of your great mercy wipe away my sins. Wash away all my evil and make me clean from my sin. I recognise my faults; I am conscious of my sins. I have sinned ..... and done what you consider evil. So you are right in judging me; you are justified in condemning me. Create a pure heart in me, O God, and put a new and loyal spirit within me.'

The Prison Chaplain, a fine Christian gentleman, has agreed to send this letter to your friend who contacted the prison to ask if I had realised the error of my ways. I hope he will feel that he can pass it on to you and that it does not cause you too many unhappy memories.

I understand that your friend told the Chaplain that you and he had worked together on a guidebook of a church near where you live. As I have been reading books about the development of places of worship I would be most interested to read it.

Finally, again I offer you my most sincere apologies for hurting you so badly. I am doing all I can to ensure that the wicked man I was no longer exists. When I am released, I want my actions to enable me to be a credit to society and not a curse. Thank you for reading this letter and may God bless you in your future life.

Dean

When he had finished reading the letters James sat and thought for a while, then he read them again and pondered some more. His next action was to phone Sylvia. When she answered he shared information with her, "Sylvia, I am glad you are home. Two pieces of news. First, Elsie is comfortable in hospital while tests are carried out. I think Laura has her mother's permission to seek alternative accommodation. I took the opportunity of saying that I think I know someone who might be interested in purchasing the flat. Laura will let us know, almost prepared to offer you first refusal. Now, more pertinent at the moment is a letter, or rather three letters, I have received from Exeter Prison. I would like to show them to you and hear what you have to say before I take any action."

Sylvia replied that she would drive over to visit him. As soon as she arrived she had a look at the exterior of the apartment block working out which way the windows of Elsie's apartment faced. Having satisfied herself that it appeared that the living room faced west and south and would therefore get plenty of sun, she sought admittance to James's rooms.

With a mug of coffee each, James showed Sylvia the letters. After reading them Sylvia asked, "What do you make of them?"

James replied, "I find them encouraging and am surprised that Dean sounds totally different to how I imagined him when he attacked the ladies. I'm inclined to think the expressions of remorse are genuine. Unless I have misjudged her, I feel that Melanie is strong enough to be shown the letter addressed to her. However, I don't feel I can show it to her until I have had a word with her parents. What do you think?"

"I agree that you should speak to Stuart and Becky before you say anything to Mel, although I do think she is remarkably resilient. Will you send Dean a copy of the guidebook?"

"Yes, if Mel agrees."

After Sylvia had gone home, James hunted through his address book and found Stuart's mobile number. Stuart was interested to hear of Dean's desire to apologise and thought Melanie would be pleased to receive his letter. He agreed to consult Becky and would ring back. Later, he asked James to talk to their daughter and to let her know that they knew about the letter.

"We think we have found the stone on which the altar for the abbey church was placed," were Melanie's first words when she arrived in the late afternoon in a state of excitement. Conversation focussed on the archaeological dig for the first few minutes, but eventually James steered it round to the letters.

"You have had an eventful day, as, I suppose, have I. Yours was obviously exciting, mine was more serious and I should like you to listen carefully. I had a letter, or rather three letters, this morning in an envelope marked Exeter Prison."

"Is it about the man who attacked me?"

"Yes. The first, marked 1, was from the Prison Chaplain. I'll read it to you." James then read Paul Divine's letter.

"He says that Dean has written to me. Is it alright for me to read it? Have you read it?"

"Yes, I have and so has Sylvia. Your parents know what it says, and they want me to be with you when you read it. Here it is."

There was silence while Melanie read the letter and then she read it again out loud. "I think that's a nice letter and he does sound genuine. He really does sound sorry, and he has got interested in history. Well done him! I will certainly let him know that I forgive him. After all, and I shan't tell him this, his attack resulted in me getting to know you and then Robin. Do you think we should send a copy of the guidebook? But you said there were three letters."

"The letter addressed to you is the third. He also wrote to me and I'll read it to you; it is similar to yours."

When he had read letter number 2, James asked, "Do you want to take your letter home and write a reply in your own time and enclose a copy of the guidebook?"

"I would like to draft a reply and show it to you. Do you think I should tell him about the dig?"

"I am sure he would be interested, and it will probably give his confidence a boost to receive a reply that includes other news. If he has been studying the layout and fittings of abbeys and monasteries, he may have suggestions of what to look for. But, do you want to get yourself into regular correspondence as this is what could develop?"

"I understand. Perhaps I should also talk to Robin before I reply in any detail."

Two days later Melanie showed James her draft of a reply to Dean. At the end of her letter she informed him that a team of archaeologists were examining what appeared to be the remains of an abbey, but they couldn't tell yet whether it had ever been completed or why it had been abandoned. James suggested a couple of small amendments and agreed to send the final copy with a guidebook of Cricken and covering letter from himself to Paul Divine.

Two weeks later James received another letter from Exeter Prison. When he opened it he found that it was a letter from Dean addressed to himself and Melanie jointly.

Dear Mr Willoughby and Miss Hardy

I was so delighted to receive your letters to me and thank you, Miss Hardy, for your very kind words and for granting me your forgiveness. It means the world to me to know that you have accepted my assurance that I am trying to better myself. I think you must be very special and very courageous to be able to be positive about your future life. Just receiving letters makes me feel that there is a place for me in the civilised world.

I loved reading the history of Cricken. Fancy stumbling on that tunnel after so many years. I wonder if the abbey that is being uncovered near your village had any connection with Cricken or the abbey that owned some of the land near Cricken.

I have read several books about the foundations of monasteries and abbeys and what happened to some of them. In one book there was mention of a monastery that had to be vacated in a hurry because some sort of invasion was threatened. The abbot and the monks hid their valuables and the abbey's treasures, including communion patens and chalices, silver altar candlesticks and other precious items before they left. They did not dare to take them with them and they obviously hoped they would be able to return. The place they hid the treasure was in a sort of mini-crypt under the altar stone. It may be worth digging rather deeper near the altar in your ruin.

I am quite envious of you getting on your knees and scraping away in the soil. Do you have hours of finding nothing and then some interesting specimen appears?

Once again, my grateful thanks to both of you for your very kind words. Incidentally, did you know each other before I disturbed your lives?

God bless you both

Dean Savage

When Melanie and James had read Dean's letter, Mel grinned and exclaimed, "Do you think there could be some treasure in our dig? I shall have to mention the possibility to Archie. He is always saying that surprises do occur."

She was up early the next day and was one of the first to arrive at the dig. As soon as Dr Ditchburn had allocated tasks to his workforce Melanie approached him and told him what Dean had written in his letter. The archaeologist remarked that he had read about a hiding place under the altar stone but had forgotten about it. He then invited Melanie to dig deeper near the altar stone and see if she could find any sign of a hiding place.

For most of the day Melanie dug ever deeper without making any discovery. It was hard work because she reached below the topsoil and found herself contending with chalk. Feeling somewhat dispirited near the end of the day she probed one more time under the end of the altar stone and felt something hard. Clearing soil away she found a stone standing on end and next to it a stone resting flat on the chalk sub-layer. Fuelled by excitement she kept clearing and realised that whereas she had been behind the altar perhaps she should be checking in front. When she moved to the front it was not long before she discovered a floor lower than the base of the altar. She found an upright stone in front of the altar that connected to the floor. Following this upright stone, she found another with a metal ring in it.

She looked round and discovered that only Archie Ditchburn and two of his senior helpers were left on site. Most of the excavation had been elsewhere during the day and they hadn't realised that Melanie hadn't gone home. Seeing her excitement when she hailed them, they came and looked at what she had found. They all joined in her excitement. Archie congratulated her but suggested she cover the ring until the next day when they would concentrate on the area.

Melanie was surprised that, in spite of a high level of excitement, she slept well that night. She may have been tired from her hours of excavation, but she was still up early and had started to uncover the ring before Archie arrived. She had phoned James and Toby Schiller as they had been involved in the discovery of the site. They both arrived early to hear what lay behind the stone with the ring.

Two hours of further excavation and it was possible to remove the stone, behind which was a cavity in which they found a metal chest. There was nothing else in the cavity, so the chest was taken to the 'Find's Tent'.

With a little cleaning and oiling the bolts were drawn back. Melanie was invited to open the chest, which yielded a hoard of silver and gold objects and a large quantity of coins.

After they had feasted their eyes on the hoard, Archie proclaimed, "I am sure this will have to be declared as Treasure Trove and the Antiquities people will need to catalogue and evaluate it. That could take several weeks. I expect they will advise us as to when we can publicise the discovery. Until then I suggest we just enjoy the knowledge we have but keep it to ourselves." He then went away to make a call on his mobile phone.

There was disappointment and acceptance that the hoard would remain a secret for a few days. There were also several conversations speculating about the future location of the treasure. Archie returned to say that some eminent historians and others had asked to visit the site before the end of the day.

Melanie detached herself from the conversations into which she had been drawn and made her way to James. "SG, this is surely a momentous day, but I can't help thinking that the starting point again is the day that Dean attacked me. Won't he be pleased when we are able to tell him that he prompted the search for the treasure's hiding place. But for him, I don't think we would have found it."

CHANGING SCENES

When two unattached couples plan to holiday together even a change of scene doesn't stop them from observing some criminal activity.

One of James Willoughby's favourite pastimes was studying maps. Although he had visited several countries during his time as a dealer in antiques and collectables he had a partial, rather than a detailed, knowledge of the British Isles. When he moved into his second-floor apartment in Clarence House he had bought himself an Ordinance Survey map so that he could identify places he could see in the countryside visible from his south-facing window. Although now eighty-six his eyesight was very good and with his field-glasses he could see for miles across the Coltsbrook Valley. He was looking at an Explorer map of parts of South-west England when his buzzer sounded indicating that someone wished to visit him.

The visitor, whom he admitted, was his seventy year-old friend Sylvia Marchant. The couple had met a few months previously when James stood in as an emergency organist at the funeral of Sylvia's mother. In conversation they discovered that James had known Sylvia's late husband Ken many years before when both men were in Russia. In his antique dealings James sometimes acquired intelligence that he shared, mostly in 'accidental' clandestine meetings, with Ken who, as a British diplomat, found the information 'useful'. Following the funeral James and Sylvia struck up a friendship which resulted in them sharing several adventures.

When Sylvia learned that the occupant of the apartment below James had been taken ill and was unlikely to be able to return to her home, she expressed interest in the possibility of acquiring the vacant flat if it came on the market. It was news of her property negotiations that brought Sylvia to Clarence House. James looked at her, then commented, "Sylvia, my dear, how lovely to see you. Your expression suggests you have something exciting to tell me, but just contain yourself a minute while I put the kettle on for coffee, unless you would prefer something stronger!"

"I will be patient, but I would like a coffee, please."

When coffee was served, Sylvia was able to share her news. "I have just come from the estate agent who tells me that he has a firm offer from a cash buyer for my house, so I have set all the wheels in motion. He thinks I might be able to move within the month. The solicitor thinks there shouldn't be any problems. The only problem I can see is that you might not like me knowing how many lady friends visit you."

"I can see that you are wanting to get you own back for the times I have teased you. But that is splendid news. Will it mean a house-warming party?"

"I shall have to think about that," Sylvia responded somewhat coyly, and followed up that remark by changing the subject. "What have you been doing with maps of the South-west open? Are you planning a holiday?"

"Yes, I was doing a little research. I have been thinking about a remark that Melanie made a few weeks ago. You remember that she asked for advice as to whether she should agree with the suggestion of one of her girlfriends that they should go on holiday together with their boyfriends. She sounded less than enthusiastic about the idea. I have the impression that she is not keen on going with her parents either as it would mean leaving the dig at an exciting time."

"Of course! Finding that treasure has added some impetus to the excavation. But what are you hatching up?"

"Well, let's consider some situations. Firstly, I think Mel would like to have a holiday with my grandson Robin, but they would need a chaperone, or perhaps two. Then I thought the best time for her would be September when she has had her A level results and hopefully secured the university place she has been conditionally offered at Bath. By then Robin will have been with his current employers for eight months and probably will be entitled to some holiday time." Looking directly at Sylvia, James continued, "From what you have just told me, by then you should have taken up residence here and could probably do with a break after the hassle of moving."

"You have obviously been doing some thinking. Is your choice Devon or Cornwall or have you considered other places? And have you said anything to the youngsters?"

"No, I am only at the research stage although I have looked on the net to see if there might be suitable accommodation available. If you like the idea I suggest we see what Mel and Robin think before I go any further."

"Splendid. When do you think we can talk with them?"

"Melanie is calling to see me this evening to show me a letter she plans to send to Dean, and I will talk to her then."

"Good. I am glad she is going to respond to that young man. It sounds as though he has changed out of all recognition from the sex maniac that attacked her. I was never certain about prison as the way to correct bad behaviour, but it seems to have worked with him. Receiving a letter from her in response to his apology will have encouraged him to maintain his progress. I am proud of Melanie's positive and caring attitude, which in no small way is a credit to the way you have continued to support her from the day you came to her rescue when she had been attacked and left unconscious."

When Melanie arrived with news of 'the dig', she was able to tell James that further discoveries seemed to have provided evidence that the church and the uncompleted monastery was a Benedictine foundation. This discovery was giving speculation to the possibility of a link with the Benedictine lands near the church at Cricken. Melanie was clearly excited at the possibility of a link as it was she who had stumbled on the tunnel linking Cricken church to the neighbouring Manor House.

After she and James had spent a few minutes talking about the excavations, Melanie took a notebook from her bag and explained, "SG (short for surrogate grandad) I have drafted a letter to Dean and I would like you to look at it and if you approve would you send it to him?" James read:

Dear Dean,

Thank you for your letter and your kind words about the Cricken guidebook. I have been asked to thank you for telling me about the possibility of a hiding place under the altar of the church we are excavating. Our leader had heard of the find to which you referred, so he invited me to dig deeper by the altar stone of our dig. I spent all day digging without success and was going to give up when I made a discovery. The photo enclosed shows what I found. I am not allowed to tell you yet what was behind the stone with a metal ring in it, but I am permitted to say that what was there made experienced archaeologists and historians very excited, and they are making further investigations. So, well done you for mentioning the possibility. I have shown my friend James Willoughby what I have written, and he has said that you can tell Mr Divine, the Prison Chaplain, but that neither of you must mention it to anyone else until the results are published. I am trusting you, Dean, with this secret, because I believe that you can now be regarded as a trustworthy person. Please don't let me down.

Best wishes, Melanie Hardy

The letter above was the final version that Melanie and James agreed upon. That task completed James asked, "Mel, my dear, have you made any plans for a holiday this summer and before you go to uni?"

"No, I did not pursue the idea that I mentioned to you, that one of my friends suggested; that we should go on holiday together with our boyfriends. Mum and Dad have invited me to join them in their caravan, but it would mean missing the dig when it is at a most exciting point. Why, have you thought of something?"

"Well, yes and no. Perhaps I should say, partly. I was talking with Sylvia today. It seems that she may be able to move into the apartment below mine within a month. After the busyness a move entails, she could probably do with a break. I also thought that after you have received your results and secured your place at Bath we shall be into September, by which time I am sure that Robin will be due some holiday...."

"And we could all go together. You can be chaperones for us and Robin and I can make sure you two oldies behave yourselves. What a splendid idea! Have you thought where we can go?"

"Again, the answer is yes and no. I have mentioned it to Sylvia, and we agreed that we should leave the planning until all four of us can sit down and discuss possibilities, perhaps this weekend. I have had the map out for Devon and Cornwall and looked at places to stay on the internet. I have done no more than what I might describe as a feasibility study. What do you think?"

"I am all for it. Shall I ring Robin this evening and see if we can have a meeting on Saturday afternoon?"

"That's right. You go for it, girl!"

*

On Saturday afternoon, the four of them sat round the table in James's sitting room looking at maps and with the internet showing them lists of holiday accommodation. Firstly, they agreed on a date and decided on the second week of September starting on a Friday or Saturday for a week. Should they try for a hotel or self-catering? They decided on the latter so that they would have a base if it rained. They all liked the idea of Cornwall, not too far from the sea. When they trawled the internet, they could not locate the ideal four bedroomed property, but there were five possible cottages with two or three bedrooms. Robin suggested that if the owners were agreeable, he could take his tent and camp in the garden and then they could manage with three bedrooms. Then Sylvia asked Melanie if she would be prepared to share a twin room with her, in which case a two bedroomed property would be suitable.

After further discussion and a good look at the map they decided on a three-bedroom cottage with a two-bed house as reserve. Both were near Cornwall's south coast. While Melanie went to re-fill the teapot James made a telephone call to the owners of their first-choice property, was pleased with the information he received and made a booking with a deposit for a week starting on the second Friday of September.

Having put the phone down, James reported, "All booked. The owners live about two hundred metres farther down the lane that terminates at their farm. They can provide us with fresh eggs and milk and will leave a welcome basket in the cottage for us. They can also offer us the use of a camp-bed that can be placed in the living room if it should be too wet or windy for camping. And there is space for two cars. The Cornish coast path passes by one of their fields and there is access to a sandy beach in a small cove from the cliff next to the path."

"It sounds ideal," exclaimed Sylvia, "Did you also book good weather?" Melanie and Robin were clearly excited, but Melanie expressed concern when she asked, "How much is it going to cost us each?"

"Ah now, the accommodation will not cost you anything. It will be my treat for my three favourite people, but I will ask you to provide the food as we shall be self-catering."

"How exciting!" shouted Robin. "I could do with a holiday. Do they have a website with pictures?"

"Yes, they do," replied his grandfather, "You can look it up." He passed the laptop across and wrote the address of the website on a note pad and left it to Robin to investigate. When he had opened the website for the cottage Melanie and Sylvia looked over his shoulder to view the pictures and read the details. James asked, "Do you like what you see?" Their excitement continued and they all exclaimed that it looked perfect and considered that they were lucky it was not already booked.

After a few minutes Robin looked at his grandfather. "I have a feeling, Grandad, and a suspicion that you didn't book this in your phone call just now, but that you confirmed a booking you had already made. Am I right?"

With everyone looking at him James smiled and commented, "Robin, I can tell that your months with your firm of solicitors have taught you not to accept anything at face value. I confess that when I was trawling the net a fortnight ago, I saw this property and decided to make a provisional booking when I learned that someone else had just cancelled. I thought it looked ideal, but I wanted you all to find it and like it rather than be faced with a fait accompli. I didn't want us to miss it by not booking soon enough. I hope you will forgive me."

Sylvia cried, "Forgive you? I think we should congratulate you and thank you for your foresight. I can see that you have not lost the skills you acquired as an undercover agent in Russia all those years ago when you knew Ken. You are still a sly old fox," she added laughing.

"Undercover! I would have you know that I was a highly respected antiques dealer, known by politicians and high society people who trusted me for my fairness in all my dealings. However, I don't think your Ken, Sylvia, ever met the James Willoughby who dealt in antiques and collectables. In fact, they did pass in the street on a few occasions, and he had no idea who I was."

"But I thought you passed him information in secret."

"True, he did come by some intelligence in unusual circumstances."

Melanie, with the scent of a good story stirring her interest, questioned, "How did that happen if you never met?"

"I didn't say they never met. I will give you one example. On one occasion the art dealer got on the same crowded underground train as Ken. Later Ken found a note in his pocket suggesting he should ask the way of a road sweeper at a busy crossroads in the city. Anyone observing that meeting would have seen a rather scruffy road man talking to Ken and waving his broom about, pointing in different directions. Ken didn't waste too much time returning to the Embassy on that occasion. A few minutes later James Willoughby enquired of the doorman at the Embassy if Mr Marchant was in the building and if so would he tell him that a table had been reserved for him and his wife at his favourite restaurant."

"Why did you do that?" asked Robin.

"It is always wise to make sure that everything has gone smoothly. I needed to check that Ken was safe: the doorman informed me that he would pass on the message as Mr Marchant had entered the building five minutes earlier."

"But who was the road sweeper?" queried Melanie, "Or was it you, and if it was how did you become the real you so quickly?"

"Mel, when those two fraudsters had their pictures taken in the village square recently who did they think was behind the camera?"

Melanie realised that James was asking her to think carefully, and she responded, "That was me …. Oh no, it was an old lady. I was wearing my grandmother's coat and hat and carrying her basket."

"That's right. A reversible coat, a collapsible broom that becomes an attaché case that can hold shoe covers and a workman's cap are very useful items for a quick change."

"All very cloak and dagger stuff," interposed Robin.

"Perhaps," replied James, "Maybe you could describe the coat as a cloak, but the broom was not a dagger!"

Melanie commented, "You could write a book about your experiences."

"Never! My undercover experiences, as Sylvia described them, must always remain unreported. The Russian secret service, and those of some other countries, has a long memory and even longer tentacles. You remember the Salisbury poisonings? Nothing you heard in this room in the last few minutes must be repeated."

"I understand," said Melanie, "but does that mean you could be in danger."

"I don't think so and I hope not. Your father, Mel, has very kindly used his security know-how to check this apartment for bugs and the police will know if anyone gets in while I am not here and, of course, I have my panic buttons. Now, back to our holiday. We need to decide what else we should plan."

During the next hour they discussed the holiday and made plans. Sylvia was prepared to drive them in her small hatch-back but wondered how much luggage they could each take. Robin and Melanie decided that they would see if either of them could borrow a car from their families.

*

One Thursday in the middle of August, James was surprised to receive a phone call from a very excited eighteen year-old before he had set out to walk to the market in the village. "SG, I passed all my A levels well," cried Melanie, "and my place at Bath University has been confirmed. I am very so pleased that I can't get my words in the right order and I can't stop smiling."

"My darling girl, that's wonderful news and just what I expected to hear. I presume the grades are what you needed and how did you do in history?"

"I got A's in English and Maths and A star in History."

"That's splendid news. I'm sure this calls for cream cakes today and then a proper celebration later. Have you told Robin?"

"I had to leave a message for him as he is in court observing a parental custody case. But I am going into the village. Shall I meet you there?"

"Most definitely. I wouldn't miss out on meeting my favourite beautiful young lady when she is so happy."

When James arrived at the bakers and tea shop Melanie and her mother Becky were already seated at a table with a young man. James was introduced to the young man who turned out to be Melanie's brother Tom, whom he had not met previously. They both admitted that they had heard much about the other and it was about time they met face to face. Tom pointed out that he had heard of James before James had met Mel. "How was that, Tom?" asked James.

"I heard about your exploits as an umpire at a cricket match that I would have played in had I not been at University at the time."

"That's right. I remember Mel telling me that you play for the village team, but I certainly didn't expect to be umpiring that day. I was pressed into service when an umpire was injured."

"Well, sir, if you are interested, we have a 20 over match this evening if you feel like watching, but we have two umpires already booked."

"I might well take you up on that."

"If you really would like to go to the match, I could keep you company," said Melanie and turning to her mother and smiling sweetly continued, "If Mother will let me borrow her car I could give you a lift."

*

For three weeks Sylvia was frantically busy preparing for her move to her new apartment in Clarence House, with help from James and Melanie when they were available. At the beginning of the week before the August bank holiday Sylvia's move was achieved successfully. On Bank Holiday Monday she and James planned to go out for a celebratory lunch, but at 11.00 Sylvia reported that she had lost an earring. She explained to James, when he joined her, that she had put both earrings on the table, gone back into her bedroom for something and when she returned there was only one.

James remarked, "Was that balcony door open when you put the earrings on the table?"

Sylvia responded, "It was, but I don't think there could have been enough wind to blow one onto the floor and I have looked. They were a present from Ken, about the last present he gave me, and it is two years today since he died. I shall have to wear a different pair."

James returned to his room and went onto his balcony. He soon returned to fetch his field glasses. A few minutes later Sylvia received a telephone call. She answered the call and heard James's voice. 'I think I know where your earring is. Have you heard of the opera by Rossini called 'La Gazza Ladra'?"

"Why yes. It's 'The Thieving Magpie'."

"I can see a magpie's nest from here in a tree on the same level as your window. The sun is just at the right angle to shine into the nest and is reflecting on something sparkly. It is not going to be easy to retrieve it. My son Adam used to be a keen fisherman, but I'm doubtful if he could fish the earring out of the nest. At least all the baby birds have fledged and left the nest. We may need a tree surgeon to climb up."

"Do you know a tree surgeon who would be willing to undertake the task?"

"I think my friend Ben Foster, who is a mine of local information, may know of someone. I'll call him. May I ask; are the earrings valuable as well as being of sentimental value?"

"Yes, they are silver gilt with diamonds inset."

Fifteen minutes later James was able to report that he had arranged for someone to call in the late afternoon. When the tree surgeon arrived and climbed the tree to the nest, he was able to retrieve the earring, but also discovered some scraps of silver foil and a gold wedding band. He returned with the objects to ground level, but not without the thief displaying his displeasure at the loss of his contraband. He presented the earring and the ring to Sylvia and commented, "I suppose I could have left the foil with the bird, but it would probably become litter in a few months."

Sylvia promised to place an advert in one or two shops to see if she could find the owner of the ring.

*

On the second Friday of September four excited travellers in two cars arrived at the holiday cottage near the village of Trethallow in Cornwall. The directions they were given enabled them to reach their destination easily and they were delighted to find the cottage exactly as it had been described. They were surprised to discover that the main bedroom was L-shaped with a single bed in each wing of the 'L' and it also had an en-suite bathroom. The other two bedrooms were smaller, either side of the main bathroom and with sea views. When the ladies saw the largest bedroom, they looked at each other and said, "Why don't we share this room? Then the boys can have a smaller room each." Sleeping arrangements agreed, the cars were unpacked, all the facilities inspected, cups of tea served and then a Land Rover stopped outside. It was the farmer calling to welcome them and to check that they had everything they needed.

James and Sylvia walked out to his vehicle as he left, and Sylvia commented on the sheep she could see in a field. "Is that a small flock of Dorset Downs you have there?"

"Yes, you're right. Do you know about sheep?"

"Not a lot, but I noticed the black faces. They are a fairly rare breed, aren't they?"

"Yes, although we have several breeders in the West Country."

James asked, "Do you get much trouble from stray dogs?"

"Fortunately, no. Even the visitors seem to have taken note of the notices reminding them of the country code. We have more problems with fly tipping. Some farmers have had to spend too much time, trouble and money clearing up other people's rubbish."

*

The next three days were fine and warm. The four holidaymakers enjoyed the opportunity to relax. Together they visited Truro, went into the cathedral, noticed the older parish church over which the cathedral had been built and browsed in the gift shop before spending time looking at other shops. On the third day they discovered a viewpoint on a headland with a parking area at the edge of which was a kiosk selling teas and ice creams. The rocky coast with small coves and sandy beaches could be seen both to left and right and there was access to the coast-path in each direction.

The viewpoint was accessed from the main road by a narrow lane with passing places for just over half a mile. The lane passed through a woodland reserve shortly before ending at the viewpoint. There were several designated paths by which the woodland could be explored.

On the Wednesday of their week the two couples went on separate excursions, agreeing to meet up at the viewpoint for ice cream in the late afternoon. Robin and Melanie arrived first as Sylvia and James took a wrong turning and ended up in a housing estate. They found themselves in a cul-de-sac where a house was undergoing extensive renovation and where three or four vehicles belonging to tradespeople were blocking the turning space.

Meeting up with the others, they all enjoyed some refreshment before James and Sylvia left to return to the cottage as it was their turn to prepare an evening meal. The young couple decided they would walk back along the lane and explore the woodland. Although they had noticed two places where it would be possible to park a car where there was access to the woods, they left theirs at the viewpoint parking area thinking that it would be better not to block the way of anyone wishing to turn round.

Sylvia and James drove back down the single-track lane. At the last passing place before the main road, they met a small pick-up truck. As the lorry passed them James watched it go past and could see in the back of the truck a load of building rubbish, including an old bath and broken tiles. He wondered why the vehicle was on a road that led only to a viewpoint. As he turned in his seat to look behind them, he realised he had seen the vehicle before when they had taken a wrong turning earlier in the day.

Remembering what the farmer had said about fly-tipping he asked Sylvia to pull into the lay-by they encountered as soon as they turned onto the main road. It was his intention to see if the lorry returned and if it still had its load, but then he realised that it was travelling towards Melanie and Robin. He took out his own, rarely used, mobile and called Melanie, hoping they both had a signal. When Melanie answered he told her of his suspicion that a load of rubbish was about to be dumped illegally.

Ten minutes later, Melanie phoned back. "It's as you thought. The lorry is off back down the lane."

"Thanks, Mel. We will wait to see it turn onto the main road."

As soon as the call was finished James got out of the car and had his phone out, ostensibly taking a picture of a fine specimen of an oak tree on the opposite verge. While he was in position facing the tree the truck passed as he had his phone videoing the scene.

On returning to the cottage, while Sylvia started the task of preparing the evening meal James walked down to the farmhouse to inform the farmer what they had witnessed. Before he reached the door it opened, and the farmer appeared. "Hello Mr Willoughby, I saw you coming. I believe I met a friend of yours today. I was talking to a police officer friend of mine at lunchtime who introduced me to an officer from another force. I happened to mention your name in the context of late holiday bookings and this Inspector Robinson told me that you have been instrumental in helping in solving several crimes."

"Well, I may be able to help your force to solve another. If you like to come up to the cottage when our youngsters return, we may be able to show you some interesting video footage about fly tipping."

"Shall I contact my friend and get him along?"

"Good idea, I think he should be very interested."

An hour later the four holiday makers were joined by the farmer and his policeman friend. They were shown pictures of a lorry reversing into the woodland reserve and then dumping its load of rubbish before making a quick exit. The crime was captured from two different positions, one by Melanie from behind a screen of trees at the rear of the vehicle and the other by Robin who had climbed one of the trees. They were also shown the picture on James's phone with a clear view of the registration number. Additionally, they were able to rewind the dashcam in Sylvia's car that she had had fitted the previous week. On that they were able to view the same vehicle in the estate where a house renovation was in progress.

The following morning the owners of a house were surprised when the work on their house was interrupted by the need for two of the tradesmen to assist the police with some enquiries. Apparently, a load of rubbish really had fallen off the back of a lorry.

RUSSIA RE-VISITED

Age is no barrier when it comes to being invited to undertake a secret assignment to Russia by someone whose undercover exploits of forty years previously are remembered by MI6.

He had just replaced his house phone on its cradle when there was a tap on his front door. He opened the door to the visitor he was expecting, namely his neighbour from the apartment below his. James Willoughby and Sylvia Marchant had established a routine whereby they had coffee together every Tuesday morning, alternating as host. Although they had known each other for less than a year their memories from their previous existences went back several years.

James, now eighty-six, had spent several years in his forties and early fifties as an antiques and collectables dealer in Russia and Hong Kong as well as visiting other countries. While in Russia he had often found himself in a position to share sensitive information with Sylvia's late husband Ken during the latter's time as a diplomat in the British Embassy in Moscow. James had met Sylvia when he attended her mother's funeral, as a replacement organist when the regular organist had broken her wrist. With shared memories they had become good friends, although there was a decade and a half between their ages. Sylvia had responded rapidly when James informed her that the apartment below his was becoming vacant.

As they sat down with their coffees Sylvia perceived that James appeared a little withdrawn as though something was bothering him, so she challenged him. "Have you something on your mind, dear?"

"Well, yes, I had a strange phone call just before your arrived, Sylv."

"Don't call me that please, you know I don't like it. If you persist, I shall call you Jimmy. Can you tell me about your phone call?"

"My apologies, Sylvia my dear. Yes, and you may be able to help, if you can cast your mind back a few years to when you were with Ken in Russia. The caller was a man who said his name was Neil Buchanan and he had served as a very junior member of staff at the Embassy in Moscow when

I was in Russia. I got the impression that he is now a bigwig in MI6. He wants to talk to me about a delicate matter relating to present-day Russia, but he wants our meeting to be unnoticeable, or perhaps 'clandestine' might be a more appropriate description. He wouldn't go into any detail on the phone. Do you remember Ken ever talking about a Neil Buchanan?"

"Neil Buchanan? I don't know. I can't think of anyone with .... Or, just a moment. NB? I do remember Ken referring to someone as NB. Perhaps that was him. Of course, they often used just initials or gave officers codenames."

"I'm sure you're right. When he called he said, 'Is that Mr James Willoughby?' and then he added 'W' and the first part of my undercover codename from that time."

"Are you going to meet him?"

"Yes. It took me a while to think of a suitable location, but we settled on one that should not attract any attention. I asked him if he could sing a bit and if he knew any harvest hymns. He said he could and enjoyed hymns like 'Come, ye thankful people, come' and 'We plough the fields'. He will be joining me at 'Phillip's Rest' on Friday when I play for the vicar's little harvest festival for the residents. We shall arrive separately, and I shall introduce him to the manager as an old friend of mine who is passing through the area and has only a few minutes to spare. I shall ask Cedric if we could have a quiet room for a few minutes so that we can have a chat about old times. Then he will leave, and I will have a chat with Quentin and some of the other residents."

"It all sounds a bit 'hush, hush'. Is he wanting to quiz you about your knowledge and experience of working undercover?"

"Possibly, but he may want to know about some of the treasures in The Hermitage Museum in St. Petersburg. I shall find out on Friday, I suppose. I cannot decide whether his enquiry about my age and my health is of any significance, although he had heard of my contacts with the local police in this area."

Following the Care Home's Harvest Festival service James and Neil met in a secluded and private room in the Home provided for them by the manager. They both felt they had contrived very well to hide the fact that they had never met before. Neil wasted no time in explaining why he wanted the meeting. "We have an assignment for which we feel that you would be highly suitable, if you would be willing to undertake it. We know that this is so unusual and so improbable that we think it would work. I will explain what it is, but you must stop me if you think it is beyond your capabilities. This assignment involves people exchange. To be more precise; taking a Russian lady from this country to Russia and bringing a different Russian lady back."

"I have spent time in Russia, but that was a long time ago. I can't see how I could fit into this scheme. Could you give me any more information?"

"Certainly, if you are happy to hear more. We would like you to be the courier. This scheme, as you call it, is so remarkable that it is unremarkable and of no interest to any observer. An elderly gentleman accompanied by his nurse on his way to a private hospital for treatment we think is so natural an event that the only attentions that it might attract should be those of goodwill."

"And I suppose that a few days later he returns, again accompanied by his nurse, except that it is not the same nurse. How do we travel?"

"You have grasped what is involved. You will join a cruise ship on its way to St Petersburg on which you will have a private suite. In St Petersburg you will be met by a private ambulance that will take you to a location where your nurse will have become a Russian citizen meeting her parents and hopefully her sometime boyfriend. It is not necessary to divulge why she had been detained in the UK, but sufficient to say that she is now free to return to start a new life out of the sight and knowledge of Russian officialdom. After witnessing the happy re-union, you will be able to recover your present health and have a holiday in St Petersburg where you will be able to meet the chief curator of The Hermitage, after your cruise party have left, and show him a Fabergé egg of rare quality. The egg will have escaped attention, we hope, as it will have been included in the medication bag you will have with you. He will probably realise that you are a connoisseur and will wish to show you many fine exhibits."

James pondered what he had been told and then asked, "Where has the Fabergé egg come from and what am I to do with it?"

"That is a matter about which I am only allowed to give you a very sketchy picture. Let me say that it was extracted from hands in which it should not have fallen. We think this is one of the 50 eggs Karl Fabergé made for the Russian royal family, but whether it is one of the seven about which survival is unknown we cannot say. Wealthy Russian oligarchs are keen to have them returned to Russia. Some careful and discreet discussions have been held with a very small team at The Hermitage and an arrangement for the egg to find its way there unpublicised has been agreed. You need not know the terms of the agreement. Its arrival will not be announced until you are safely back in this country and its source or the method by which it arrived will never be revealed. We are quite happy for it to be believed that the egg was discovered in Russia."

"What about the two ladies I am to escort? Or rather, they are to escort me. I assume that there has been some difficulty about them being able to leave the countries where they currently reside."

"Again, you do not need to know any details, but I can inform you that they both speak Russian and English well and have nursing experience. I hope you haven't forgotten your facility in Russian."

At this point James laughed and responded, "I don't know how much research you have done about my recent activities, but you may not have discovered that, in order to keep my brain active, I have set myself during recent months the task of reading aloud Russian texts printed in Russian. I hope that will do."

"Does that response mean that you are willing to undertake this assignment. If so, how soon could you leave? There is a cruise ship leaving Southampton on Wednesday of next week. That is in 5 days' time. We should require you to visit London, ostensibly to view a gallery, on Sunday or Monday, but actually for a briefing. Expect a package to be delivered tomorrow. It will give you all the information you need to be able to join the cruise with your nurse. I will leave it to you to explain to family and friends that need to know that you will be away from home for a few days. Now, I must be on my way. We will say our goodbyes in the corridor."

When they left the quiet room, James spotted Cedric and thanked him for the use of the room. He continued, "It was so good that we had a few minutes to catch up on several years of news." Then turning to Neil, "I am so glad you could spend a time on your journey. I hope you find your cousin well when you reach Cornwall."

Neil replied, "I was really pleased to have the opportunity to have a chat and I also enjoyed being able to participate in Harvest Festival. Perhaps we should try to make sure we don't leave too long before our next meeting."

Neil left the building alone while James went to speak to some of the residents. When he reached his apartment half-an-hour later, he sat down, reviewed the morning's conversation, then put his head in his hands and said to himself, 'Now, what have I let myself in for. What will Adam, Sylvia and, indeed, Melanie say? How much can I tell them?'

James woke several times during the night and felt far from refreshed when he rose on Saturday morning. So many thoughts were chasing each other round in his mind and they all seemed to end with an unanswerable question. He had his breakfast and then sat looking over the valley outside his living room window. He realised that he would be unable to make any plans until the promised package arrived with more information. He did not have to wait too long as shortly after 9.00 am his intercom buzzed and he learned that a courier was waiting in the lobby to give him a parcel.

Returning to his room he spent the next hour and a half reading and re-reading the information and instructions contained in the pack. Most of his questions seemed to have been answered, including how much or rather how little he was allowed to tell his family and close friends about his assignment. He noted that he was not to travel incognito but that he could use his real name, although he had been given a new codename. He was also given the names of his 'nurses'. On the outward journey he would be looked after by Irina and his return companion would be Lara.

Just before 11.00 there was a knock on his door. Wondering who it could be, he was somewhat relieved to discover Sylvia and Melanie, his eighteen-year-old surrogate granddaughter, on the other side. When his visitors were greeted and seated with cups of coffee James expressed surprise and pleasure in their visit. "What a pleasure to have the company of my two favourite ladies. Is there a special reason for the visit? Are you going to tell me about your first few weeks at Bath University, Melanie?"

"Yes, I will tell you about that," replied Melanie, "but when we met in the village this morning Sylvia told me that you had a strange meeting yesterday at the Care Home. We were hoping that it wasn't anything unpleasant or sinister. We are pleased to see that you haven't been kidnapped."

"No, it wasn't anything like that, but rather a compliment that someone had remembered that I had some expertise when I was dealing in antiques in Russia. I have been asked to undertake a commission next week and I shall be away for a few days."

"Next week!" exclaimed both his listeners. Melanie continued, "You're not going to Russia, are you? Will you be going alone, and will you be safe?"

"I think I can trust you both to keep your lips sealed. Many years ago, perhaps as many as a hundred, a valuable Russian artefact disappeared. It appears to have turned up in this country amongst other items that had found their way into the wrong hands. Very quiet diplomatic discussions have resulted in an agreement to send the item back to its country of origin. The difficulty has been to think of a way of doing this unnoticed. The solution is to send it with a long retired and hopefully forgotten antiques dealer whose arrival in Russia would go unremarked. So, you see where I come in, and Sylvia, you will see how MI6 thought of me."

"SG, won't you be in danger, especially if someone leaks your mission? I couldn't bear it if you were captured, hurt or imprisoned. How long will you be away? What if your plane crashes? I know you're very clever and I guess you avoided being noticed many times as an undercover agent, but that was a long time ago when you were much younger."

James thought he had never seen Melanie look frightened before, so he tried to reassure her. "I will not be flying but travelling by ship with many other holiday makers. I know that the Foreign Office will be monitoring my progress, but I think I might also have a chat with your father, Mel, to see if he has any device that can keep track of me. For anybody else who wonders where I am, they can be told that I have decided to take a little holiday to visit some old haunts to see how much they have changed in the last forty years."

It was then Sylvia's turn to sound worried. "When you arrive won't you stand out as a foreigner? Surely it will be difficult for you to move about unnoticed."

James stood up and went to his bedroom. While the ladies looked at each other with puzzled frowns on their faces he transformed himself. The figure that shuffled back into the living room was wearing a long black overcoat of a distinctive style and a Russian hat. He was muttering to himself in Russian. Seeing the ladies he broke into almost indistinguishable English, "Where gone my friend Jims?" Then continuing threateningly, "What you done him? Why not here? Who you?" Picking up a coffee cup, he smelt it then continued, "This English stuff – why no Russki coffee?"

Both ladies stood up and backed away unsure whether this man had been hiding in the bedroom all the time they had been there. James removed his hat and glasses and resumed his normal voice, rather than the guttural accent he had been using. "Am I at all convincing?"

Sylvia responded, "Quite realistic, I think I might have met you in Russia, but can you maintain that performance? Will people there speak differently now?"

On Monday James travelled to London using the train ticket he had been given. He was met at the barrier at the end of the platform and escorted by taxi to a meeting where he was given further information as well as guidance on how to keep safe if something did not go to plan. Two days later while he was walking, case in hand, towards the village centre a car pulled up beside him and the driver, seeing his burden, offered him a lift.

When the car reached its destination, a secluded country house, James was met by NB and introduced to Irina. A small ambulance was used to transport James and Irina to Southampton where a wheelchair from a cruise ship was brought for James. A polite female steward escorted the 'invalid' and his 'nurse' to their private hospital cabin. A security guard had already brought their luggage on board.

Two hours later the cruise passengers began to embark and after a further two hours the ship sailed into the Solent. During the next four days James and Irina stayed in their cabin, including while the ship called at two ports when many passengers went ashore. They read, talked, did a little exercise and generally amused themselves, but James was always resting at the appointed times when the steward called with meals and checked whether they had any other needs.

In their chats James learned Irina's story. Although a businessman her father was quite active politically, but when Irina was twenty-three and already trained as a nurse, her father found that his political persuasion had become unpopular, and he deemed that it might be a good idea for the family to take an extended 'holiday' in Bulgaria where he had some contacts. After two months they made plans to return to Russia. The day before their departure date, Irina went shopping to buy a present for her boyfriend. While walking down a street she was grabbed from behind by two men who roughly pushed her into a car.

That was followed by seven years of hell while she was abused and used as a slave. She was traded from one owner to another several times and after moving through five or six countries she ended up working eighteen hours a day in a warehouse in England where she was given very little food and just a cupboard to sleep in. When the warehouse was raided by the police she was found in an emaciated state. She was gradually nursed back to health. As she recovered, she began to help with the nursing care of other unfortunates who had suffered similarly. Investigations into her family background discovered that her parents were living in Russia, but as her father was still recognised as being unsympathetic to the state the Russian authorities were not interested in assisting her repatriation. Hence an undercover scheme to return her to her family was devised.

As soon as the ship docked in St Petersburg, after a cursory inspection of their papers, Irina and James, again in a wheelchair, were quickly transferred to a waiting ambulance with their luggage and driven away to an isolated and quiet, tired old house a few miles outside the city. In Compton St Philip Stuart Hardy informed his daughter and Sylvia Marchant that the first phase of the journey had been completed safely.

James and Irina were received kindly by an elderly couple but continued their patient-nurse relationship for several hours until they felt that they truly were in a safe environment. It was more than twenty-four hours before a visitor arrived with a programme for their next three days. Irina was given a telephone number by which she could contact her parents to arrange for them to collect her. James was invited to wait for another day until a car arrived to take him to a hotel in St Petersburg, where he would spend the night before making his own way to The Hermitage the next day. He was given an entrance pass for the museum and a letter of appointment to see the head curator. The plan was that after conducting his business and perhaps taking an opportunity to view some of the treasures on display he would return to the hotel and wait for a car to return him to the old house in the country.

The joyful re-union of Irina with her parents and the boyfriend, who had never given up hope that she would return, went smoothly. After taking a tender and tearful farewell of James, Irina, her parents and boyfriend departed. Irina's final words to her 'patient' were, "I shall never forget you, James: thank you so much."

When the promised car came for James it was late in the day and already dark. Expecting to return after two nights at most he left most of his belongings with his hosts. In less than five minutes the car joined a main road. James made a point of observing the route taken and noticed place names and landmarks. On reaching the hotel he was immediately shown to his room and refreshments were brought to him in his room.

In the morning, rather than relying on room service, he found his way to the dining room where he was shown to a table in a cubicle and served with breakfast. While having his breakfast he realised that there was a conversation going on in the neighbouring cubicle. He was soon thankful that he had not let his knowledge of Russian lapse as the talk was about himself. It was clear that his mission was not secret, and plans were being laid to waylay him on his way to the museum. Listening carefully, it became clear that his identity was known, but they did not know what he looked like. They planned to watch until he left his room and follow him.

As he had taken the precaution of not leaving the valuable package in his bedroom, he quietly left his table while the two in the next cubicle still talked and slipped out of the hotel. He had left his coat behind but had with him the precious cargo and Russian currency he had been given. After mingling with shoppers for a while he came to a gentleman's outfitters, where he was able to purchase a coat and hat in a different style and colour to that he had left behind. Next, he found a store that had a counter with costume jewellery, some containing semi-precious stones. He bought a couple of necklaces for Sylvia and Melanie. He thought that if he were to be robbed his bag containing his recent purchases would most likely be snatched. As he had time to spare before his appointment with the curator, he entered a coffee shop and ordered a Russki coffee. It was good to rest his feet for a few minutes and consider his situation, while he was aware of the 'egg' virtually boiling in his bag under his coat.

James wondered how long it would be before his disappearance from the hotel would be noticed. Twice he observed two men scanning pedestrians, once outside the store he had visited and again, the same men, when he reached the main entrance to The Hermitage. He found a quiet spot to plan his next move. He knew of a side entrance, but would it be open, and would he be conspicuous if he tried to gain admittance there? He then noticed two queues at the main entrance, one for ticket holders and the other for casual visitors. He decided to be a casual visitor as the men's attention seemed to be focussed on the queue for ticket holders.

When he reached the desk, he showed his papers to the young lady and whispered, 'there are two men by the door watching for me.' She understood immediately, opened a side door and ushered him through it while also pressing a button, which probably provided a security alert. The door was quickly closed behind him. He had hardly had time to look around him before a young man appeared and politely invited James to accompany him. Without entering any of the parts of the building open to the public he was conducted to a room where he was warmly welcomed by a well-dressed man with a hearty smile who professed to be very pleased to see him. James assumed he was probably in his late fifties. He introduced himself as Igor Ivanovitch, the head curator of the museum.

"I am delighted to meet you, Mr Willoughby. May I call you James? And please call me Igor. May I offer you a little refreshment? I hope you had no difficulty in finding us."

"Many thanks for your welcome, Igor. I have visited your exceptionally fine museum on several occasions in the past, but my last visit was nearly forty years ago. I had no difficulty finding you, but I believe my meeting you was not to everyone's liking." Seeing concern expressed on Mr. Ivanovitch's face he told the story of his morning.

"I am so sorry that you had such a worrying experience and congratulate you on the way you responded. Without making any comment or judgment on your activities when you worked in this country, I can understand some information I was given that you were well versed in making yourself elusive if necessary. Perhaps that skill has not left you and I sincerely hope that it doesn't desert you before you reach your home in England. You are clearly a brave man to accept this undertaking and bring us an object which will give such joy to those who view it. Before you leave here, we must discuss and make provision for your safety until you leave our shores."

"That is most kind of you and it must be nearly time for you to behold what I have brought, but I believe we have to have a little conversation using predetermined words, known only to you and me and our masters who have arranged this meeting."

"Exactly James and I have to start. So here goes ...."

When the conversation had been completed and security requirements had been fulfilled James took off his coat and revealed the bag hanging round his neck. He removed from the bag a box that had two locks on it and placed it on a table. Igor took a key from his desk and inserted it in one of the locks, then James removed a wallet from his pocket and removed a key from that before inserting it in the other lock. Igor turned his key once clockwise, James turned his twice, Igor again turned his, this time three turns and finally James turned his twice anti-clockwise. There was a click and then James opened the box and removed the object inside.

When Igor, in response to an invitation from James, undid the wrapping, both men gasped when they saw what was inside. It was a porcelain and glass model of a royal Russian sledge drawn by two horses. On the sledge was a beautifully decorated egg. The ensemble was mounted on snow made of glass and encased in a tinted glass case. The whole piece was exquisite and demonstrated superbly the superlative skill of the artist Karl Fabergé.

Igor exclaimed, "This is magnificent. We have some fine Fabergé eggs, but this is as fine, if not finer, than any I have seen. I guess this must have been removed from one of the royal palaces when the Romanovs were deposed and subsequently executed in 1917. Thank you, James, for bringing it. I must now make sure that it is kept secure until it can be displayed in the correct environment. I have been asked to give you this item for the British Museum." It was a beautiful piece of glass produced by the famous French glass maker René Lalique.

Having carefully stored the egg safely, Igor took James for a tour round some of the finest items on display in the museum. After they had marvelled at the splendid exhibits Igor turned to practical matters. "Clearly you cannot return to your hotel, so may I invite you to come home with me for the night and then we can see how you can return to your safe house in the morning?"

"That is extraordinarily kind of you, and I think I would be wise to accept. I made a careful mental note on the way to the city and if there is a bus that goes to the nearest village, I think I could complete the remainder of the journey in daylight on foot."

Igor was able to identify a bus that would take James to the village. In the morning he caught the bus with several other passengers. On arrival at the village, he began on foot to retrace the journey he had made by car two days earlier. He had turned off the main road, which was quite busy, into a narrow lane with a large tree on each corner. There was no traffic on this lane, and he was able to walk in the road, but nearing a bend he left the road in case a vehicle came round and found a track behind a hedge. He was no sooner out of sight than a car passed him travelling in the same direction. About a mile further on around another bend he came to the isolated house. Parked outside was the car and two men were gesticulating and conversing in loud angry voices with the elderly lady. James spotted a way to the back of the house, where he found her husband feeding the pigs. Seeing James, he quickly motioned to him to wait in an outhouse, telling him he should hide from the men in the car.

Back in Compton St Philip Stuart Hardy was growing increasingly anxious about James's safety as for two days he had been unable to pick up any signal from James's tracking device. He was not to know that, in his haste to leave the hotel, James had left the device in the pocket of the coat he abandoned. Stuart had no idea whom to contact to express his concern and he did not wish to alarm Sylvia or Melanie. As James was not due home for another four days, he resolved that all he could do was wait and hope that for some reason the device had malfunctioned.

MISSION ACCOMPLISHED HONOURABLY

An unlikely candidate is chosen for a special task overseas: when he completes the commission successfully in spite of unexpected difficulties he receives a surprise award.

When he had opportunity and time to do so Javed Khan, the manager of the Cricken Manor House Hotel, liked to observe guests who had called to take afternoon tea in the hotel. On this afternoon in November there were two couples, independent of each other, that occupied his attention.

The pair that had arrived first were two elderly ladies, who Javed thought may be sisters. They had booked in for a two-night stay and after finding their room had returned to the lounge and ordered afternoon tea. One returned to their room to fetch something and on her way back noticed a book on the reception desk. Seeing that it was a guidebook about the hotel and the neighbouring church she couldn't resist the temptation to buy one.

When the other lady looked at the guidebook, Javed heard her say, "Look at the names of the authors, Sis, Melanie Hardy and James Willoughby. Didn't you know a James Willoughby at University?"

"Yes, I did," replied Sis. "I don't think it could be him. After all he was about three years older than me. He's probably dead by now or in his dotage. I think he studied history or Russian or possibly both. However, as a historian it could be the area in which he has worked. If it is the man I knew I wonder who Melanie Hardy is. You know James never lacked attention from the girls."

"Yes, and I believe you had quite a crush on him."

The other visitors, who arrived at that moment, were a young couple of whom Javed had become quite fond. He had first met them when the young man's sister had her wedding reception in the hotel. Since that day he had seen them many times as they were involved in the search and research of an early tunnel that connected the original manor house to the church. They were too late to hear the conversation of the two ladies, for it would surely have amused them as they were Melanie Hardy, the co-author of the guidebook, and her boyfriend Robin Willoughby, grandson of James Willoughby.

Javed welcomed them and was about to tell them of the conversation he had heard when he noticed that their demeanour was not the sunny smiles they usually had for everyone. Rather, they were quite downcast and carried worried expressions. He was wondering if he should ask them if they were anxious about something or if they had had bad news. Before he could do so two things happened. First George Owen, the hotel owner, entered the room to have a word with him and almost simultaneously Melanie's mobile phone rang. Javed tried to listen to George while continuing to watch Melanie. Suddenly Melanie let out a shout of delight and turned to Robin, quite unaware that she had alerted the whole room and yelled, "He's safe, he's alright and he is on his way home. Oh, Robin, I'm so relieved, I thought something had gone dreadfully wrong." She collapsed into Robin's arms, tears of joy flowing down her face, the pent-up emotion of the last few days released like a dam breaking.

Realising that every eye was turned on them, Robin stood up and said, "I am sorry that we have disturbed your peaceful afternoon, but you may have realised that we have just received some wonderfully good news when we had been dreading hearing the opposite."

Melanie, seeing the two men coming towards their table, held out her hands to them, and explained, "James has been to Russia for a few days. To begin with my dad was able to track his movements and then suddenly we lost touch. It has been nearly a week since we knew anything about him or his whereabouts, but Dad has just had a call from him on the ship on his return journey. I am sorry that was all a bit garbled, but I am so relieved to know that nothing bad has happened."

After a further chat by the four of them, George and Javed moved away to continue their conversation that had been interrupted. Robin turned to Melanie, "We must let Sylvia know about Grandad."

"Of course, we must. She has been in a terrible state, worse than me. I've got her number. I'll phone her now." While she phoned, she continued, "You know she has been distraught since she heard that he was missing. I think she loves James as much as I love you and that's a lot." When the phone was answered and before Sylvia could speak, she cried, without preamble, "Good news, he's safe and on his way home."

The voice at the other end replied, *"I'm sorry, who are you and what do you mean, whom do you want to talk to?"*

"I want to speak to Sylvia Marchant, have I got the wrong number?"

"This is Mrs Marchant's home, but I am sorry she is resting at the moment. Perhaps you could ring ...."

Realising the phone was about to be put down, Melanie interrupted with, "This is Melanie, please tell Sylvia that I have some news about James. I'm sure she will want to know."

"Can't it wait, she isn't at all well?"

"I know she isn't well, that's why I have to give her news that will make her feel better."

"Oh, well. It seems that she has woken and is asking who is on the phone." Melanie heard the voice saying, *"It's someone called Melanie and she has some news."*

"Melanie!" came Sylvia's voice, *"Is that you? Norma said something about news. Is it about James?"*

"Yes, it's wonderful. He phoned Dad from the ship and says he is on the way home. I think he phoned Dad because something clearly went wrong with the tracking and presumably James knows why."

"Oh, that is wonderful, an answer to prayer. Oh, Praise the Lord. Do we know when he will be home? Oh, to see him again, dear man. Thank you for letting me know. I feel better already."

When the phone conversation was over Melanie turned to Robin with a conspiratorial look on her face and affecting an American drawl to her voice said, "She sure is going to give him some special welcome when he arrives."

Javed was pleased to note that conversations at the tables had resumed as before, so when George left the room, he returned to Robin and Melanie and told them of the conversation he had overheard from the two elderly ladies. Next, he went for a walk round the tables to check that everyone was happy. When he reached the table with the two ladies, he stopped to have a chat and told them he was pleased to see that they had shown interest in the hotel's guidebook. He told them, "It is only a few months since it was written. Melanie Hardy, one of the authors, is in the room today. She was here for a wedding and discovered the entrance to a tunnel that leads to the church. We have had great excitement finding out about the old manor house and the church."

"You say that Melanie Hardy is here now?"

"That's right. She comes here occasionally with her boyfriend and sometimes with her boyfriend's grandfather who is the co-author. It was Melanie who yelled out a few minutes ago when she had a call to say that James is on his way home from a few days abroad."

"I knew a James Willoughby when I was at university. If he is still alive, he must be at least eighty-five by now. I wonder if we could meet the young couple to see if they think he might be the James I knew."

"I'll ask them if they would be happy to join you at your table, if you like."

When Robin and Melanie reached the ladies' table, Robin was first to speak, "Good afternoon, I am Robin Willoughby, and this is my girlfriend Melanie Hardy. I understand that you think you may have known my grandfather."

One of the ladies replied, "Yes, that's right, but please join us. I am Doreen Prendergast, and this is my sister Iris Fowler, but we were originally Iris and Doreen Green. Both our husbands have passed away so now we have holidays together. It is Iris who knew James Willoughby at university."

Iris took up the tale, "Yes, such a charming man although he was older than me, probably by about three years. Looking at you, Robin, I can see several similarities of how he looked at about your age."

Melanie joined the conversation, getting out her phone, "I have pictures of SG when he was young and as he is now. Would you like to see?"

Iris peered at the pictures on Melanie's phone and exclaimed, "Oh yes, that's James as I knew him. Look, Sis, looking just as he was, oh, sixty years or more ago."

"I don't remember him. I don't think I ever met him."

"But you did, you came to my twenty-first birthday party. James also, he came to that. All the girls wanted him at their parties, but strangely he never seemed to have a particular friend, which may be why we all gravitated to him, hoping that he would choose us for his girl. Not only was he handsome, but he was always kind and seemed to have time for everyone. He always seemed to be well informed about everything that was going on and yet if you were looking for him he had a habit of being elusive, as though he could disappear if he needed to."

Melanie commented, "That sounds very much like SG. He had obviously already acquired skills that he used so successfully when he was in Russia. I wonder if he had to employ them while he was away this time."

Doreen asked, "Why do you call him SG? He isn't one of 007 James Bond's mates, is he, with a codename?"

"Oh no. At least I don't think so. It is the codename I have given him. It stands for Surrogate Grandad. My own grandfathers died before I was four. James rescued me just over a year ago when he found me unconscious after I had been attacked. He has been a great friend to me and as a result of knowing him I met Robin."

Robin continued the story. "When one of my sisters was getting married and my other sister was engaged, I thought I would be on my own so I asked if Melanie could be invited to the wedding. The wedding ceremony took place in the church near the hotel and the reception was held here. Mel went exploring, got lost and found an old part of the original manor house. She fetched Grandad and me and between us we discovered the entrance to an old tunnel. It's all in the guidebook that the two of them wrote."

Iris immediately had a question, "How exciting! Is it possible to see the tunnel?"

"Not yet, I'm afraid. We have to raise funds to make sure it is safe for visitors. We have to obey health and safety regulations. But we hope we shall be able to have a grand opening sometime next year."

Iris turned to her sister, "We never guessed when you stuck a pin in the map that he should come to such an interesting venue – a recently discovered old tunnel and news of an old university friend." Then addressing the young people, "Do you know when James is due home? I should so like to meet him again."

Robin again replied, "We don't know for sure, but according to his schedule he should be back in this country sometime next Monday or Tuesday. After that he may not come home straight away. How long are you saying here?"

"We have booked until Monday morning, but we might be able to extend our stay for a day or two if the hotel can accommodate us. Would you be able to let us know when you have more information?"

"I am sure we could. As soon as we know when he will be with us, I shall have to make plans to fetch Melanie back from university at Bath, even if it is only for a few hours. If I don't fetch her, she'll be hitching a lift somehow. She won't want to miss seeing Grandad and hearing about his trip."

Before daybreak of the next Tuesday, the cruise ship on which James was travelling docked at Dover. As passengers awoke, they realised the ship was already alongside even though dawn had not yet fully broken. By the time the loudspeaker system had informed passengers of disembarkation details, James, in the guise of an 'invalid' with his nurse, had been driven away in a private ambulance.

Shortly after lunchtime James phoned Sylvia, his son Adam and Stuart, Melanie's father, to tell them he expected to arrive home sometime between 4.00 pm and 5.00 pm. As soon as he heard the news Robin contacted the Cricken Manor hotel with a message for Iris and Doreen. He said he would try to make arrangements for them to meet James the following morning. Next, he borrowed his father's car and set off to Bath to collect Melanie.

Although Sylvia had offered to fetch him home, James insisted that he would travel by car and taxi. He duly arrived just before 4.30 pm., but not without Sylvia catching sight of the taxi from her window. She was in the vestibule of the apartment block before James had time to get into the lift to access his rooms on the floor above hers.

Somehow keeping her emotions in check Sylvia suggested James put his luggage in his apartment and then descend to hers for a cup of tea and a chance to relax after his journey. When he came down the stairs, James found Sylvia's door open. She was waiting for him. When he was inside the door, she flung her arms round him, kissed him and exclaimed, "James, dearest, it is so good to have you back. It seems such a long time and I was so worried when Stuart lost track of you. Mel has been so worried as well; we have been trying to comfort each other but we have been like a couple of silly schoolgirls crying over the loss of their first love. I could understand such behaviour of an eighteen-year-old, but at seventy I thought I had more control."

James continued to hold her, gently stroking her hair, as he responded, "What a lovely welcome and it is good to be home. I have had quite an adventure, my love, but what I need now is a cup of proper tea and then a few minutes rest. I think we are likely to have visitors this evening who will want to know all about my trip." It was another couple of minutes before they let go of each other. Had she been there to witness their meeting Melanie would surely have approved of the special welcome extended to her SG.

By 7.00 pm James had an audience gathered in his living room all eager to hear about his 'holiday' in Russia. Present were Sylvia, Melanie and her parents Stuart and Becky, Robin and his parents Adam and Rachel. "To start with," began James, "I think you all know that I was asked to undertake a special and secret assignment. I have had a debriefing this morning and I have been told what I am allowed to tell you. You are the only people who may hear this, except Adam; you can tell your sister and the other grandchildren who are not here, providing they as well as you do not mention it to anyone else. There is certainly one life that could be in danger if any one of us fails to keep it secret. Do you all understand?"

James then looked long and sternly at every member of his audience in turn. "If any of you feels that you might, even accidentally, tell someone else, you should leave now."

James waited another couple of minutes before starting his report. "I told you that I had been asked to go to Russia to deliver a priceless artefact. It almost certainly belonged to the Russian royal family who were executed in 1917 and was made by a renowned master craftsman for the Romanovs. I was asked to take it because I had lived and worked in Russia as an antiques dealer and my knowledge and dealings were respected while I was there. As it turned out I was remembered by some staff at The Hermitage Museum in St Petersburg.

"What I didn't tell you was that delivering the artefact was only my cover story. To avoid discovery, I was also chosen because of my age. My second cover story was that I should be an invalid being taken to a private specialist hospital for treatment accompanied by a nurse. We travelled on a cruise ship but none of the other passengers ever saw us. Only our special stewardess, one other steward and the captain knew of our presence on board. The clever part of the scheme was that my return journey nurse was not the same person who accompanied me on the outward journey. They were both nurses, both were Russian and they both spoke Russian and English fluently. Only a handful of people in the secret services of both countries knew of the scheme."

James stopped at that point and looked at each of them. Three of the ladies had their hands to their mouths and all were clearly spellbound and aware of the risk behind such an operation. James continued, "There was obviously an element of risk to the venture and the planners had considered what action they may need to take if anything went wrong, for example if I really was ill. They planned to monitor my progress regularly. Nevertheless, I decided on a second line of defence by asking Stuart also to track my movements. Initially, Stuart, I think that worked well, until about the third day in Russia. I'll come to that shortly.

"The journey to St Petersburg went smoothly. My nurse, Irina, and I kept to our cabin, during which I learned her story. She was about thirty. Having completed her nurses' training her family spent a few weeks in Bulgaria where she was kidnapped, after which she spent seven years in slavery until the British police discovered her when they raided a warehouse. As the Russian authorities regarded her father as a dissident they were not interested in any repatriation for his daughter.

"When we docked, we were immediately taken by ambulance to an isolated farmhouse in the country where we were looked after by a lovely elderly couple. We were soon able to assume our normal identities, while we waited further instructions. On the third day Irina's parents and her boyfriend, who had never given up hope that she would be found, came to fetch her. Their reunion was one of the tenderest scenes I have ever witnessed.

"In the late afternoon of the same day, I was taken by car to an hotel in St Petersburg, so that I could make my way to The Hermitage on my own the next day. At breakfast the next morning I was shown to a table in a cubicle in the dining room. Shortly after two men occupied the next cubicle. Listening to their conversation I discovered that they planned to abduct the courier and rob him of his valuable cargo. They knew my name and my room number, but they did not know what I looked like. They clearly didn't think the courier was an old man. They decided to wait for me to leave my room and start my walk to the museum. Fortunately, I was wearing my heart monitor, or rather the box containing the valuable artefact, round my neck. So, I left the dining room and went straight out of the hotel without fetching my few belongings and my coat. Stuart, your tracking device was in my coat pocket. That explains why you lost track of me. I'm sorry but I didn't know what might become of it.

"I made my way to the museum making three or four diversions, including shopping for a new coat and hat. I was very pleased that my memory of the city served me well. I reached the museum in time for my appointment, having twice seen the two men scrutinising passers-by. Although I had been given a ticket I didn't join the queue for ticket holders, but followed the casual visitors, where the lady on the desk was very quick to usher me out of sight.

"I concluded my business with the head curator very satisfactorily. The precious article I handed over was truly magnificent. I might tell you about it another day. When I told the story of the two men, I was invited to stay the night with the curator, Igor. The following morning, he directed me to a bus that would take me to a village close to the farmhouse.

"I left the bus in the village, walked along the main road until I was able to join the narrow lane that led to the farmhouse. As I approached a bend, I left the lane and found a track on the other side of the hedge. I was only just out of sight when a car passed. When I eventually came in sight of my destination I saw the car stopped in the middle of the road and two men and the farmer's wife in heated argument.

"I decided to keep out of sight and managed to make my way to the back of the farmhouse where I met the old man. Spotting me he promptly told me to hide in an outbuilding. Inside were some overalls and an old peasant's hat. Quietly we made plans. I had noticed an elderly tractor hitched to a trailer containing a load of straw. The tractor had a large bucket attached to the front. With Boris in the trailer with pitchfork and loaded long barrelled shotgun I hastily revised my tractor driving knowledge, from the time when, as a young teenager, I used to drive my grandfather's tractor on his farm. We drove across a field and emerged on the lane about 200 metres beyond the farmhouse, before driving back to the farmhouse.

"The two men, whom I had seen the previous day, were still arguing with the farmer's wife who was about to strike one of them with her broom when around a bend came a tractor. We had to come to a stop almost touching the car. Boris got down from the trailer, pitchfork in hand and demanded that the men move the car. By now I had worked out how to lift the bucket on the front of the tractor and raised and lowered it a few times. I also held up the shotgun and uttered a few expletives I had remembered from my previous sojourn in the country. I don't know what the men made of my language, but Boris confessed afterwards that he had been amazed at the breadth of my vocabulary. Standing up on the tractor I could see over the hedge where I could spot two cars coming along the lane from the main road. Shouting that police cars were coming I resumed my seat, 'accidentally' firing the shotgun so that stones flew up from beside one of the men's feet.

"I must commend the athleticism of the two men who returned to their car and reversed and spun the car round before driving away at speed. In their hurry they probably never saw the police cars. For that matter, no police cars came to the farm, but about five minutes later a car did arrive being driven carefully and sedately. The farmer's wife welcomed the driver and a young lady and took them indoors. Boris and I decided that the tractor had worked hard enough so we put it back in the field. When we re-joined his wife the two visitors were drinking coffee with her. We were introduced to the young lady, Lara, who was to be 'nurse' for the next part of my journey.

"Having listened to an account of the altercation they had just missed, together with my reason for returning by bus, the car driver retired to make a phone call. When he returned, he told us to collect our belongings as he had been instructed to take us to another refuge. He also invited Boris and his wife to join us for their safety, but they declined so that they could stay with their livestock. Boris said he would reload the shotgun.

"We were transferred to alternative accommodation where we stayed two nights with charming hosts. I learned that when she was a student Lara had married a fellow student, an Englishman. He had returned to England when his course finished and joined his father in the family business. Enough to say that the family business enjoys a high profile in this country but is not sufficiently recognised in Russia for Lara to obtain the necessary exit papers to leave her country. Unfortunately, after her husband had left something caused students in her university to stage an uprising. As a result, authorities had placed a blanket ban on all requests to leave the country.

"Our cruise ship arrived in St Petersburg for its last visit until next April. When passengers disembarked to join guided tours to various places of interest, Lara and I arrived by ambulance and were taken to our private cabin while there was little other activity on the ship. Once we were safely underway and Russia had disappeared into the distance, I was able to make a phone call to Stuart. I phoned Stuart in order to set his mind at rest, for I assumed he would have no idea what had happened to me. I was afraid that, depending how Stuart had reacted and how much of his concern he communicated, some of you would be imagining all sorts of scenarios.

"Now, I think that should bring you up to date. I am pleased to be back with you all and now I think I could do with a drink. I don't think there is anything else much to tell you, but I'll answer such questions as I am allowed to."

Adam spoke first. "Dad, we are all so pleased to see you. As I expected this to be an evening for celebration, I brought a couple of bottles with me. I hope you have enough glasses." Robin and Melanie jumped up to respond.

Becky was next to speak. "You went all that way. Did you have no chance to do any shopping?"

"I am grateful that my masters equipped me with some emergency spending money. After I had bought my new coat and hat, I found a store where I was able to make some small purchases. There were two reasons for doing this. I wanted to bring something for you all, as well as Ruth and Michael and other members of the family not here this evening. I thought if someone was going to try to rob me, they might go for the bag containing my shopping. I was also determined to bring something for my two best girlfriends. I was not robbed so everything has come home with me. However, I also brought one item that I no longer have. That was an exquisite piece of glass sculpture made by the famous French artist René Lalique: a present from The Hermitage to The British Museum."

James went into his bedroom, returned with the presents and distributed them to everyone. He came last to Stuart, "This is not a present but something that belongs to you. When I reached my cabin my coat that I had abandoned in the hotel was waiting for me. In the pocket still was the tracking device."

Melanie asked, "Has your nurse Lara been re-united with her husband?"

"I expect so, but I haven't had that confirmed yet."

As everyone was accepting their celebration drinks Sylvia slipped out of the room. She returned with a cake she had baked with a 'welcome home' message on the top.

Pieces of cake were passed round, and general chatter ensued as everyone realised just how special had been the assignment with which James had been entrusted and how well he had achieved it. Before the evening was ended James had to escape to his bedroom to answer a phone call. When he returned, he informed the gathering that the call had been from his contact at MI6. Lara had been re-united with her husband and the family wished him to know that they were most grateful for his part in bringing her home.

James was pleased to enjoy a few days of relative idleness, while Sylvia made sure he had plenty of rest. They both recognised that the separation they had endured had brought them closer. In the second week of December when Melanie and Robin had called to see them in James's apartment and Melanie had reported on her first term at university, James produced a letter he had received. He explained that the letter contained news that would be made public in the New Year, but that he was permitted to share it with them. He had been told that his name would appear in the New Year Honours List. The citation would say that he had been awarded a knighthood for services to his country when his actions had helped to maintain peace between peoples.

Melanie looked at him, then exclaimed, "That means I can stop calling you SG and address you as SJ, for Sir James." She followed that up, by turning to Sylvia and cheekily saying, "And if you marry Sir James you will be Lady Sylvia."

Author's Note

I hope you have enjoyed reading about James's adventures in the sixteen stories. No doubt you will have formed some impression of his character and personality. Although you will have learned some details of his past life, or indeed his double life, you may wish to know more of other incidents in which he may have been involved. As well as wanting to know more details about his early life of which only hints are provided by his old schoolfriend QQ and Iris who knew him when a student, you may wonder if he has other tales to tell about his activities in Russia or elsewhere in the world. Do you have questions about his life during the months and years beyond the time when these accounts finish? In other words, are there to be any more adventures?

I currently have no plans to write any more, unless James informs me of any other adventures which he wishes me to record. I do recognise that I have left you with unanswered questions. As I have now reached the age at which you first met James, and I have other writing plans still to be fulfilled, I wish to work on those before James fills the screen in front of me again. If I am spared long enough, I may return to James: that is if other writers haven't been granted my permission to do it for me or if a film director doesn't get the idea of turning the stories into some sort of soap opera.

What issues were left in the air? The obvious one is about the relationship between James and Sylvia. I am conscious that some readers may find Melanie's final statement teasing. Is it just a spur of the moment comment by an excitable teenage girl or has she detected a spark that she feels needs help to become a flame? Or could it be that Iris might reveal something from James's university days that causes Sylvia to have some misgivings?

Some readers may wonder if there are further revelations to be announced when the tunnel connecting church and manor house is opened to public viewing. Looking further ahead how will the relationship between Melanie and Robin develop and will James live long enough to welcome more Willoughby great grandchildren? And the treasure discovered in the archaeological dig – what of that?

Having been involved in one publication, namely the guidebook of the church and manor house, will Melanie feel that she wants to try to write James's biography? That would require James to sit still long enough to answer all her questions and I suspect that I would be expected to provide the details.

Finally, I wish to record my grateful thanks to friends who have regularly given their time to read or listen to my literary efforts, particularly Margaret Hearing, Dawn Clift, Geraldine Canniford, Cathie and Tony Seigal and Alison and John Crawford. I must also state that the comments I receive from friends who ask questions such as, 'Are you still writing?' or 'When is the next book to be published?' or even, 'You could write a story about that, Nigel' are a great encouragement.

Nigel Power

www.ingramcontent.com/pod-product-compliance
Lightning Source LLC
Chambersburg PA
CBHW040223170726
48295CB00014B/793